SHOWDOWN AT PINOS ALTOS

MELODY GROVES

WOLFPACK PUBLISHING
— EST 2013 —

Showdown at Pinos Altos
Paperback Edition
Copyright © 2023 (As Revised) Melody Groves

Wolfpack Publishing
9850 S. Maryland Parkway, Suite A-5 #323
Las Vegas, Nevada 89183

wolfpackpublishing.com

Paperback ISBN 978-1-63977-745-7
eBook ISBN 978-1-63977-746-4

SHOWDOWN AT PINOS ALTOS

CHAPTER ONE

NOVEMBER 1863—PINOS ALTOS, NEW MEXICO TERRITORY

JAMES COLTON DUCKED BEHIND THE COUNTER, his wooden bar sheltering him from the barrage. A second beer bottle sailed over his head. *Crash!* Behind him, the bar mirror exploded, shards pelting him like hail in an eastern New Mexico thunderstorm. Pieces landed on his shoulder, one lodging in his lengthy hair.

"Dammit, Big Dan! Son-of-a... Knock it off!" James launched himself over the wooden bar top and jumped on the miner's back. Despite the forty-pound difference, James bulldogged Dan Baker. Both men crashed to the floor and sprawled against the bar.

Perched on top of the muscled man, James wheezed. "I said stop!" He pinned Big Dan's hands above his head. "Just stop." Men's whoops and hollers echoed against the wooden walls.

Punches flew and bodies careened through his Buckhorn Saloon. One chair sailed across the floor.

James met the glassy stare of another large man who'd had one too many but was still able to throw a powerful roundhouse. "Yee haw!" the man shouted.

Groans. Bottles crunched. A chair splintered against the bar. James ducked again. Attention diverted to more raucous patrons, he loosened his grip on Dan. Then, like a bucking bronc, the miner reared.

Flying backwards, James rolled across the floor and slammed into a wall.

Blurred images barreling across the floor. Chairs shattering. Headache thundering. Despite the throbbing, he located his arms and pushed up. Right into a canvas pantleg. His gaze inched upward into a bearded face, those brown eyes dancing with mischief. Arms, covered with dirt-encrusted shirtsleeves, filled James' view. Before he could scramble to safety, two Herculean hands crushed his shirtfront lifting him to his feet.

"Wait! Wait!" James clutched the forearms. He stared into a face he fought to recognize. A mining friend of Dan's...Jake something.

"Dance, Bar Man, dance!" The man swung James around like a rag doll, then released him. James flew over two tables, rolled across a third, then careened into the bar—again.

He rubbed a growing goose egg on his forehead. If he didn't get this fight under control right now, he'd have no saloon left. Not even enough for Indians to raid if they ever came back. He struggled to his knees and squinted against the nauseating gas lantern lights. The front of the bar afforded little protection, but it was someplace to lean against. From here he had a good vantage point. Feet, legs and people two-stepped across the length of the barroom.

James pushed to his feet then edged around the wooden counter. His Hawken shotgun rested just under the bar. He groped for it until his hands touched the stock. He had vowed never to use it on a man, unless defending his life or that of another person. And this was no exception. James pointed it skyward and squeezed the trigger.

The thunderous roar brought down parts of the wooden ceiling, as well as immediate quiet. The various miners, prospectors and muleskinners glared at him.

James glared back. "There. That's better." He wagged the Hawken at the crowd. "Now, pick up them tables. After you do that, I'd appreciate you going elsewhere. It's closin' time."

"Aw, com'on, Colton. What'd we do?" Big Dan stepped in front of the empty shotgun.

"Hell," another miner shrugged. "Just havin' some fun." He scooped up his hat from the floor then rubbed his jaw. "For just a pup, you're as ornery as a dang she-bear."

James lowered the Hawken. "Just have your fun someplace that don't cost me money." He scanned his wrecked saloon. "Gotta be fifty, hundred dollars' worth of damage. Now where'm I supposed to get that kinda money to replace what you broke?"

"Ah, hell, Colton, you got money you ain't even spent yet." Big Dan pulled a slack-jawed miner up to his feet.

"Just borry from your highfalutin' big brother." A cowboy tucking in his shirt leaned closer to James. "I hear tell them big town sheriffs are rich."

"Closing time." James pointed outside.

Miners, cowboys, two still holding cards, and a few painted women pushed their way through the swinging saloon doors. Mumbled curses for ruining their evening's entertainment shot back into the Buckhorn. Further curses were echoed by the few men still inside. Cold, high-mountain night air of Pinos Altos swirled around James while he stood at the doors waiting for the rest to pick up their debris and leave.

The last customers grumbled goodbye as James kicked at a broken chair leg lying in the doorway. Big Dan picked up his wide-brimmed greasy hat, which had started life white, plopped it on his head then turned to James.

"Plumb sorry 'bout that, neighbor. Just couldn't help myself. Feelin' right good." Dan slapped James on the back, sending him a foot forward. "Heard that no good Indian's headin' this way. I'm gonna be the first to kill 'im."

With Big Dan's help, James righted the closest table, pushing glass with the side of his boot. "Which Indian?"

Big Dan's eyes narrowed into slits. His forehead creased. "Ain't you heard? Mangus Colorado's kin. Sittin' Horse...Sittin' Stallion...somethin' like that. Nastiest hombre this

side of the Rio Grande." He buttoned his coat then reset his hat.

Pieces of glass crunched under foot. James picked up a beer bottle neck, turned it in his hand. He frowned at Dan. "Why d'you want him dead? I heard Colorado was the only Apache trying to make peace around here. His kin may want the same thing. With him dead, it'd be nothing but raids and killings."

Dan wobbled toward the door. "Plenty of raids goin' on right now. Or ain't you been listenin' to people in your own establishment? Plenty of talk about killin'. And it ain't us doin' it neither."

James sighed, set his shotgun on the bar, righted a chair then scooted it toward a table.

Big Dan clamped his paw around James' shoulder and leaned in. His whiskey-laced words assaulted James' nose. "Since we're next-door neighbors, I remember you telling me 'bout the time you spent captured by Cochise. Wasn't so pleasant or that long ago." He breathed out more whiskey. "Now you lookin' for more of the same?"

Healed whip lashes and mended bones tugged at James' memory. He ran a previously broken finger over his scarred left cheek. James forced words over painful memories. "Yeah, more'n two months of pure hell. But I'm not willing to kill the Apache just for defending what they think is theirs."

"What'd it take for you to kill one?"

"Already done that, Dan." James turned, then kicked chair and bottle parts. "Already done that."

His last customer's fading footsteps, the swinging doors slamming closed, weren't enough to drown out his screams as Cochise's war chief tortured him.

The memories, always the memories.

"Heard about the fight, James."

James spun around, grabbed his assailant's arm and brought his clenched fist back ready to pound the Indian into pulp.

"It's just me." The soft voice. Morningstar. His wife. "You all right?"

The last bit of moisture in his throat pushed down, James lowered his fist and nodded. "Fine." He loosened his grip and pulled her into an embrace. "I'm *so* sorry." His eyes squeezed shut.

Morningstar wiggled out of his embrace. "My fault. I know not to come behind you like that." She gave him a quick kiss. "What a mess."

James looked over her shoulder at what was left of his first business venture. An Apache raid would have been less destructive. He sighed again then thumbed over his shoulder. "Gotta get a new mirror."

Morningstar slid an arm around James' waist and nuzzled into his chest. "James Colton, what's wrong? Besides the brawl, I mean."

He held her at arm's length. Those shining ebony eyes always read his thoughts, his feelings. Could she read how much he loved her? How lucky he was? He drew her once more against his chest, her warm body soothing his nerves. Her light lilac scent eased his throbbing head. He held her tighter.

While they stood, eyes closed, he vowed—for the millionth time—not to let the memory of Cochise and his second, One Wing, take over his life. After months of hard work, he'd managed to put them in their place and he was determined to keep his past in the past.

"Cochise again?" Morningstar stepped back and held his trembling hand.

"I'm all right." He pulled his hand away and hid it behind his back. "Just caught off guard. Probably tired."

Morningstar glanced around the saloon. "I'm sure you are. I'll help clean up."

While sweeping and listening to broken glass screech across the plank flooring, James thought about his recently purchased saloon. Biggest one in Pinos Altos and it was doing a fine business. He knew he could afford to replace the damaged furniture. It was the aggravation more than the money.

Why'd they always fight in here? Why not on the street or down at one of the others saloons? He already knew the answer. For years, the citizens barely survived starvation and relentless Apache attacks. Life turned into an ordeal. Now, however, with food in their bellies and the Indians agreeing to peace, everyone was celebrating. Life was good again. And the Buckhorn was the town's first saloon, built five years before. Why not enjoy a place that feels like home?

CHAPTER TWO

JAMES SAT AT THE KITCHEN TABLE, STARK shafts of morning light stabbing the tabletop. He wanted to find something good in this day, but nothing came to mind. This morning was no different. He blamed himself for not being the man Morningstar thought she was marrying a year ago. Their wedding night had quickly become his wedding nightmare. Turned out, he certainly wasn't the man he thought he would be.

Cooking breakfast smells filled the room, but even such a satisfying aroma did nothing to assuage his contempt for himself. For Cochise. For the torture he'd endured.

If things had been different, by now Morningstar would be a mother, he a father. They'd be a family. Something he always assumed he'd have. And if things had worked right, maybe by now they'd even be starting a second baby. Something Morningstar wanted more than anything. Children. The one thing he couldn't give her.

"You're looking awfully high strung. You feeling good?" Morningstar set the plate of eggs and ham in front of James and one at her place. She sat across from him.

James ran his hand through his hair then tossed a few papers on the table hoping to cover the frustration he knew lined his face. "Just figuring the loss from last night's fight." He rubbed stubbled cheeks. He'd shave after breakfast. "Mirror's gonna cost a bundle."

"What'd the freighters say this morning?" Morningstar sipped her coffee.

James sprinkled salt then pepper on his eggs. "Four months at best. Comes out of Mexico, and with all this fighting between the Mexicans and Apache, who knows if it'll even get through." He spoke over his food. "Price went up, too. Told 'em I'd think on it."

Fork gripped in hand, James stared at his coffee cup. Silence filled the tiny kitchen. He pushed food around on his plate.

"It's just a broken mirror." Morningstar reached across for his hand.

His wife deserved to be happy. Dammit, if she couldn't have children, maybe she could have something else. James offered a substitute.

"Been doing some thinking," he said. "Since you don't have little ones pulling at your apron strings, would you want to become a nurse? You could get proper training from your pa."

Morningstar's fork tinged against her plate rim. Her eyes met his. "A nurse? I've already done that. I want to be a *doctor*. Attend the Women's Medical College of Pennsylvania or New York Medical—"

"New York? Penn..." James frowned. The idea had sounded better in his head than when the words spurted out. He sure as hell had no idea what he'd do if she agreed.

A couple sputtered starts and stops, then Morningstar beamed. "It's what I've always wanted! Imagine! Me. A full-fledged doctor. Just like my pa." She jumped up and rushed around the table where she threw her arms around James' neck. "I'll do it! I'll write Pa and tell him the good news."

James had to think... and fast. Make his words just right. "But it's gonna take what? Three, four years? What'd happen to the saloon? We just got here."

"Andy can take over while we're gone."

"Can't ask my brother to stay here that long. Besides, we don't know where he's at."

"Can't be that hard to find him." Star shrugged. "The saloon's already making money. He could save up and—"

"Maybe we oughta think on this some more." James wrapped his arms around his wife and pulled her onto his lap. The tempting closeness served only to bring frustrating memories of last night, and the night before, and...

"Already thought about it, James. This town needs a doctor."

"It's got one."

"A midwife. Miners don't go to her."

Nobody he knew and certainly nobody who'd admit it. "I know you've learned a lot from your pa," James said. "Even though he's not your blood kin, you sure picked up his skills."

She turned wide brown eyes on James. "I helped him even when I was a child and since I know what I'm doing, and I doctored in Kansas during the raid..." She spoke as if she'd already planned. "You know...if you don't want to go with me, I could go alone. Find a nice family to room with."

"Alone?"

She tossed him a half smile. "Just think about it. Please?"

That was the least he could do for someone who'd given him so much. Given security and love when the bottom fell out of his world. He raised eyebrows to her. His unspoken way of agreeing.

James laid his napkin on the table, stood with her. "I don't deserve you."

"Shush now. Enough talk like that." Morningstar met his gaze. "What you need is to go down to Mesilla, order that mirror. Talk to Trace." She took her seat across from James. "You can close up for a few days and we can leave tomorrow at first light. Can't wait to tell Teresa! I know she'll be as excited as I am."

Great. Two women yapping about children and school. Now he'd *really* have to talk to his brother.

CHAPTER THREE

JAMES AND MORNINGSTAR COLTON MADE THE
trip in two days. Mesilla, New Mexico Territory's largest
city, was home to James' brother and many, many
memories.

Admiring the endless turquoise sky as he drove their
wagon past the adobe farmhouses and cotton fields on
the outskirts of town, James reflected on his first weeks
in the West. Days after he'd been hired by Butterfield
Stage Lines to ride shotgun with his driver brother, four
masked outlaws had robbed the stagecoach's strongbox
as well as the passengers' valuables. He remembered
spending weeks hunting for his stolen watch—a quest
which almost cost him his life.

Statuesque cottonwoods stood sentinel lining both
sides of the Rio Grande. Their golden copper leaves,
tinged with green as if refusing to give way to autumn,
rustled in the late-afternoon breeze.

The team slowed to a walk. James and Morningstar
entered the plaza riding past the Mesilla Mercantile
taking up half of the west side, Griggs Feed and Grain

the other half. Lemon's Grist Mill, south of the mercantile, bustled with activity.

He studied his wife perched next to him, her dusty face, red cheeks glowing with the cool November air. How could he be more in love with someone? In a long, odd turn of events, if James hadn't been captured, he'd never have met Morningstar. So *damn* Cochise, but *thanks* Cochise.

"Always a bittersweet time, isn't it?" Morningstar's voice cut into his thoughts.

James drew a deep breath. "More sweet than bitter." He looked over at her. How would she react to Trace's daughter, Faith? Last visit as they left, he had to practically tear the baby out of her arms.

Before any more thoughts assaulted him, James reined up in front of his brother's house. Situated three blocks from the plaza, Sheriff Trace Colton was still close enough to town to respond to any problems, but far enough away to enjoy a smattering of privacy.

Teresa greeted them in the front yard. "Trace figured you'd be coming soon, James. Morningstar, so good to see you." After rib-shattering hugs, she led them into the plastered adobe house. The walls breathed a warmth and sense of family James envied.

"Where's that good-lookin' husband of yours? The one looks just like me?" he scanned the room. "Figured he'd be home by now, feasting on your delicious fried chicken." He followed Teresa into the kitchen. No brother. He then moved into the living room. Lowering himself into a rocking chair, he leaned back. This chair fit his back better than his springboard wagon. Sure felt good to be still for a while.

Morningstar handed him a cup of freshly brewed

coffee, then both women joined him. Teresa took one end of the couch and Morningstar the other.

Teresa sipped her coffee. "Trace took Faith over to Bergstrom's stable. She wanted to see ponies."

"She's talking?" Morningstar held her cup halfway to her lips. "Already?"

Nodding, Teresa smiled. "A few words here and there. She's also walking, 'bout two months now. She's everywhere."

James studied his wife's face. Tears filled her eyes, and he spotted hands trembling. Morningstar buried herself in the coffee cup. He wanted to hold her, tell her they'd have children of their own—someday. Instead, he sat. Truly, nothing he could say would change things.

In the silence, he regarded his sister-in-law. Indeed, Trace had married a fine woman. James drained his cup, stood and stretched his lanky frame. Marriage had added a few pounds, but his six-foot body was still trim and muscled. At twenty-two, he possessed the physique of a farm boy who'd known hard but satisfying work. As he brought his shoulders back, he felt the familiar tug of scars. Many scars.

"Gonna walk down to the Corn Exchange Hotel, get us a room, Star." James turned his attention to Teresa. "I'll find that brother of mine and drag him home. 'Bout time he paid you some attention." He set the cup on the table.

Teresa stood. "He's going to be glad to see you, James. He's missed you." She grinned. "But don't tell him I told you."

James gave Teresa a wink and his wife a kiss. "Be back soon." He pulled the door shut and stepped into the crisp afternoon air.

* * *

SITTING NEXT to his wife at the dinner table, James reached under and held her hand. She squeezed back. The faces of his brother and Teresa glowed over their daughter. In fact, he'd never seen his brother happier. Faith squirmed in her highchair and picked apart a biscuit. How many crumbs could one roll have? James grinned at his niece. She certainly was beautiful. Her light brown hair reflected the Colton family color. Everyone had some shade of brown. His was darker than the other brothers'. He hadn't seen his youngest brother, Andy, in some time, but guessed his hair was still lighter.

Thoughts turned to Andy, last in line of the Colton dynasty, four years younger than James. Had Andy found whatever he was looking for? When James and Morningstar returned from Kansas two months ago, Andy had already unpinned his deputy's badge and taken off for adventure.

"Let's retire to the living room, shall we?" Teresa released Faith from the highchair. The fifteen-month-old raced into the other room and planted her little body against her pa's leg.

Trace picked up the youngster and brushed the hair out of her eyes. "Pa and Uncle James are gonna tend the horses, Button. Be right back." Planting a kiss on her forehead, he set her on the floor.

James ruffled his niece's hair then followed Trace. Cool night air drifted around him as he stepped outside. He thought about how much tiny Faith had changed Trace's life. Would he ever experience that kind of change?

In the barn, the brothers forked fresh straw into the stalls. Trace patted his horse's neck as she pulled at a flake. He glanced over his shoulder. "Couldn't stay away, huh?"

"Just wanted to be sure your sheriffin' is up to snuff." James combed his dun's mane.

Shooting a good-natured glare at his brother, Trace flipped a blanket over the back of his pinto and picked up a currycomb. "Sheriffin' is just fine, little brother. I toss an occasional drunk in jail, nothin' too exciting. Hell, a good bar fight's the highlight of the week." He ducked under his horse's neck and leaned against the warm animal.

James curried his horse's rump. "So, things are working out, huh?"

Trace tilted his hat back on his forehead and grew serious. "It was the right thing to do after we got back… from Cochise's." He stared at the barn rafters. "Yeah, it was the right thing to do."

Only horses munching disturbed the silence. Trace pointed the comb northward. "Heard from Andy a while back. 'Couple weeks now." He shook his head. "Decided to be a prospector and pan for gold up in those Mogollon Mountains."

Both brothers chuckled. Trace slid his hand down the neck of James' other mare. "I remember him saying he was 'gonna get rich' then buy champagne and drink it all."

"Nothing he won't go see or do, is there? Tries everything once."

"Suppose he's ever gonna grow up?" Trace draped a horse blanket on a stall rail.

"Hope not."

While smoothing a light blanket over the back of his favorite mare, James' thoughts turned to his wife.

Drawing in a long breath drew Trace's attention. His brother's eyes reflected the kerosene lantern's glow.

"Got some news for you." Trace rubbed the back of his neck, then his eyes trailed to his brother.

James stepped closer. "Can always use good news."

Trace shuffled his feet, studied his hands then brought his gaze into his brother's eyes. "Teresa's gonna have another baby."

Blinking a few extra times, James managed strangled congratulations. A year of frustration knotted his stomach. He searched the barn rafters for solace.

"What're you thinking?" Trace squeezed his brother's shoulder. There was closeness, a bond, which no amount of anger or time could separate.

"I'm truly happy for you, brother. I am." James fought the frustration pressing in on his brain, roiling in his guts. He searched the brown eyes he'd known his entire life.

Trace stared back, eyebrows knitting. "What then?"

James swallowed, engulfed by his sense of failure. "I can't give Morningstar children. That's what she wants more than anything." The words tumbled from his mouth, no way of stopping them. "Those Apache...that—"

"It's all right." Trace gripped James' shoulder.

"No. It ain't!" He jerked from Trace's tight embrace, his voice bouncing off the stable walls. "Hell, I still have all my parts—at least Cochise didn't cut 'em off. It's been long enough now. Should be able to be a *man*. But I'm not."

James spotted sanctuary across the narrow barn. He stormed toward it then pressed his forehead into a splintery wall. His fist slammed against the wood.

"Don't spur yourself. Morningstar loves you no matter what. Forever."

"Only until a *real* man comes along." James spoke more to himself than to Trace. He hung his head, studying the dirt floor, supper rising in his throat. Why was this so damn hard?

Trace glanced at the floor and then his brother. "There's more?"

James shoved both hands into his coat pockets and stared into the warm barn. "Am I not enough for her? Now she wants to run off to medical school. Leave me and run off." He lowered his voice. "To New York."

"Leave you? Medical school?" Trace's dark eyebrows knitted. "That's rather sudden. What gave her the idea?"

Hesitating, words formed their own thoughts. "I kind of did."

Trace's knitted eyebrows rose. "Ah hell, James. Don't worry." He wagged his head. "New York? She's not going anywhere. Only a select few women get in. She'd better get that notion out of her head."

"Not Morningstar. When her mind's made up—"

"No school's going to accept her. We both know that. And consider the cost. I loaned you all I could for the saloon. So, between the two of us, we don't have the money. Besides, we don't live back East. Relax."

"Maybe I could sell the Buckhorn."

Trace leaned against a barn post and glared.

Refitting his hat, James let out a stream of air. "Poor Star. She can't have kids or medical school." His heart sat heavy in his chest. "She knows I love her, but she'll find somebody who can give her one...or *both*."

"Never." Trace's voice soothed James' raw nerves. It was the same tone James had heard so often when they were held in Cochise's camp. The tone that kept him going. "She's crazy about you. Hell, even if she did leave, you're strong enough to survive." He stepped back. "What're we talkin' about? It'll all work out. Trust me."

Relaxing, James kicked at a dirt clod. "You're probably right." Space to think right now would help settle his stomach. It certainly wasn't Teresa's good cooking causing the rumbling.

Trace elbowed James. "Want dessert?"

No. Nothing would go down right now, but James refused to give in, to spoil this evening. "Suppose she's got blueberry pie?"

"I *know* she does." Trace thumped his brother's chest. "Race ya!"

The Colton brothers sprinted across the back yard, around the house and onto the front

porch. They crashed into the door at the same time.

Teresa and Morningstar stood just inside the door.

"If you boys're gonna roughhouse," Teresa said, hands planted on her hips. "Keep it outside."

Morningstar pointed over her shoulder. "The baby's asleep, so—"

"We're just here for blueberry pie, Star." Trace stepped into the house after the women backed up.

James gripped his brother's arm before getting too far inside. "Damn good to see you." He used his hat brim to whack Trace's chest. "Damn good."

CHAPTER FOUR

JAMES STEPPED ONTO THE PLANK BOARDWALK under the *portal* in front of the Sheriff's office. Two days had galloped by while he located and purchased a mirror for his bar. He was lucky. One had just come in from Mexico *and* in one piece. The mercantile owner promised to keep it safe until James was ready to haul it back to the Buckhorn Saloon. Things were truly looking up. The price was half of what the freighters in Pinos Altos were charging.

He surveyed the dusty adobes ringing the plaza. Mesilla, home to three thousand American citizens, offered entertainment only imagined elsewhere. Live stage plays, two newspapers and thirteen saloons kept people busy. Even a few discreet bordellos operated near the plaza.

In addition to buying the mirror, he'd followed Trace on his rounds, helping break up one nasty barroom brawl.

But now, late afternoon sun spread its final warm glow melting the rugged adobe town into a golden-brown village. A gentle breeze edged with winter ruffled the brown hair hanging under James' hat. He sighed. Despite a few bad memories, he loved this bustling town, its freight wagons rumbling through day and night. Pinos Altos was home for now, but what about the future? Trace appeared content, would probably live here forever. Maybe James should talk to Star about relocating back to Mesilla. Maybe, just maybe with Teresa close by, Star could watch Faith and the baby. No more talk of becoming a doctor.

Sweetening the temptation, Swede Bergstrom had offered James his old job back. While doing light work at the livery wasn't too appealing, he'd be closer to his brother. And maybe, eventually, brother Andy would settle down here, too.

Although the "baby" of the family, Andy was not spoiled. He'd been expected to do as much work as the other brothers. He'd chopped, carted, fetched, and branded just like everyone else. Pa taught his four sons to work hard—real hard. So far, James realized, all four boys had turned out well. Each had had a few talking-tos from the school marm, but then, who hadn't?

"You gonna warm up the *portal* all afternoon?"

Trace's deep voice spun James around. Boot catching on a warped board, he tripped, plowing face first into his brother's chest.

Trace grabbed James' shoulders to steady him. "Glad to see you, too. But you don't have to hug me every time you see me."

Pulling out of the strong grip, James kicked at the loose plank. "Once again savin' me from a fall. Thanks."

"That's what brothers are for." High crowned black hat readjusted, Trace closed the office door. "Gonna make a few rounds, head on home to supper. Deputy's gonna watch the place. Wanna come?"

"Yeah, if anything to keep you out of trouble, older brother. I hear you're a real rabble rouser."

"Says who?"

"Everybody. You make trouble wherever you go." James' grin spread ear to ear.

Trace tugged his brother's hat down over his eyes. "Just jealous, little brother. Just jealous."

The Coltons sauntered toward the line of adobe buildings on the south side of the plaza. 'Transportation row' housed a blacksmith's, one of the newspaper offices as well as head- quarters of the San Diego-San Antonio Stage Lines. Sam Bean's Saloon now occupied the offices of the defunct Butterfield stage.

James' chest tightened, his mouth dry as desert as he edged past his old stage office. He envisioned himself, a terrified nineteen-year-old, walking toward the gallows, then stopping right here in front of this window. His stomach churned. During that same time, Trace lay near death from a bullet wound, and James was about to die, swing until he stopped kicking. The scratchy rope tightened around his neck. His shoulders ached—

"You all right?"

James jumped at the voice in his ear. Trace's face. He fought to return to the present. "What?"

"Welcome back." Trace planted an arm around his brother's shoulders. "Memories. Hate 'em." He nudged James toward the other side of the plaza.

A final glance into his former life, then he pushed memories aside. James licked his dry lips.

On Trace's heels, James stepped into *The Mesilla Times* office. He grinned at the man behind the wide wooden desk with the nameplate *Editor* on top. James waved a greeting. "Howdy, Tommy."

"I'll be gawd-damned." Thomas Littleton stood, limped around to the front of the paper-littered desk and perched on it. "Look what flea-bitten, mangy coyote managed to drag itself in."

James' grin widened.

Littleton reached out, grabbed James' hand and pumped it. "What the hell brings you to town? Come to see what life's like in the big city, boy? Need some culture?" He lit a cigarette, pulled in the first drag, offered the rolled tobacco to James.

Shaking his head, James glanced around the office. "Fine place you got here. Anything you print worth reading?"

Littleton blew smoke toward James. "You know, Sheriff Colton. If this smart-mouthed son of a bitch wasn't your kin, I'd knock his disrespectful ass clear across the plaza."

Trace drew his hand across his face to wipe off the spreading smile. "You two better kiss and make up. James is a saloon owner now. You just might want a free drink some time. Keep threatening him, he'll likely charge you double."

"Hell, Trace, he waters down the whiskey. I hear tell they do that up there in the sticks." Littleton leaned into Trace. "They don't know no better. You know—them backwoods boys."

James brought his shoulders back, his mind racing with pithy comebacks.

Thomas Littleton slapped James on the shoulder and emitted a smoky spiral. "Damn good to see you, boy."

James breathed in the odor of smoke mixed with ink, listened to the clacking of someone in the back setting type. He let his gaze rest on the landscape painting behind Littleton's desk. Snowcapped mountains, a wide meadow in the foreground, a river snaking through the entire picture.

The river. Reminded him of his three-day ride to Mesilla to stand trial for murder. Shackled and caged in the jail wagon. His first encounter with this Thomas Littleton and two other deputies. Their endless chatter during the trip. James felt for the knot on his skull where a third deputy cold-cocked him.

Torturous confinement. Even worse, the absolute terror of his near drowning as the jail wagon lodged against debris swept along in the torrent of the Mimbres River. Trace, who drove the wagon not knowing it was his brother he was carting back to hang, had saved him.

"Close your mouth, boy. You're snoring." Littleton spoke into James' ear. "Never seen a picture before?" He cocked his head toward the painting. "No words on there, so you don't have to strain your brain too hard." Littleton thumped James' shoulder. "Hell, boy. You need to get to civilization more often."

Swallowing the lump in his throat, James glanced at the man leaning against his right shoulder. Easily twenty years older, Littleton was more of a father figure than friend or brother. Certainly crustier than James' own father, he was definitely full of life. No doubt Littleton used language Pa wouldn't.

The editor turned his attention to Trace. Listening to Littleton chat with his brother, James returned to the past. Trace had saved this newspaper editor also. Close to unconscious, Deputy Littleton had wedged himself in the corner of the waterlogged, overturned wagon and was near death when Trace tugged him out. Leg broken in two places as the wagon toppled over, Littleton fought for months to recuperate. He walked with a decided limp, ending any career in law enforcement.

Three years ago. James remembered Littleton being the only deputy who had treated him with any decency. After they had both healed up, they became friends. For some reason, Thomas Littleton had taken a shine to that boy about to be hanged and had been one of the first to congratulate him when the judge over-turned the guilty verdict.

"You gonna stand here all day learnin' to read or buy your old friend a drink?" Littleton stubbed out his cigarette, waved to the man in the back of the room. "Tomorrow, Tubbs."

James glanced at the man bent over some kind of printing machine, ink smeared on his face. A hand hovered over the contraption. It waved.

Slapping James on the back, Thomas grabbed a jacket from the hook on the door frame. "Ol' Jeff's a helluva print setter. Helluva printer."

The three men stepped into the darkening plaza. A few oil lamps lit the boardwalk in front of stores now shutting their doors for the day. Composed of hard-packed *caliche* soil, the streets around the plaza ringed the wooden bandstand dominating the center of the square. Weddings, funerals, baptisms, *quinciñeras* and any other excuse for a social gathering spilled out from the church on the north side of the plaza and ended up there.

Biting his lower lip, James remembered his almost-wedding with Lila in that church. He'd missed it by days. If that Apache hadn't captured him and Trace, if—

"Damn if you're not as slow as a mule in winter and stubborn as one, too."

James shook his head and stared at the man standing

inches in front of him. "Sorry, Tommy. Gotta stay focused."

"Damn right. Focus on buyin' me a drink instead of whatever's whirling around in that crazy head of yours." Littleton pulled the front of James' coat.

James swatted the hand away. "Wonderin' why you're so downright ornery. How'd the town ever let you run a newspaper?" Walking side by side with the businessman and Trace made James' shoulders relax. This felt good.

Before entering the Crystal Saloon, Trace buttoned his coat closer around his throat and thumbed over his shoulder. "I better run home and tell Teresa we'll be 'bout an hour." Trace glanced into the sky at the new evening. "Damn cold. Thought November wasn't supposed to be this chilly."

"A drink'll warm you up when you get back. We'll keep your chair warm." James opened the door and stepped into the amber-shadowed barroom. Blue smoke lowered the ceiling and swirled around his head as he peered into the dim room. Odors of whiskey and tobacco mingling with stale beer assaulted his nose as he made his way to the one empty table back in the corner. Using thumb and forefinger, he rubbed his stinging eyes which threatened to send tears down his cheeks.

He blinked, swiped at a drop on his cheek, then plopped into the hard chair. James couldn't help but grin. A drink with a friend and his brother would round out a satisfying day.

James, Trace and Thomas spent a quick hour swapping stories, spinning yarns and enjoying themselves. Two beers relaxed James into telling tales true and somewhat true. Not one for too much exaggerating, his new look on life since being captured by Cochise added spice to his stories.

Arms extended overhead, Trace leaned back and yawned. Scooting his chair away from the table, he pushed his body to his feet. "Better get home to supper, James. Those women of ours can be downright mean when we're late."

James turned to Thomas. "Lucky you're single. There's no wrath like a wife whose husband's not on time." He stood, shook hands with the newspaper owner. "Been good seein' you again, Tommy."

Thomas Littleton stood and embraced his friend. "You're all right for a hardheaded, crazy, ex-jailbird, ex-Apache captive saloon owner." He smacked James on the back. "You'll do to drink with."

Pulling himself away from Littleton, James extended his hand then shook with the newspaperman. "See you again before we leave."

Trace and James threaded their way through the men and few women gathered around tables and people elbow to elbow at the bar. Swinging the doors open, both men shivered in the cold breeze. They buttoned their coats and flipped up the collars around their necks. Shoving hands into pockets, the brothers headed for home.

"Trace, there you are!"

Both Coltons whirled around at the shout several yards behind them. They waited for the man sporting a long coat and shiny badge to catch up.

"What's wrong, Sammy?" Trace studied the shadowed face of his deputy.

"Knew you'd both want to hear right away." Sammy Estrada glanced at James and nodded. Taking a deep breath, he swung his gaze back to Trace. "Just got word the Apache raided that little mining camp up in the Mogollon Mountains."

Fighting to make sense of the news, James focused on the panicked face of his older brother.

"Good Lord." Trace ran his hand over his mouth. "Any survivors?"

Sammy wagged his head. "Not at this point. Sorry to have to tell you. I know that's where your brother was last you heard."

James furrowed his forehead. "Dead? Andy's dead?" He clutched Trace's coat sleeve and shook his head. "Hell, he's just a kid."

"I know." Trace whispered as he stared into darkness.

James' heart thudded. *Apache*. Knives in his throat... rawhide bands strangling... A tight grip on his shoulder brought his focus back into the present. Trace's hold tightened.

James gave a quick nod to his brother then focused on Sammy.

"One more thing." Sammy looked over his shoulder toward the jail and hesitated. "There's talk the Apache are heading south, toward Pinos Altos."

"Ah, hell!" Mouth suddenly dry, James' words rasped. "My house...my bar..." His eyes trailed to Trace's paling face. "My friends?"

Trace planted a firm hand on his brother's back. "At least Morningstar's safe. She'll stay here 'til we get back."

James fought panic. Arrows...screams... He straightened his shoulders back into the present then pulled in cold air. "Go tonight or wait 'til morning?"

"Morning. We'll pack, get our gear and supplies ready tonight, head out at first light." Trace turned to Sammy. "Mind things while I'm gone."

"You bet. Want me to get an extra deputy?"

Trace nodded.

Sammy patted James on the upper arm. "Andy'll be all right. We gotta believe."

James heard nothing but a dull pulse and meaningless words.

"Let's go, James." Trace took two long steps then turned around to his deputy. "I'll be back soon as I can. Check in on Teresa and Faith for me. Just make sure they're doin' all right."

Sammy nodded and waved as the Colton brothers trotted home.

CHAPTER FIVE

Sputtering flames licked the blackened log in the center of the campfire. James swallowed the final sip of coffee, tossed out the remaining few drops, then set the tin cup beside the pot. Fingers stiff, he held them close to the fire's warmth. "Gonna get damn cold tonight, Trace. Want more wood on the fire?"

"One or two. We got plenty for morning." Trace handed James a long stick.

Breaking it in half, James pushed both pieces into the fire and examined the orange-red sprites dancing back to life. He arched his back and winced. "Eighty miles. My poor ol' body can't take another three days in that saddle."

"We'll stay in those saddles 'til we find Andy."

"I know. But I'd give almost anything for a nice soft bed right about now."

Inky blackness surrounded James as he listened to the gurgle of a nearby stream. He pulled his blanket closer around his shoulders. Stars always littered the sky. James squinted into the dark and frowned. Nothing but black.

Then, as if teasing him, one silver stud peeked out from under its cloud quilt then winked back into obscurity.

Trace lay back on the hard ground and rolled into his wool blanket. "We got what... thirty more miles to Santa Rita? Suppose they got a soft bed there?"

"I'm counting on it." James raised his eyebrows as he arranged himself on the ground. He pulled a rock from under his hip and tossed it away.

Close enough to the fire without being singed and head pillowed by his saddle, James relaxed, tugged at his blanket and drew up his knees. Eyes opening and closing, he struggled to stay awake long enough to make sure his brother was asleep. Since the news of Andy, Trace hadn't slept more than an hour. James had wakened often, and each time found his brother either thrashing side to side, adjusting his blanket, or poking the campfire with yet another stick.

James eyed the still body of his brother lying next to him. He detected a snore. His own eyes no longer able to stay open, drifted shut. Cold nipped at his cheeks. It would freeze tonight. Pulling the blanket into a cocoon around him, he slept.

That captive Indian girl trembles in front of me, both of her arms clutched by vicious Apache. Her terrified eyes plead. Is she afraid of me? I'm a prisoner like she is. I'm not going to hurt her.

Bruises on her frightened yet stoic face. How many fists have plowed into her slim body? She's young...thirteen, fourteen at most. She's not Apache, certainly not from Cochise's tribe. Pima? Part Mexican? She's obviously regarded as worthless, something to be used then tossed aside like a gnawed bone. I know exactly how she feels. I'm sorry for her.

Vice-like grips on my arms loosen, the strangling horsehair ropes around my wrists drop away. Questioning the action but

enjoying the freedom, I glance over my shoulder. Where's Trace?
He'll know what's happening.

Gone. My brother is gone. I'm all alone.

A barrel-chested Apache rips off my shirt and tosses the
material to the ground. A knife tip jams into my back. The steely
point pokes my skin. Another blade appears and jabs my neck.
Although it hurts like hell, I refuse to cry out.

Not this time.

One Wing grunts and points at my britches as the knives are
retracted. I frown, not understanding what they want. Another
Apache grabs my pants and yanks them down. As quickly as that
happens, the captive girl's dress is ripped from her. We stand face
to face.

Embarrassed.

Confused.

Naked.

I try to stare only into her spiritless eyes but my gaze slides
down. Another sharp knife tip pokes my back. I glance from face
to face gathering around me and the girl, reminding me of a pack
of wolves corralling their prey. Hundreds of snarling visages,
their grins wicked and eyes glowing, stare at us.

One Wing releases my arm. Pushed, the girl plows into my
chest. Her body shivers against mine. Indians' taunts fuel my
anger.

"Take her, James Colton. You claim to be a man. Be a man.
Take her. Right here, right now."

Mouth open, I stare at the girl. I shake my head, mumble an
apology to the young woman in my arms and promise she'll be
safe. I couldn't do that to her. She's innocent... And I'm inno-
cent, too.

Apache close in. The circle around us tightens like a noose.
Her breath caresses my ear. I hear Apache urgings. Her heart
beats against mine. Flesh on flesh.

I push her away. Indians force us back together. We are as close as we can get. Her body is warm. Hot.

I run my shaking hands across her bare back. Her skin...soft, welcoming. I fight the taunting, yet the closeness excites me. Stirrings grip my stomach and rumble even lower. Giving in to the urgency, my hands slide down—

"Wake up, James. What's wrong?"

Eyes flying open, James bolted upright. Blanket clutched to his chest, he sat struggling to cover his clothed body. Desperate to make sense of his world, he swung his head side to side.

A firm handclasp on his shoulder, James recoiled at One Wing's face inches from his.

"James?"

The voice—not Indian. The face—not One Wing.

Blinking, James drew in breath, bringing form and shape to the fire's glowing embers and to his brother's face.

"Another dream?" Trace released his grip.

"Same one." James ran his hand through his hair and across his lips. "Can't get Dark Cloud out of my mind."

Trace nodded and let out a thin column of frost while scooting next to his brother. "From what you said, if it hadn't been you, the Apache—"

"Yeah. But I shouldn't have." James looked away as his words spiraled down to a whisper. "I always wonder, if she'd lived, if she'd—"

"Bear your child?"

James nodded and straightened his back. "Wonder what it would've been?"

"Wouldn't 've been anything. Leave it be, James."

"Can't help—"

"Are we gonna have this conversation again? Quit spurring yourself. There was nothing you could do except what happened." Trace spoke in a low whisper, picked up a twig and tossed it into the fire pit. "If it really did."

James balled his fists. "I told you it did. After Cochise sent you away. Why can't you believe me?"

"I do. It's just that your thinking isn't always clear. One Wing about destroyed you, and I think at times you get confused, is all."

"I'm not confused about this. I was forced to take her as my wife. A young Pima. She was small…helpless." James pulled in frigid air. "I wanted to be an honorable husband. I even took her beatings for her."

"I remember you taking some of mine, too." Trace's gaze fell to the ground.

James stared into the campfire's pulsating embers and nodded. His words were soft, slow. "We laid together every night even though there wasn't a place on me she touched that didn't hurt. But it was a pain I could endure because I needed her so bad." He squeezed his eyes tight. "I needed…her."

James filled his lungs, opened his eyes as tightness gripped his throat. "Then they killed her."

"What've you told Morningstar?"

"Nothing. What *can* I tell her? That I physically loved another woman?" James picked up a twig and threw it at the fire. "That we actually consummated our marriage— several times?" He swallowed over a knot. "Something I can't do with her."

The coals' glow reminded James of a life that's ready to catch fire but, without proper tending, dies. However, his brother's body next to him felt safe, his strength comforting.

Trace picked up the wool blanket and dropped it into

his brother's lap. "Get some sleep. Long day ahead of us."

James lay back, pulling the cover over his body. He turned on his side, then fought the blanket bunched under his chest. Even the saddle, used as a pillow, fought him. He fidgeted with it, hoping it would support his head and neck instead of causing pain, like now.

A couple deep breaths and he relaxed into what he hoped would be blessed sleep. He shut his eyes.

That woman, that memory, danced in his mind, haunting his thoughts. Before that time with Dark Cloud, he'd never seen a woman naked, much less touched one.

Feeling her body press into his, bare skin against bare skin, warmth flushed him. Aroused, James' guilty thoughts turned to Morningstar, soft and sensual, too. Why couldn't he—

"Dammit, Trace." James sat straight up. "Dammit. Put some coffee on. It's gonna be a long night."

* * *

TOPPING A STEEP RISE, the Colton brothers reined their tired mounts to a stop. White clouds of steam erupted from the horses' nostrils, crystallizing before evaporating into the thin mountain air. James threw back his shoulders and breathed in frosty gulps.

Rows of gentle hills stretched to the west, giving way to towering mountains standing purple in the distance. In front of James, the trail led down the hill, winding through a narrow valley, spilling out into the mining village of Santa Rita.

He pointed his chin toward the rugged Black Range Mountains. "Sure is pretty."

"Pretty damn cold if you ask me," Trace snorted. "What'd they mine around here, anyway?" He patted his horse's neck then shifted his rear in his saddle.

"Copper, silver, a little gold, I think. Mexican and American miners been coming up here about sixty years." James shook his head. "Damn hard work if you ask me."

James thought about men breaking their backs for just a glimpse of that elusive metal. Men would kill to hold it in their hands.

Uncorking his canteen, Trace took a quick swig, then handed it to his brother. He peered into the grayed sky while James sipped. "Think it'll snow?"

James glanced upward and pulled his coat closer around his body. "Most likely. Already snowed in Pinos Altos twice this winter. Folks say that's unusual." He returned the canteen to Trace.

"It is for me, that's a fact. Don't get snow but never down south." Trace replaced the cork then hung the canteen around the saddle horn then cut his eyes sideways to his brother. "You gonna be all right going back to Santa Rita?"

James took time forming his answer. He'd thought about it on the way over and knew he was a stronger man than two years ago. The past was the past. "Yeah. We've stopped there a couple times on our way to Pinos Altos, but...well, I try not thinking about that beating." He clenched his jaw. "I was such a fool."

Glancing away, Trace wagged his head. "You nearly died."

James cringed at the memories. "Thank God Lila found me when she did."

Half a minute of silence surrounded the brothers.

Trace raised his eyebrows and looked at James. "At least one good thing happened there."

"Like what?"

"You found out you're a better poker player than you thought."

"Yeah, *I* win all the money, then *they* take it." James swatted at Trace's arm. "Don't need you reminding me."

A grin raised a corner of Trace's mouth. He nodded. "We'll stay overnight and never come back. All right?"

"I'm fine. Really. Long as they got good, hot coffee, I'll be even better than fine."

"Don't care if it's good, I'd just settle for *hot* about now." Trace blew on his hands. "Still

got two hours ahead of us."

James gigged his horse and gave a quick nod. "Might make it before dark or snow, whichever comes first."

CHAPTER SIX

ANDREW JACKSON COLTON REWRAPPED THE tourniquet around his upper right arm and winced. The white world in which he lay swirled and twisted with each frosted blink. Pulling one end of the red-stained material with his clenched teeth, he promised himself he'd get out of this alive.

He thought back to days earlier. After losing what he figured was a full day to unconsciousness, he had managed to dig himself out of his chrysalis snowbank. Like an uninitiated butterfly, he had emerged into an illogical world. A horrific nightmare. Problem was, he couldn't fly away like that butterfly.

Everywhere he looked, up and down the narrow valley in the Mogollon Mountain range, corpses littered the rocks and bushes. Miners and prospectors, his friends—even adversaries—murdered, mutilated, scalped. Blood dotted the white landscape reminding him of his ma's red and white polka-dotted dress she wore to fancy doings. Frozen red spots vibrated against the crystalline white.

Days ago. He recalled the bone-chilling war cries, the screams as arrows found targets. Blood. Chaos. Apache materializing out of rocks and trees. No one'd had time to escape or defend himself.

Running.

Scrambling.

Terror.

After the arrow slammed into his arm, Andy remembered succeeding in breaking off only the shaft, the arrowhead planted deep in flesh and muscle.

He didn't pass out from the pain then. Not right then. It took a glancing blow to his head to cause that.

Thoughts back in the present and shaking so hard his teeth chattered, he flapped his arm against his body then pushed himself upright. The energy drained as he found his knees.

Collapsing, his face pushed snow into a tiny drift. *Can't rest...get to the cabin...wood...stay warm...*

A lusty snowflake glided inches from his face then drifted past his exposed right cheek. The flake twirled around his head. More snow blanketed his entire body with its chill.

CHAPTER SEVEN

ALL DAY LONG, THE CLOSER TO SANTA RITA James and Trace rode, the more people they met coming toward them. Families, their wagons packed high, horses and mules struggled up one hill and down the next. Single men, walking, riding, their saddlebags full, flicked warning frowns at the Coltons.

One man held up a hand and stepped into James' path.

"You don't wanna be goin' that way, fella." He jerked a callused thumb over his shoulder. "Best turn right around and hightail it outta here, fast as you can."

Trace leaned down closer to the man's bearded face. "Indians?"

"Cochise. Mangas Coloradas," the man nodded. "Bad hombres. Nobody to mess with."

Studying the man's weathered face, James detected fear with a tinge of defeat. He had to know even though Santa Rita held mainly bad memories. "Anybody still there?"

"Not for long." The man shifted the pack on his shoulders and put one foot in front of the other. "Better git 'fore that crazy mankiller comes after your hair."

James held his brother's gaze. "Can't. Gotta find our brother first."

Shrugged shoulders and a grunt trailed behind the man as he marched south. "Suit yourself. Your funeral."

More wagons and people in the distance. Some running, most at a good clip.

Throat like desert sand, James swallowed hard before speaking. "Should we turn back? I mean, no need three brothers dying." Once the words were spoken, he hated himself for saying them. No way in hell they'd leave Andy out there all alone. What the hell was he thinking? Maybe to save Ma and Pa the agony of losing three-fourths of their sons. Maybe to save Morningstar and Teresa the pain of burying their men. Of Faith and the baby not having a pa.

Apparently, those same thoughts were running through Trace's head as he sat, gazing at the purple hills and then his hands. A few deep breaths brought his shoulders up and then down. He rubbed his eyes then turned them on James.

"If you wanna go back, I won't stop you."

"Not without Andy." James pulled his hat down lower on his forehead and set his heels into the sides of his horse.

* * *

EVEN IN THE late afternoon gray drizzle, Santa Rita didn't look the worse for wear. No black smoke roiling from Apache attacks. No people screaming and running for their lives. No Indians whooping and hollering up and down the streets. In fact, it was quiet. Too damn quiet. Nobody was out and about.

James and Trace rode unmolested down the center of town and pulled up in front of the Glory Hole Hotel, same one James had used for a short time three years previously. After dismounting, the men entered the lobby expecting to find people hurriedly packing and rushing about. As they'd found outside, it was empty.

Trace dinged the bell on the counter expecting a hassled man to come barreling in ready to assign them a room. They waited. Nobody. Trace dinged again. Again nobody.

"Hello? Anybody here?" Trace leaned over the counter then wandered the lobby. James went the other way.

Empty. Deserted.

"What d'you think? Should we get a room or get outta town like the man said?" James leaned on the counter noting the room keys lying helter skelter on top.

Trace shrugged, then swiped his gloved hand across his face. "Feel kinda like a sitting duck in here. But it's a helluva lot warmer than outside." He glanced around the lobby again. "What d'you think?"

"Let's get a room on the bottom floor. Be easier to jump out the window if we have to," James said. "Leave at first light."

Trace selected a lower number key and headed off in search of the corresponding room.

Once they'd located the room and brought in their saddlebags, the brothers led their horses a block down to the stable.

A man met them at the wide barn door. "Horses'll get cold tonight if you don't put a blanket on 'em."

After putting the horses side-by-side in stalls and snugging blankets over their backs, James regarded the mustached man who looked to be Mexican. Much shorter and slimmer than either Trace or James, the man had a determined look in his chestnut-brown eyes.

"This is not a safe place to be," the man said. "Best to leave at dawn."

"That's what we plan to do," Trace said. "How much we owe you?"

"*Nada.* Nothing. Tomorrow, I leave, too." The man shut the stable door against the waning daylight. "My wife will feel better by then and we'll leave."

James shook his hand. "*Vaya con Dios, señor.*"

* * *

STANDING Pony raised his arm and saluted the rising sun. His band of warriors gathered behind him, reflected his actions and sang to the almighty Mother Earth, asking for victory against anyone who wasn't of the People. Through their whoops and songs, they praised the spirits who would protect them during their next foray.

Fervor wound down. The men encircled Standing Pony, waiting for their leader to speak. He met each warrior's gaze.

"My Apache brothers, the time is here. Many Mexicans and their army, Americans and their families, are stealing our land. The land our fathers' fathers hunted on. Land on which we live and die. Our blood, our very souls are one with this earth."

Standing Pony watched the faces of his warriors. He knew they would follow him anywhere—even into death.

"While our mighty leader, Cochise, fights other

enemies, let us defend our land, our people, our very existence against those who would take it from us."

Cheers and chants drowned out further words. While his warriors crowed, Standing Pony's gaze encompassed the land. Mesas and a smaller mountain range rose in the distance. Behind him, the Mogollon Mountains glowed with a mixture of winter sun and miners' blood. Victory for him—his Chiricahua tribe—lay in those mountains.

The miners of that camp had been easy to kill. Too easy. There was nothing to sing, boast or even brag about. Those Americans lay down and died without a struggle. Standing Pony knew the rest of the fighting would not be that easy. Between him and those mesas sat several villages, all waiting to be overrun by "hostiles," as he'd been called.

All right. Call us hostile, I'll show you hostile.

Fist thrust skyward, Standing Pony challenged his warriors. "Today, we ride west. Kill everything in our way. This land will be ours once more."

* * *

DRIFTS of early morning white powder greeted the Colton brothers as they pushed open the hotel doors. Both men stood on the veranda and jammed gloved hands into their coat pockets.

Trace frowned. "Hell! Damn snow. Why couldn't it wait a few more weeks?"

James studied the steel sky. "Socked in pretty good. Might not be able to go at all today." He faced his brother. "What do you say we find breakfast? My stomach's pressing against my backbone."

Trace blew a column of frost. "All right. But, we're leavin' today. Come hell or high water."

"Or ten feet of snow." James planted a gloved hand on Trace's back and nudged him toward a café, which he hoped was open. "It'll be all right, Trace. We'll find him."

CHAPTER EIGHT

LAWRENCE, KANSAS

LUKE COLTON GAVE A FINAL SQUEEZE TO TWO-year-old Adam, wrapped in his arms. "Be a good boy for mama."

"Yes, sir." Adam's words lisped, but Luke knew exactly what his son had whispered.

One more hug, then Luke handed him to Ma standing on the boardwalk. Were those tears in her eyes? Torn. He was so torn about traveling to Mesilla. Here he was, the last of the four brothers to leave. Ma and Pa needed him. And hell, he had his own family, all right here in Lawrence. However, he needed to see his brothers. Have long talks with them. Get out of Kansas for a while. But for how long?

It all depended on Sally. Would she find room in her heart to forgive him? The lying about not riding with Quantrill when, in fact, he'd ridden alongside the feared Confederate Raider for months. Hell, he'd been one of the leading henchmen. The deceit. Never mind the women. Not only was it darn cold outside now, but it was also downright frigid in his house. Only his son and baby daughter were glad to see him.

After the burning of Lawrence in August, Luke vowed to change his thinking. To amend his rowdy ways. He'd become the man he should have been and make his family proud. Especially Ma and Sally. What about Pa? Even rebuilding their house together hadn't shored up the shaky relationship.

So he needed his brothers' help. Their words of wisdom.

"All aboard!" The stagecoach driver hollered at the people gathered on the boardwalk. He leaned over from his perch on the seat and pointed to Luke's tapestry carpetbag. "If that's goin', toss 'er on up here."

Luke's Pa, Joseph, picked up the bag and handed it to Luke. Their eyes met. "Have a good trip, son." He extended a hand.

Luke tossed the bag up to the driver, then shook with Pa, the grip firm. He pulled his coat tight around his chest and buttoned the top. Even with little Adam in her arms, Ma hugged Luke like her life depended on it.

"Take good care of yourself, Luke," Ma whispered. A tear rolled down her cheek. "Give everyone a big hug and kiss for us. Tell them we'll see them all soon. And we love them."

Nodding, Luke turned his attention to beautiful Sally, baby Hannah in his arms. He loved her now more than ever, but probably it was too late. She'd been the one to encourage, no... *insist*, he visit his brothers. He wanted to hold her one more time. Tell her how sorry he was—again—but she kept her distance. An icy distance. Luke leaned in close and kissed his daughter's cheek. At almost one, she sure looked like her ma. Blue-green eyes, blond hair.

"Gotta go!" The driver bellowed down at Luke.

This was it. What he'd lost sleep over for the last several nights. His gaze traveled from face to face, then he stepped up into the coach. It rocked with his weight. Three other passengers, two men and one woman, scooted their feet for him to step over. The door banged shut. His heart rose into his throat.

A "hee haw," a hearty lurch, and they were off. Luke leaned out the window and waved until the coach turned the corner. Finally, he settled back against the hard seat. It would be a long ride—a week at least, if everything went according to schedule.

After cursory introductions with the other passengers and then awkward silence, Luke had plenty of opportunity to think uninterrupted. He reflected on his twenty years of life as the never-ending Kansas plains rushed past. The horses' mile-eating gallop brought him closer and closer to his brothers and to the reunion he envisioned.

Stuck as number three in the order of four boys, he'd always felt odd man out. Six years stood between him and Trace, the oldest of the brood. Might as well be six hundred. Trace liked him, he was sure, but not as much as he liked James. Those two were inseparable, had been as long as he could remember. On the other hand, he and Andy were close, but their relationship didn't come anywhere near to matching the two oldest. What could he do to make Trace sit up and take notice, be as proud of him as he was of James?

James. Luke reflected on the brother less than two years older. What a good time they'd had a few months' ago when James and lovely Morningstar had come to

Kansas. Their long visit had cemented his and James' relationship. They looked alike and thought alike, but by being alike, they'd had their fair share of heated arguments. "Acting the maggot," as grandpa liked to say in his Irish lilt. "Acting the fool," Pa would say. Things hadn't changed since they were boys.

Dusty prairie miles rushed under the stagecoach wheels as Luke thought. He couldn't wait to see Trace and Andy. They hadn't come to Lawrence last summer with James. Trace was sheriff of Mesilla and Andy about to become deputy—now that he'd turned eighteen. Powerful jobs. Had it gone to their heads? Were they swaggering around town showing off their badges and harassing people? No, not his brothers. No doubt they were busy fixing a broken wheel or helping old ladies across the dusty plaza.

Trace was the level-headed, responsible brother, always watching over the younger three like a mother hen over her brood. Would he still be level-headed? He'd been captured by Cochise and held prisoner for two months along with James. Those Apache proved relentless in their efforts to control the brothers. He'd been told whips, knives, ropes, fists and bone-crunching kicks had kept them in line.

One afternoon a couple months' back in Luke's barn, James had revealed his more than seventy scars from Apache captivity and abuse eighteen months before. Were Trace's scars as severe? Did he still wake at night screaming, like James? And what about Andy? He'd been wounded last spring by a Union bullet. Hell. Even little brother had scars.

Luke had scars of his own. He'd survived being shot by Quantrill who accused him of being a turncoat during the burning of Lawrence. While his house had suffered damages, it remained standing, unlike Pa's that James and Pa had rebuilt. But even that trauma paled in comparison to what his brothers had endured. How the hell had his brothers survived? He'd heard stories about Apache treatment, hadn't given it a great deal of thought until he'd learned of his brothers' capture. Would Trace tell stories? Would they be like what James had said?

Removing his hat and running his hand through straight brown hair, Luke gripped the dusty hat brim and wondered what he would have done had *he* been captured by Cochise. The conjured images churned his stomach. Or was that the rocking coach?

Determined to change his thinking, he eyed the woman sitting directly across from him, their knees touching. These Concord coaches afforded little comfort. He'd read somewhere the designers allowed fifteen inches of bench space per person. Thank goodness it was not a full load this trip. There was a little room to spread out.

Her dark eyes and hair, the way she held her head, reminded him of James' wife, Morningstar, who was pretty in an exotic sort of way. Was this woman part Apache like Morningstar? Luke still had trouble under-standing why his brother would marry an Apache after being so severely abused by them. Maybe it was because Star, as the family called her, was from a different tribe and adopted as a baby by a Tucson doctor. Or maybe it was his way of coping with the memories.

Star loved James with all her heart. At least that's what Sally had said. Luke was certain, however, he'd caught her a time or two looking at him in something other than a sister-in-law manner. Her eyes would narrow just a bit. Those lips curled up ever-so-slightly on the ends. Her cheeks blushed a light pink over golden skin. Once he'd heard her giggle when he said her name. Was it playful flirting?

James and Morningstar. Would he get to visit them in Pinos Altos, and spend time at their Buckhorn Saloon? Maybe he'd do a little gold panning in the nearby creek. Plenty of gold had come out of there. Or maybe he'd even head up into the Mogollon mountains James had written about. Remembering Morningstar's face brought a smile to his. Would Trace's wife, Teresa, be as beautiful?

Sally. He'd promised he'd be true to his wife. After all, they'd taken the marriage vow more than two years ago and she had been a good wife. Attentive, understanding, a great cook and even better under the covers, he couldn't complain about her. He was darn lucky, in fact, to have her. So, what the hell was he doing running away?

He again glanced at the woman across from him. Mrs. Santori she'd been introduced as. Traveling with her husband and his brother to Denver. Luke calculated they'd all ride together until reaching Trinidad, Colorado on the Santa Fe Trail. At that point, he would stay on the route turning south to go over Raton Pass and down into Santa Fe, then eventually Mesilla. His companions, however, would change coaches in Trinidad and head north to Denver. So, for the next five or six days, he'd have a real pretty woman to look at.

Prairie swales lulled him into peaceful rest. The late afternoon day turning gray, he closed his eyes against the cool November air.

CHAPTER NINE

MORNINGSTAR PEERED UP AT THE OVERCAST SKY and pulled her woven shawl closer around her slim shoulders. A walk around the plaza then to the post office would be a pleasant distraction from her worry about James. A slight breeze tugged at her skirt. *Please let the men, her man, be all right, be safe and come home soon.*

She thought about Andy, the first time she met him, over a year ago when he'd ridden into Tucson with James. She laughed remembering Andy had asked her for a dinner date and she turned him down in hopes the older brother would ask. It took a few more days and all the courage she knew James could muster.

Strolling down the street, she remembered falling in love with James the moment she saw him. Something about him fascinated her. Here was someone in desperate need of help — to allow him to accept his past abuse by Cochise's tribe, accept the scars he carried, but more importantly, to be able to trust in love again.

Morningstar's eyes darted to the ground then returned to the plaza. James was pretty well mended now. Certainly, he had moments of self-pity and frustration at the way his life changed, but he was better at putting events in perspective now. And his recent visit with his folks in Kansas smoothed rough spots. He was, indeed, much healed.

Morningstar smiled and nodded at two Mexican women walking past, their gray shawls protecting their heads from winter's chill. The bundled women smiled back. Her thoughts returned to James. If he could just be the man, the lover he wanted to be, maybe the torment would end. Then they'd have children. Lots of children. But what *was* the problem? Was she not woman enough? She shook her head. No, James had assured her it wasn't her. It was him. But there was something else. Or was it some*one* else?

The boardwalk creaked as Morningstar stepped up on it. Her eyes cast right and left before locating the post office tucked in the back of the mercantile on a side street. Once inside, she smiled at the warmth. The small stove, perched in one corner, radiated a welcome heat.

"What can I do for you, young lady?" The silver-haired man behind the wide counter produced a sincere grin, two dark spaces in front where teeth normally stood.

"I'm Morningstar Colton—Teresa Colton's sister-in-law. She's not feeling well today and asked me to pick up the mail."

The postmaster reached over and shook her hand. "Sheriff Colton's kin? Well, pleased to meet you. I'm Abraham Kinnear. Just call me Abe." He leaned closer. "So, Mrs. Colton's under the weather, eh? I hear she's expecting another young 'un."

Morningstar nodded, annoyed by his curiosity, but

willing to be polite. "Yes, that's right. She'll be fine. But chasing a baby is mighty tiring."

"Sure is." Abe stared out the window, half a grin growing on his face. "I 'member when Annabelle and me first started our family. Two little ones at once. Boy, howdy, they was a hand full. Then the Lord blessed us with three more, one right after another." A twinkle appeared in both eyes. "Wife made me sleep in the barn for two straight years after the last one was born."

Morningstar couldn't help but laugh. She was sure that wasn't true, but after five children, the poor woman was probably exhausted.

"You got kids, Mrs. Colton?" Abe picked up a letter and placed it on a stack of envelopes at the end of the counter.

Morningstar forced a tight grin and shook her head. "Not yet. James and I aren't ready for children. We've recently moved up to Pinos Altos and he's opened a saloon. A family will be next, I'm sure."

Abe turned his back and riffled through a stack of letters. He spoke into the envelopes, words softened by the adobe walls. "Don't mean to pry, but being as I'm the postmaster, I hear all sorts a interestin' things about people. Ah... here they are."

Gripping three letters, Abe held them up. "James' wife you say?"

Morningstar nodded and extended her hand to accept the mail.

Letters still in hand, the postman again gazed out the window as if staring into memories. "I 'member when your husband first got back from Cochise's camp. Broken man he was. Everyone figured him and his brother gone for good. But when they come ridin' into town with their friends, your husband appeared more dead than alive."

His shoulders rose as he wagged his head. "Looked 'xactly like a close-to-dead Injun."

Morningstar stared out the same window.

After a beat, Abe continued. "'Course he warn't no Injun. Yup. Pretty banged up he was. Sheriff Colton, too. But that James... bumps, bruises, and whip cuts. Run head to toe. Them Apache sure worked him over. Ain't never seen nothin' like it... and don't never hope to again." Abe's eyebrows reached for his hairline. "Course Lila runnin' off didn't help his disposition any. We all thought he'd drink himself to death before he joined the army."

Abe spun and faced her, snapping back to the present. "Lordy, Mrs. Colton. My mouth. Sometimes just runs away with me. I apologize."

Morningstar's heart beat a little faster. Here was someone else who'd known James before. Abe confirmed everything she'd heard. Could it have been Lila who caused her husband's problems? Was *Lila* the someone else?

"No apology necessary Mr. Kinnear," Morningstar's words sounded padded, as if enveloped in cotton. "I know he had a rough time."

A second study of the postmaster revealed no new information, although he looked as if he'd be happy to sit and talk all morning. Knowing her hands trembled, she tucked them into her skirt pockets. Slow breaths calmed her.

She glanced down at the mail still clutched in Mr. Kinnear's hand. Remembering the real reason for her errand, she felt around in the pocket and extracted an envelope. "Almost forgot. I'd like to mail this, please."

Mr. Kinnear peered at the address. "Tucson, eh?"

Irked at this man's inquisitiveness, bordering on

downright nosiness, Morningstar brought her shoulders back. "My parents. My pa's the town doctor." She nodded. "Now I do need to get back to Missus Colton."

"Of course." Abe handed her the letters. "Hope to see you again, Mrs. Colton, and tell the other Mrs. Colton I hope she gets to feelin' better real soon." He ran his hand through his hair and chuckled. "Kinda confusin' with two Mrs. Coltons."

"Thank you, I'll give her your message. Good day." Morningstar stepped into the chilly morning air and scanned the return address of the three letters. One caught her eye. Luke Colton. Third brother in line of the Colton dynasty. Father of two children. *Why did he and Trace have kids and James doesn't?* She gripped the letters until her fingers turned white. *Andy probably has some, too.* Scolding herself for being bitter, she realized that wasn't a nice thing to think about unmarried Andy. He was more responsible than that.

By the time she reached Teresa's house, Morningstar had worked herself up into something close to anger. She blamed Cochise, Butterfield Stage Lines, Lila, even Trace for James' inability to produce children. What would happen if they could *never* have a family? Would she stay with James no matter what? And what if she found someone who could...? Luke, for example. Since the brothers looked alike, the baby undoubtedly would look like James. She pushed that thought out of her mind as she opened the door and stepped into the warmth of the house.

"Anything interesting, Star?" Teresa called from the kitchen.

Morningstar swallowed then answered. "Mr. Kinnear is certainly a busy body." She pulled off her shawl, draped it over the back of the rocking chair, shoved more thoughts of Luke farther away, and fought to subdue her bad mood and lusty ideas. "That postmaster ought to be with Pinkerton instead of the post office."

A soft chuckle sailed out of the next room followed by a child's laugh. "He sure should. We get any mail?"

Morningstar clutched the letters and followed the giggles into the kitchen. Relaxing, she ruffled Faith's hair. Seated in a highchair, the baby munched on a fresh tortilla. Crumbs decorated the kitchen floor, the baby's lap, and her face. Morningstar brushed white flakes out of Faith's hair.

"Trace got a letter from Luke. Sorry, I peeked." She offered the short stack to Teresa who held up her floury hands.

"Would you open it and read?" Teresa glanced at the bowl of flour and water waiting on the counter. "He's your brother-in-law, too. It's all right. Plus, you've met him. I haven't." She plunged her hands into the doughy mess.

Morningstar opened the letter and read out loud.

Dear Trace and Teresa,

Ma and Pa send you their love and wish they could hold little Faith. They're hoping to visit you next year if you can't get home first. The farm is doing quite well which is the reason for this letter. I have much to talk about, too much for this missive. Therefore, if you have no objections, I will be coming for a visit the twenty-ninth of November.

I wanted to be there for Andy's birthday, November first, but affairs at home wouldn't permit travel then. I will be coming alone, as Sally will stay at home with the children who are still too young to travel such a distance.

Until then.

-Luke

Teresa stopped kneading and looked at Morningstar. "Visit, huh? Trace'll love that."

"The twenty-ninth." Morningstar folded the letter and replaced it into the envelope. "That's next week."

"Correction. Four days from now. We'll never be able to get word to him that Trace isn't here."

Morningstar tapped the letter against her palm, lusty thoughts returning. "Guess we'll have to entertain him until the men return." A wide smile grew. "Just think, Teresa, soon as they find Andy, all four brothers will be reunited." Images of Luke paraded through her head. What were the chances he'd be coming now? Maybe it was fate.

CHAPTER TEN

"WE CAN'T WAIT ANY LONGER, JAMES. WE NEED to get goin' now." Trace checked his horse's cinch and tightened one more notch. His gloved hand ran down the animal's warm neck as he led him out of the Santa Rita stable and into the biting mountain air. Trace patted his favorite horse, swung up into the saddle, and then eyed his brother emerging from the barn. "Snow or no snow, Andy's in trouble. You comin' or stayin'?"

"Now that's a damn fool thing to be asking." James mounted his horse and reined him left down the street. "You can't go alone. First, you'd get lost half a mile out of town, and second, I don't want just anybody breaking into my house, sleeping in my bed." He raised his voice. "Besides, the fine residents of Pinos Altos just might mistake you for somebody what left home in such a hurry, he forgot to take his right name with him. Hell, Trace, they're liable to take a potshot at you."

Trace trotted ahead then slowed. He eyed his brother now riding beside him. "You oughta use your breath for breathin', 'stead of mixin' it with tongue oil."

Shrugging, James tossed a wide smile at his brother.

At the outskirts of Santa Rita, the Colton brothers spurred their horses into a gallop. Snowdrifts kept the strides short, but the strong animals managed to plow through.

However, within a couple of hours, the horses' heads drooped, their breathing and gait labored. Slowed through the growing drifts and ice patches, the horses were forced to pick their way toward Pinos Altos.

Surrounded by aspens and steep hills, James eyed a stand of towering Ponderosa pines. Sleet pellets stung his face as he stared into the sky. "Damn snow! Way it's picking up, it's gonna be full dark before we get to town." He grumbled into his coat and stuck one hand under his armpit.

Trace leaned over and ran his hand down his horse's neck. He gave a quick pat. "We're gonna have to rest these horses soon. Don't know about you, but I'm ready for grub. I'm starving." Snow coated Trace's hat. "You bring extra jerky?"

"Is that all you think about? Your stomach? Hell, nothin' but cold's in my gut. No room for hunger. But we're closing in on Pinos Altos. Another couple hours and we'll be in my house, nice and warm, hot food in our bellies." James used his chin to point. "Jerky's in the saddlebag."

"Ayyeee!"

Apache erupted from every crack and crevice, every bush and tree. War cries, threats, and whooping reverberated throughout the hills and, like enraged hornets, swarmed toward the Colton brothers. An arrow whistled past Trace's head.

"Head for those boulders!" Trace spurred his horse

toward an outcropping farther north. James spotted the rocks and urged his horse into a gallop.

As he kept riding, James glanced left then right. Three different Apache mobs rode toward them, their mounts at full-out gallops. His stomach spun. Breaths spurted. Images of his captivity by Cochise flashed through his mind. But he vowed, *not this time.*

Trace leaned over his horse's neck as he rode and yelled at James. "Follow the trail left. Turn here!" Left rein in hand, he yanked straight down.

Turn too sharp and ice too slippery, Trace's horse slid. Both rider and animal spun then crashed against a snow-covered boulder. They hit the ground with an earth-shaking *whump.* Trace strained against the eight-hundred-pound horse flailing on top of him, but his leg remained pinned.

Alongside now, James jumped from his horse and rushed to his dazed brother, the face paling with each labored breath. "All right?" He knelt by Trace, scooped his shoulders off the ground and pulled.

Under Apache screams, Trace groaned and struggled to dislodge his leg. He pushed against James and the frozen ground, but his horse's thrashing kept his body pegged. Trace mumbled a string of oaths and moans. He twisted.

"Careful. Leg could be broken." James glanced at two Apache lurking behind a bush. He aimed his Colt and fired. One Indian clutched his chest and fell. The acrid odor of gunpowder sank with the heavy snowflakes.

"Get me out." Trace grimaced as his leg scraped between the saddle and ice-encrusted earth.

Frantic to release his brother, James adjusted his hold on Trace, yanked and wrenched. Seconds dragged until one powerful pull extracted Trace. Hoisting him to his feet, James steered his brother past the fallen horse, an arrow now at full attention in its neck. He shoved Trace onto the one remaining mare.

James swung up behind, wishing Trace's horse hadn't been too hurt to carry him. Riding two-up was hard on horses. He took a quick breath and another glance at the Indians. Close enough to identify the red and blue war paint striped across faces, James recognized the markings of Cochise's tribe. He spurred harder than he knew he should, pushing his horse into a faster gallop.

Clouds, snow, ice crystals assaulted his very soul. Blinding white boulders and trees swirled in front of James. Memories swam.

James leaned forward into his brother's ear. "If they capture me—"

"What?" Trace massaged his leg and gripped the saddle horn.

"If I'm taken prisoner, promise you'll kill me. Right then."

"They won't—"

"*Promise* me. On grandpa's grave, Trace. *Swear it.*" James' arms around his brother tightened as he guided his horse along the snow-packed road hidden behind a stand of Ponderosa pines.

Mouth opening then closing, Trace nodded. "I promise, but only if you do the same for me." He shouted above the war cries. "You've got my word."

"It's a helluva thing to have to pledge, brother." James leaned forward and urged the horse to outrun those Apache. "You got mine, too."

The fact they were riding double and that the Indians' horses carried only one rider and with no saddle, James knew they had no chance of outrunning the enemy. The best he could hope for would be taking out a few of the warriors before both he and his brother were killed. Or worse. Captured.

Boulders, trees, and frozen bushes whipped past as they followed their tracks back toward Santa Rita. James felt his horse slip coming into the draw. The narrow trail up the opposite steep side glistened with ice. The horse couldn't make it up the other bank, certainly not with two men on her back.

Chancing a quick look behind him, James reined to the right as they reached the bottom of the gully. Horse plowing through swollen snowdrifts, James led her between boulders.

Trace glanced around behind his brother. "We're losing 'em. 'Bout half are heading on south."

Knot in his throat, James managed to speak over it. "Maybe they're circling around." He shook his head. "We're not gonna outrun 'em. Best get to that outcropping and take a stand."

James felt his older brother's chest heave. "How you doin', Trace?"

"Hurts like hell!"

Up ahead to his left, James spotted a jumble of boulders. A rock fort. Some place to hole up and pray for reinforcements.

Arrows flew from every direction, plinking into trees and snow. Bone-chilling war cries pierced the air. James spurred the horse up the narrow draw. Frozen junipers and pines flanked boulders perched along the edge of the arroyo. Over his shoulder, James counted just a handful of warriors on their heels. *Where are the others?* His gaze swung the other way. *Takes only one arrow to kill.*

James drew in a quick breath and urged his horse farther up the draw.

"Here. Stop." Trace's husky words cut through James' panic. "Over by those rocks." He waved toward boulders, the fort on his left.

James tugged on the reins, felt his horse slide across ice but somehow manage to stay upright. The moment his feet touched ground, James slid on ice also, but muscled his brother off the horse and nudged Trace forward. "Can you walk?"

A nod and grimace. James pushed aside branches of a low-hanging pine, snow weighing down the limbs until they touched ground. The branches scraped discordant designs into the white powder. Trace clambered up the rocky slope behind his brother.

James pointed up and to his right. "Maybe those damn Apache'll have as hard a time navigating as we do." White blinding him, he felt for hand and foot holds as he yanked Trace up with him.

Scrambling under branches then rolling through a snowdrift, James shoved his brother into the safety of two boulders leaning together. The A-frame provided sufficient cover but limited visibility. From this vantage point, his view was clear up and down the draw. But, completely blind from behind and above, James prayed the Apache would give in and just go home.

Home. His home. If Indians were this far south, they had already rampaged through Pinos Altos. All his friends, the miners, the families would be scattered, possibly even dead.

He pushed those thoughts to one side, checked his gun and thanked Pa he'd tucked away extra powder and caps in his shirt. Dry and handy just in case. His pa had taught him well. James made a mental note to thank Pa as soon as he got back. He chilled. *If* he got back.

James glanced at his brother's ashen face. Maybe the leg wasn't broken after all. He'd walked on it.

An arrow zipped past. James ducked. Two gunshots echoed down the narrow ravine. He frowned. "Those Apache must've got rifles from the miners. Don't remember Cochise having them before."

"Maybe stolen from the Army." Trace aimed his Colt and fired. An Apache clutched his head, stumbled and fell. "I don't plan on getting closer to find out."

James watched a party of Chiricahuas march up the gully to his right. They didn't bother hiding. He reloaded with practiced precision then jabbed his brother's shoulder and pointed.

Trace finished tamping the powder and glanced left. "Uh oh." He jerked his head toward another Apache band stalking up the snowy ravine. He twisted left then right. A few Indians perched on their horses, waiting for the final kill. "We're surrounded, James. Gotta make a run for it."

James spun around and faced his brother. "Run? Run where? Either way they've got us."

Trace studied the rocks behind them. "Up. Maybe one of us can make it." He eyed his brother. "You're in better shape than me. You go. Send help if you can."

An arrow ricocheted off a rock inches from James' face. He flinched. "We go together or not at all. Not leaving you here." James squeezed the trigger and watched a piece of rock shatter over a warrior's head.

"One of us should live, James. It's gotta be you." Trace yanked at his brother's coat. "Now go!"

Planting his foot against Trace's strength, James

gripped his brother's arm. "I said 'no'." He fought for air and stared into eyes he knew so well.

With a resigned sigh, Trace reloaded his gun. "All right."

"They got us." James stared at his gun as he tamped powder into the chamber. He examined the weapon end to end. Air filled his lungs as his shoulders straightened. "We made a pact. Can't outrun or outshoot those Indian. It's... time."

Trace blinked at James.

James narrowed his eyes. "You loaded?" He hardened his heart. No time for regrets and second thoughts. The gun grew icy then burning hot in his hand. "I won't be captured again."

Eyes filling with moisture, James shoved the gun barrel against his brother's head.

"Wait!" Trace pushed it away. "I haven't forgotten. Just ain't time yet." He eyed his brother, then aimed at an Indian, pulled the trigger. The brave crumpled. Tossing another quick glance at his brother, he reloaded. "Just a bit longer."

"They're not taking me alive!"

"I know." Trace fired again. "I agree."

Apache close enough James could easily make out features, his grip on his weapon tightened. Was his brother right? If they killed Trace before he could carry out his promise, James would have to kill himself. A bullet through the heart would be quickest. Less chance of missing.

Sheltered by a boulder at the lip of the triangle, James hunkered down. Indians now on top of them, James closed his eyes and wiped the dripping sweat. War cries bombarded his senses. Was that Trace screaming behind him? Had he been hit?

James glanced left and spotted Trace's mouth set in a tight line under his resolute stare. A look of determination on his brother's face filled James with renewed confidence.

"*Ándale, muchachos!*"

Confusion collided with relief. Not Apache orders. Sounded Spanish. James peered out of the overhang and into a sea of ice. Nothing but fleeing Apache scattering to the winds. The ones on foot bolted for their horses and headed for the forest.

More unfamiliar screeches, hollers, and yells. James searched the gulch for the source. Bullets rained from above. Apache melted into the snow-packed terrain. Ice patches shattered and lead dots peppered the snowbanks.

"*Basta, cabrons! Vayase!*"

James furrowed his forehead and studied his brother. While Indians were known to speak Spanish, this didn't sound like Apache. More like the real thing.

Wiping his forehead with his free arm, James nudged his brother. Heavy snowflakes blanketed the ground as James dared to peer out into the frozen forest. "What d'you think?"

"We're still alive." Trace's eyes swept the boulders.

"Who do you suppose they are?" James craned his neck to catch a view of the men above him.

"Army of Mexico, *gringo.*"

James frowned at Trace. Could it be? The Colton brothers eased out for a better view and stared up into a cavernous rifle barrel.

Behind the barrel stood a complement of soldiers. One man, poised next to the rifleman, met James' gaze and gave a sharp nod. James noted the brown-green of the Federale's uniform, silver medals decorating the front of his jacket. Black hair hung below his hat, a full, neatly trimmed black mustache shadowed lips curling up on one side.

The man's shiny eyes matched his hair. James lowered his gun, raised his other hand above his head and watched his brother do the same. The cannon-sized barrel of the .50 caliber Henry rifle loomed inches from his face.

Oozing out from every crevice, men looking much like this Mexican filled the spaces between rocks. Trace gazed from man to man. James eyed a young soldier on his left.

"Step out into the light, *señors*, where I can see you. Easy, easy." The man plucked the weapons from James and Trace then jammed the guns into his belt under his coat. "Keep your hands up."

James eased down to the bottom of the ravine and helped Trace hobble to a rock and sit. "My brother's leg is injured, might be broken. He can't stand."

"*Qué lastima.*" The man wagged his weapon at the brothers. "You were at a distinct disadvantage, *señors*. Two *gringos*—too many Apache to count. If it had not been for our army, you would be full of arrows by now." He turned to the other men. "*¿Qué no?*"

The soldiers looked at each other, heads bobbed. "*Sí, mi capitán.*"

A solemn voice from behind the leader spoke out. "Shoot them now? Or tie them up and use for target practice?"

Chuckles, guffaws and suggested alternatives erupted from the uniformed men.

"Do you need practice, Carlos?" The leader grunted to a man on his right then turned to his lieutenant. "*¿Qué piensas, Segundo?*"

Another Mexican soldier, taller and leaner than the captain, stepped next to him. "I think, *Capitán*, with the *Indios*, we have had plenty of practice for today. Besides," he licked his cracked lips. "Your soldiers here, well, they can shoot flies off whores at fifty paces."

James swallowed hard.

Eyes narrowing, the soldier stared at James and raised his pistol. "I say shoot them now."

Rifles and pistols clicked ready.

James stole a quick glance at his brother's pasty white face. Hands itching for his seized gun, he studied the man identified as the commander. Hard lines etched the weathered face, the body stood lean and disciplined.

Trace rubbed his leg and stared up at the captain. "No need to shoot us. We're just passing through."

The leader eyed the Colton boys then turned to the soldier next to him. "How many bullets to kill these *gringos, Segundo? Cinco, siete?*"

"No, *Capitán*. Only two. One for each of them." He sighted his cocked revolver at James. "Between the eyes."

The leader nodded. "*Es verdad.*" Rifle trained on Trace, he glanced at his second in command. "You're an excellent marksman, *Segundo*. You rarely miss—except that one time." He shuddered. "What a mess you made of that *hombre*."

The leader winced as the other soldiers shook their heads. Two held their stomachs while the rest grimaced. *Segundo's* eyes cast downward as he nodded.

A grin crawled across the commander's wind-reddened cheeks.

Long seconds dragged by before the Federale commander lowered his rifle and held up a hand. "No need wasting good bullets. Put away your weapons, *hombres*. The *Indios* are gone for now." He jerked his head toward the Colton brothers. "These *juetos* are harmless."

James let out a stream of frosted air. Shivering from cold and nerves, and now that he'd survived Apache and what appeared to be the Mexican army, the next task was to get his brother back into town, to a doctor who could fix his leg.

Snow, frigid sheets of white, urged into frenzy by gusty air, battered the men.

"*Señor*...Captain?" James unbuttoned his coat and draped it around Trace's shoulders.

"*¿Sí?* Captain José Mendoza, Army of Mexico." No hand was extended.

"Captain Mendoza, I gotta get my brother to a doctor right away. If you're the Mexican army, either kill us, arrest us, or let us go."

James' request prompted long, riotous laughter from every soldier. A few thumped each other on the back. One leaned against a rock and held his side.

The captain, cradling his weapon, slapped James' shoulder. "*Gringo*, if we'd meant to kill you..." he cocked his head toward his men, "we'd let the Apache do it."

The soldiers chortled and nodded. A few elbowed each other and grinned.

James trembled. Memories. He pushed them back into the shadows of his past. "Thanks for stepping in when you did, *señor*. Your timing couldn't be better."

"*Sí*, for that I agree with you. You both are free to go. Here are your weapons." Mendoza extracted the guns from his waistband and returned their revolvers.

"*Gracias*." He shoved the .45 back into its holster, its weight familiar on his hip. The Colt's weight relaxed him a bit.

"Thank you also." Trace held out his hand and accepted the Mexican's gloved hand.

"*De nada*. We are headed for Santa Rita. I understand a doctor is there." The captain turned his back on Trace, spoke over his shoulder. "You can ride with us if you wish." He pointed up toward the top of the ravine. "*Vamanos, muchachos*."

CHAPTER ELEVEN

ANDY GRABBED FOR HIS HEAD. THE BRASS BAND marching through it thumped and thundered, indistinguishable noises turning into a cacophony of mismatched screeches. Prying one eye open, he slammed the lid shut and grimaced at the light assaulting his face. Soft, pathetic moans escaped his lips.

"Mornin'." A voice from obscurity sung deep, melodic tones. They wafted through the stillness. A soft chuckle followed.

A hand slid under Andy's throbbing head and cradled it. Rough metal rubbed against his bottom lip.

"Sip of water'll get dem eyes open."

Something wet dribbled down Andy's chin. He tried opening his mouth. Nothing but pain. His lips moved but his jaws held tight. Roaring ache stretched across his face, even into his ears. Now desperate for water, he clutched at the receding canteen. "Ummbbm…"

"That's 'nuff for now. Best not drink too much all to once."

"Ummmbbb..." Andy struggled for words, one arm flailing for the water.

"Ain't gonna get much said. That face of yours don't look too good. All streaky black and blue." The man cocked his head. "Jaw's probably broke."

From under half-raised lids, Andy stared into an ebony face offset with yellow eyes. Coal black irises glistened. After several blinks, the face took form inch by inch. Thick, curly hair perched on top a lean face, weathered, but not ancient. Crinkles gathered around the eyes. A broad, flat nose pointed down toward lips now rising on either end. The rounded chin sported a sparse beard, one which hadn't seen a razor in weeks.

"Name's Dawson." The face, now connected with a body, sat on Andy's cot, the canvas sagging close to the plank flooring.

Andy squeezed his eyes shut and rubbed his throbbing temples with his left hand. No matter how hard he tried, his entire right arm refused to move.

"Dug that arrowhead outta your arm. In deep. Thought that cussed critter'd never let go."

Andy heard most of the words, felt the man's body next to him, a hand on his forehead. *Just like Ma when I was sick.* Forcing his eyes to once more open, he stared at the face inches from his.

"Damnation." Dawson wagged his head. "Your fever's high 'nuff t'heat this here cabin all by itself. Don't need no firewood."

He patted Andy's bare shoulder, then held the canteen just out of Andy's reach. "You'll get strength back soon enough. Then you can work like the rest of us." Dawson frowned into Andy's face. "Yeah, work and sweat, sweat and work. They say that's all we good for, just like mules." He snorted. "We'll show 'em different."

Andy waved his left hand until the canteen swung in close enough to snag. He gulped the icy water like he was on fire. Andy drank until the black man again tugged the canteen out of his grasp. He nodded a thanks, lay back and regarded the man now standing over him.

Dawson's eyes swept up and down Andy's body. "You're a strong one all right. You'll do just fine." He jerked his thumb over his shoulder. "Soup's 'bout ready. Want some?" Dawson met Andy's stare. "What's wrong?" His eyes narrowed into cold slits. "Ain't never seen a man of color before?"

Surprised by this man's challenge, Andy shook his head then nodded. Sure, he'd seen plenty. He and James had spent time playing poker with Buffalo Soldiers when they were in the Army over in Tucson. If memory served, he'd lost close to two weeks' pay to one very large, very black soldier.

The beefy aroma of stew caught his attention and rumbled his stomach. Extending his left arm, he held out his hand to shake. Andy's lips warped into a half smile. Words proved difficult to form. Not only was his head still throbbing, but his swollen lips and stiff jaw made speaking close to impossible. He worked his jaw and mouth around until he thought he could make sense, then managed to put sound with it. "Andy."

Dawson gripped the extended hand. "Nice meetin' you, Andy. My cookin' 'ain't t'best, but it's all we got. Me and the jerky hid while them A-pach' was busy. That dried old meat makes right tasty soup. I'll get ya some."

Managing a couple of spoonfuls before exhaustion took over, Andy lay back. His entire body relaxed. Fighting heavy eyes, he set the bowl on the floor knowing he should eat all, but his stomach sent signals he'd had enough for now. His eyes closed.

Fire in his arm. Andy's eyes shot open. He winced. While the pounding in his head had lessened, jolts of pain shot from his shoulder all the way down to his hand. He lifted the red-stained material encasing his upper arm and stared at the jagged wound, black stitches lacing the swollen skin together. Eyes trying to focus, he searched the tiny room for the man who'd saved him. The room stood empty except for Andy and his throbbing arm.

The cabin door squeaked open. A blast of frozen air exploded into the room. Behind that, in stepped Dawson, arms loaded with sticks. Shoving the door shut with his foot, he shot a glance at Andy.

"Damn! Colder than a witch's behind." Dawson looked at Andy as he laid the wood side by side. Neatly stacked from largest on the bottom to smallest on top, the pile would last several days. "Ain't used to this kinda cold. This here Mogollon's colder'n anywhere I been. Back where I come from, snows only onst in a while. Every other year if we be lucky."

Elbow taking his weight, Andy watched the man who'd saved his life methodically break smaller sticks into ten-inch lengths then lay them into the tiny fire. The room stifling, Andy kicked off the wool blanket covering him.

Sweat plastered his heavy cotton pants to his legs. Andy knew he'd pass out from the heat if he didn't get some cool air. Now. Swinging his feet over the side of the cot and planting them on the floor, Andy pushed up the rest of his body.

A roughly hewn sawbuck table, the stack of firewood, and Dawson tilted as Andy tried to make sense of his world.

Long seconds passed before objects stayed in place.

Then gathering every ounce of energy available, Andy pushed off from the cot and stood. He aimed his pointed finger toward the door and stumbled across the room.

Icy air assaulted his lungs and shirtless body as he lurched into the clear blue day. All around him, snow whitewashed the landscape. Rough boulders smoothed under the crystalline canopy. Layers of ice glistened on top of the stream curling down the valley.

Andy gulped gallons of cold air until he could focus on his world. Head clearing, he noticed a particularly odd-shaped snowbank. Curious, he limped around to the other side. An arm protruded from the white.

Blood-curdling screams. Chaos.

Death.

Images of terror flooded his memory.

Shivering, he plowed through a knee-deep snowdrift and squatted down by the arm. He swept off snow and ice until most of the man was visible.

Andy hung his head.

This was someone who had told him only a few days before he would be leaving soon, richer than when he arrived. A family man. His kids could have shoes now, he'd said. But instead, there he lay—frozen in agony.

CHAPTER TWELVE

"IF WE RIDE FAST, TRACE, WE CAN CATCH UP with those Mexicans." James pointed south. "We'll be safer going back to Santa Rita."

"Already told you, just like I told that Mexican captain, I'm not going back to Santa Rita for no damn doctor. Leg's feelin' better. It ain't broken." Trace tugged on his boot and stared down at his brother kneeling beside him.

Ripping his snow-covered hat from his head, James smacked it against the rock his brother perched on. "Damn! If you're not the most hardheaded man I know. We're two, maybe three hours from Santa Rita. We can get you checked out, find a good horse, hot food and a warm place to sleep tonight."

"Sounds inviting, doesn't it?" Trace removed James' coat and tossed the warmth to him. "You go right ahead there, little brother. But I'm heading on up to Pinos Altos then Mogollon."

"We can go tomorrow. Weather'll be better."

Trace glared at James. "Those hours could mean the

difference between Andy living and dying. Now, I'm not willing to take the chance we could've saved him if we'd kept going." He shifted his glare to the icy sky and dropped his voice. "Dammit, James. I can't let Andy die."

"Might not be up to us, Trace. I just don't want us freezing to death—or worse." James lowered his voice to a whisper. "Andy may already be dead."

"Already had those thoughts." Trace pushed off from the rock and balanced on one leg as he tried his weight on the other.

Snow swirled. James gripped Trace's arm and shook his head at his horse. "She can't carry two very far. With this snow and ice, we'll be lucky if she gets five miles."

"Only need ten more after that." Trace steadied himself against his brother's shoulder and searched up and down the gully. Trees and boulders blended into a whirl of white cotton. "Get the gear off my horse. I'm gonna see if I can wrangle one of these Indian paints they left behind. I know I can ride him. At least that's one thing I learned living with Cochise."

James tugged at his brother's coat sleeve. "Stay put. I'll go get the horse and the gear. No need you walking more'n you have to." He glanced into his brother's hard-ened face. "Still say we go back to Santa Rita." Trace's narrowing eyes dulled with pain, but his lips remained set in a tight line. The same tight line that always signaled—*discussion over*.

* * *

JAMES' eyes snapped open. A deep, throaty growl rattled to his left. Mind groggy, he fought to identify the sound —or even where he was. Another growl—deep, more menacing. Close.

He lurched bolt upright, unable to see anything in the freezing darkness. James reached for the Hawken rifle always nestled beside him, but instead, grabbed a handful of his brother's leg. Relieved, but feeling a bit silly, he realized where he was. Inside. Home. Trace, deep asleep at last, snored next to him. Filling his lungs then letting out a frosted breath, James shivered harder.

James eased back down. He cursed the roaring fire they'd built in the fireplace when they'd laid down. It must've gone out in the night. The wool blanket pulled up around his neck warmed him, then noticing his frozen nose, James hid his entire face under the covers. Squeezing his eyes shut, knowing he had to get as much sleep as possible, he willed himself to sleep. He twisted onto his side, but Trace's heavy breathing intermingled with deep snoring kept him awake. His eyes closed then opened. He forced them shut.

Sleep, that elusive commodity, just out of reach, tantalized and toyed with his consciousness. Was he asleep and dreaming or awake and wishing he was sleeping?

Lying there deciding which it was, his thoughts turned to hours earlier. He and Trace, riding into Pinos Altos well after dark, had followed small bonfires lighting a few houses along the road. Several families huddled around the flames and nodded as the Coltons rode past. James recognized most of them and waved. Stomach tightening, he dreaded what he would find when he reached his house.

Much to his surprise, his home was intact. Indians had ransacked the place, but it was still in one piece, nothing even burned. He and Trace had righted the bed, replaced the mattress and found enough blankets to settle down for a much-deserved night's rest. They'd agreed to check on the saloon the next day.

James watched the graying bedroom take form as his brother mumbled something and sat up.

Trace ran his hand through his tangled hair, words now developing into complete thoughts. "Knew if we waited long enough, hell'd freeze over." He rubbed his eyes and peered at James. "Just didn't think it'd be this soon." He yawned.

James thumped his brother's leg careful not to thump too hard. "Think you can hobble well enough to help me find some wood? A fire'll take the chill off. Might even cook breakfast before we go."

A roaring blaze in the fireplace warmed the men's bodies as well as their dispositions. Life looked a bit more inviting after filling their stomachs with bread and jerky and toasting their backsides near the fire.

Trace extinguished the flames while James rummaged through the kitchen, finding a single can of beans, two of peaches and a hardtack loaf.

"Look at this." James stood at the kitchen door and held up a can retrieved from under the table. "Those damn Apache broke all the jars, opened all the cans and took the rest of the food. Hope they choke on it."

Spilled flour, sugar and coffee spread over the floor as if the Apache had used them for paints. The house—their canvas. Swirls of coffee led into the bedroom. Scattered across the living room lay sharp pieces of glass intermingled with green beans, like tiny trees, victims of overzealous woodcutters.

Trace nodded and joined his brother in the kitchen. "I'm just thankful you and Morningstar left when you did." He lowered his voice. "Don't know what I would've done if you and Star—"

"It didn't, so don't think like that." James squeezed his brother's shoulder and handed the can to Trace. "After we check on the saloon, it's only a day and a half up to Mogollon."

Trace rubbed his leg and looked down at the broken dishes littering the kitchen.

James gripped both of his brother's shoulders. "Trace? Look at me." He waited for eye contact. "I know what you're thinking and you're wrong. You are *not* responsible for Andy gone missing. It's not your fault the Apache attacked."

Clouds of vapor hung between the brothers.

James gave the shoulders a hardy shake. "I'm serious as hell. There's nothing you could've done *then*. The important thing is you're doing something *now*." James knew he had Trace's full attention. "And what you're doing is right—you're being the best big brother anybody could ask for."

Trace looked away. "This gonna be one of those *female* talks? You know...all mushy?"

"Hell no," James said. "Nothing gal 'bout me." He puckered up to spit on the floor, but what would Star say? Instead, he stuck out his chest and swaggered across the room.

Laughing, Trace stuffed the last can into the canvas possibles sack and tied the string around it. "Got any more bullets?" He shook a box of cartridges. Silence.

"Damn! Looks like they took those, too," James said. "We'll stop by the general store. Maybe Harvey's got extras." He picked up his rifle and checked the chambers. Both loaded. "Ready?"

"Let's go." Trace limped ahead of his brother. Buttoning his coat and pulling his hat lower, he pushed open the door. Biting, blustery wind slammed it shut.

Reflexes on high alert, he managed to jerk his foot inches away before being crushed.

Shoulder jammed against the door, James shoved it open.

"Dammit, anyway!" Trace rammed his muscled body into the storm and hobbled to his horse. "What the hell's up with this weather? Apache cause that, too?"

James tied the leather sack to his saddle horn then mounted his horse. Poor thing was as cold as he was. Although both horses had been in a barn all night with a blanket over their backs, still, they were chilled.

Kicking his reluctant dun into a walk, James rode beside his older brother and thought about what life would be like without Andy. There'd always been four brothers, at least for nineteen years. What would it be like with only three?

CHAPTER THIRTEEN

TERESA COLTON JUMPED AT THE SHARP KNOCK on the front door. Morningstar stopped from washing the plate and turned.

Teresa set down the dish she'd been drying then wiped damp hands on her apron. "Kinda late for a visitor. Wonder who it could be?" Glancing at the baby perched in the highchair, she stepped into the living room.

More knocking—louder the second time.

"Who's there?" Teresa leaned against the door.

"Sammy Estrada. Sorry to bother you, Mrs. Colton."

Teresa tugged open the door and produced a smile for her husband's deputy. "Please come in. It's too dark and cold to be standing outside."

"Thanks, ma'am." Sammy knocked dirt from his boots, jerked off his hat, then gripped the head covering with gloved hands.

"Can I get you something hot? Coffee?" Teresa studied the deputy's eyes. Eyes, which most times sparkled, took on a serious cast tonight. Something wasn't right. He wouldn't come by just for a visit. He'd already checked in earlier today.

Sammy flashed a quick grin. "Smells great. Coffee'd be fine, ma'am. Just half a cup." He slid into Trace's rocking chair as he'd done so often before, balancing his hat on his knee until Teresa handed him a cup. She sat on the sofa across from him. Morningstar held the baby and perched beside her sister-in-law.

Awkward silence. Sipping noises. The baby jabbering.

Sammy took a long sip, then spoke over his cup. "Missus Colton, both of you, I have two reasons for stopping by tonight." He glanced from woman to woman. "First, to make sure you're doing all right."

Morningstar smiled. "That's really sweet of you. We're fine. Appreciate your concern. What's the second?"

Empty cup in both hands, Sammy studied the inside, then brought his gaze up to Morningstar. "I'm sorry. A fella come into the office a few minutes ago and said Pinos Altos was hoorawed by the Apache. Happened a couple days ago. A few houses burned to the ground, but the snowstorm kept the damage to a minimum."

Morningstar cuddled the baby, holding her tightly. "James? Were he and Trace there? Have you heard?"

Sammy shook his head. "No word about your husbands, but the fella said only one person was killed. And it wasn't either Colton."

"As long as the men are safe, we can always build a new house." Morningstar brushed a stray strand of hair from Faith's forehead.

"That's the plumb truth, Mrs. Colton."

Teresa's calmed nerves flared as she realized he had more to say. Was it more news about her man?

Sammy's shoulders straightened. "He also said after

the Indians hit Pinos Altos, they rode south to Santa Rita. Imagine, a town that size bein' attacked." Sammy groaned up to his feet and handed the cup to Teresa. "Most ever' body survived that raid, they'd left town soon enough, but apparently the Mexican Army, the *Federales,* got involved. Guess they're still determined to push out the Indians. Been that way for at least sixty years."

Morningstar stood. "Why can't everyone just get along? The Apache believe that the land belongs to no one. We all live together, as one—the earth, the people, the animals."

Teresa touched Sammy's arm. "How'd the town fare?"

Sammy pursed his lips. "Wasn't too much of the town left after the shooting stopped."

Inching toward the door, he pulled his coat tighter around his chest. "I'm afraid those men of yours rode right into a swarm of trouble. 'Tween the Apache, Mexicans and snow, they'll be lucky to get back anytime soon." Sammy gripped the door handle. His gaze hit the floor then returned to the women. "Sorry for the news but wanted you to know first off. If there's anything I can do to help, please just ask. I'll be right here."

"Thank you, Sammy. Let us know if more news comes in." Morningstar followed him to the door.

"You can count on me, ma'am. *Buenas noches.*" Sammy stepped into the darkness.

CHAPTER FOURTEEN

JAMES TWITCHED AWAKE. MUSCLES IN BOTH arms screaming, he managed to move the right one, but the other remained squashed under his brother's sleeping weight. He nudged Trace. "Hey, roll over."

He flexed his free hand. Prickles of pain shot up his arm as feeling flowed back into his fingers. Trace snored on.

Powdery fluffs of white covered Trace's boots. His exhausted rumbles echoed from wall to wall in the tiny cave. The rocky overhang, closed in on three sides, had protected James and his brother from the brunt of the weather, affording a brief respite from the icy breeze and snowfall.

James poked his brother again. "Wake up. Sun's already up." Pushing against Trace's shoulder, James succeeded in releasing some of the pressure on his left arm then slipped it out. He rubbed the arm and crimped his tingling fingers.

Rolling onto his side, James peered into the awakening turquoise-sky day. He squinted against the glare, and from his vantage point, nothing but white blanketed the entire landscape. White also blanketed his boots. How much farther to Mogollon? In a perfect world, they'd return to Pinos Altos right now, sleep in his warm house again, and then Andy would ride in like he had no cares in the world. Andy's pockets would be filled with gold nuggets.

James shook his head. No such miracles existed. He let out a sigh to hide disappointment at reality. "Trace. Sun's shining and time's wasting. Let's go." James shook his brother's shoulder until the breathing changed. "Good morning. Weather finally gave us a break." No wind, no hail or sleet threatened him. But it was cold. Damn cold. He pulled his stained leather coat tighter around his shivering body and sat up, the top of his head brushing the stone ceiling.

Trace rolled left and plowed into rock. A red knot raised on his forehead. "Damn!" He massaged the tender skin and opened his eyes. "Damn! What the hel—?"

"You're ornery like a bull calf in a cactus patch." James patted his brother's leg then crawled out of the rock cave.

"Feel like one, too." Inch by inch, Trace sat up, rubbed his eyes and forehead again. He squirmed out into the glaring sun then plunked his high-crown black hat on his head.

Arms extended overhead, James reached higher, then twisted his twenty-two-year-old body to the right and left. Snaps and pops. His back released its hold. James surveyed white-peaked rocks and icy patches of ground unfolding before him. Everywhere he turned—white. Glistening snow and ice crystals spread over the country like a fancy lace tablecloth draped over mesquite bushes. Delicate frozen threads hung from trees and bushes.

"Look at all that snow." James spoke over his shoulder as his brother stretched, grumbled, then reached back into the cave and retrieved his leather saddlebag.

James fumbled the strip of beef jerky Trace slapped into his chest. Retrieving it from the snow, he brushed it off and then chewed. The brothers ate in silence and stared at the snow-covered terrain. Morning sun bounced light off snowdrifts, hillocks thick with bushes, and jagged peaks stood purple in the distance. Shading his eyes from the light, James glanced into the clear sky. Silhouetted against the stunning blue, a hawk glided high above, casting about for his own breakfast. Just like us. Searching for something you gotta find, but sure as hell isn't easy.

His gaze shifted earthward. Would the path, hidden under all the white, lead them to Andy?

Last piece of jerky stuffed into his mouth, Trace reached into the shelter and extracted the saddle, which doubled for his pillow, then marched off for his horse tethered nearby.

James choked down his breakfast and regarded his brother brushing snow off both horses. No usual joking, no pleasant words. Eyes narrowed, stiff shoulders. Worried enough for the both of us, James thought.

Swinging the creaky leather saddle over his own horse, James tightened the cinch strap and adjusted the bridle, then tossed saddlebags over the horse's rump.

Groaning, Trace stepped up carefully into his stirrups, settling into the saddle. He blew on his gloved hands and stuck the right one under his left armpit. "Get a *move* on,

James. I'm freezin' my ass just waitin' for you." Trace's words spurted ice. His breath hung in the air like iron spears.

One foot planted in his stirrup, James glared at Trace. "Wait just a damn minute." James swung up onto his horse and guided his right foot into the leather stirrup. "What's crawled down your gullet?"

"Nothing!" Trace flicked the reins over the sorrel's neck and gigged his sides. Instead of leaping into action, his mount placed one hesitant foot in front of another and, like a turtle, inched forward. "Damn fool horse. Let's go!" Trace snapped the leather again.

"He's not gonna go very fast. Might as well let him pick his way toward Mogollon."

James maneuvered his pinto alongside his brother's. "Besides, don't want him breakin' his leg. Yours almost broke is bad enough."

Muttered words intertwined with grumbled curses were all Trace gave his brother. They rode in silence. Reaching a sharp curve in the narrow canyon floor, Trace pulled to a stop and threw a quick glance in James' direction. He waited for James to catch up.

Trace hung his head and studied his lap taking half a minute to meet James' gaze. "I apologize. I'm sorry. It's just that—"

"It's all right."

"Hell, it's not all right. Shouldn't treat you like the enemy. It's just... I miss Teresa and Faith. And... what're we gonna find? How could Andy've survived? Hell, it's been at least a week since the attack." Trace swept his arm presenting the panoramic view. "Even if he escaped, how'd he be able to get out of this?"

"We'll find him. He'll be all right." James eyed his

brother. "Look. It's cold. And your leg's hurt. Not much to eat. You banged your head." He reached over and in the most understanding, brotherly fashion, smacked Trace on the back. "Just look at it this way..." He shrugged and spread his hands palms up. "What else can go wrong?"

CHAPTER FIFTEEN

"Next stop's Mesilla." The stage driver shut the door and peeked through the window. "Should be there in a couple hours."

Luke smiled at the good news. The snap of the whip and the "Step up, mules!" command of the driver propelled him toward the final leg of his journey. He touched his hat's brim and nodded to the two ladies arranging themselves on the hard seats. Could be mother, daughter.

One was younger, much prettier than the other. Her dark brown eyes met his a time or two, then she'd turn her head away as if embarrassed to be caught.

Enchanting. Her light brown complexion set off by those stunning eyes and hair. Luke thought about his own wife now eight hundred miles left behind, then wondered what lay ahead. The driver's words thundered across his brain. *Mesilla.* Two hours more and he'd be with two of his brothers again. Luke pushed aside lusty thoughts of the pretty woman across from him and concentrated on the journey and the impending arrival.

He couldn't wait to see the look on everyone's faces—Trace, Teresa, and Andy—as they all hugged on the boardwalk. Just like when James and Morningstar came to Lawrence. Would there be tears? And would James and Star be there as well?

As they swayed in the coach, various shades of brown rushed by. Light green mesquite bushes punctured the beige of the desert sands, stretching as far as he could see. Since the last stop, fifteen miles north of Mesilla, the sky was the only color to stand out against brown sand dunes, brush, and rabbits. A few miles to the west, a row of finger-like tree branches silhouetted against the blue sky. Ancient cottonwoods ran along the Rio Grande, the area's lifeblood. To the east, the rugged Organ Mountains stood proud, like sentinels, and defined the Mesilla valley.

Adobe houses, some coated with flaking white plaster, became more frequent nearer to Mesilla. He'd read about the Southwestern-style houses, the small, boxy dwellings of mud and straw mixed together, how they provided warmth in the winter and respite from the summer's paralyzing heat. Here they were scattered everywhere.

Leaning out the window as the stage turned the last corner on this portion of the route, Luke knew Mesilla was home. Something about brown on brown, even the brown skinned people he noticed on his journey, appealed to him. No wonder Trace and now Andy loved living here.

Adobe houses. Plenty of horses. Bustling plaza, complete with wagons and people, filled the area. Shops and signs proclaiming items for sale hid parts of the buildings. Luke searched the people as he rode. Nobody looked familiar. Where were those brothers of his? More than likely already at the stage stop waiting. Luke hung out the window and gawked.

The stage jerked to a skidding stop, settling in front of the San Antonio and San Diego Mail Line office while dust billowed up under the wooden wheels. The shotgun guard jumped down from his high seat, and then opened the door. Luke helped the two female passengers navigate the cramped quarters and waited for them to exit. After they alighted, he grabbed his hat and the now-empty sack of food his wife had packed.

Luke stepped from the stagecoach, stretching his body. Twisting and turning, he wanted to rub his numb rear end, but instead settled for his back popping into place. He nodded to the driver who, still on top of the coach, dropped the last of the carpetbags to the guard on the boardwalk. Luke shielded his eyes against the sun. "Great trip, sir."

The driver navigated across his seat, set his foot on the wheel then jumped to the ground. He dusted his gloved hands. "Yup. Any trip without broken wheels or red-devil Injuns a good one." He disappeared into the stage line office.

Luke located his red and black tapestry bag next to the guard's foot. "Thanks again for the ride. I enjoyed it." He nodded to the dust-encrusted man.

"Slow and steady. Just the way we like it." Running his hand across his mouth, the shotgun guard pointed down the street. "Gotta find something to slake my thirst, friend. Wanna come?"

Luke shook his head. "Thanks anyway. Supposed to meet my family here. Guess I'm early or they're late." He searched up and down the street hoping for a familiar face. A pound of disappointment pressed on his chest. This wasn't the greeting he'd envisioned at all.

Sheriffing duty at the last minute had probably come up.

"All right, suit yourself." The guard nodded to Luke and marched off. He stopped and turned back around. "If ya change your mind," he pointed west, "Sam Bean's Saloon has the coldest beer."

"Thank you for the tip." Luke nodded.

"Must be Luke Colton."

Booming words in his ear spun Luke around. Locating the owner of the voice, he stared into a face he didn't recognize. "Why's that?"

"Look just like your three brothers." The man extended a hand and a grin. "Sammy Estrada, Mr. Colton. I'm your brother's deputy, right hand man so to speak. Pleased to finally meet you."

"And you, sir. He's mentioned you in his letters." Luke returned the genuine smile. Maybe Andy was second deputy.

"All good, I hope." Sammy picked up Luke's bag.

The third youngest Colton brother scanned the crowd. "Where's Trace?" Too long of a pause from the deputy melted Luke's smile. "Something wrong?"

Sammy touched Luke's arm, nudging him toward the plaza. "Walk with me…"

Three long blocks and spurts of superficial chitchat later, they stopped in front of Trace's white-plastered adobe, its porch running the width of the house.

A brown-haired woman flew out the front door, across the wooden porch and down the stone walk. The grin was wide. "Luke Colton!" They met halfway where she hugged him and then held him at arms' length. "I'd know you anywhere. I'm so glad to finally meet you." She turned to the deputy. "Now the family's complete."

Luke took in wide brown eyes, pinked cheeks and

upturned lips. "You gotta be Teresa. You're exactly what that lucky brother of mine described." He nodded toward the deputy. "Sammy tells me I couldn't have come at a better time. Not only do I get a long visit with you and your new daughter, but I also get to see Morningstar again. And visit with all three brothers when they get back."

"So glad you're here!" Teresa beamed at Luke.

Luke glanced over her shoulder expecting Morningstar and the toddler to rush out also. "So, where *are* the other two?"

Hand flying to her mouth, Teresa shook her head. "Forgot my manners, I'm so excited. Please, both of you, come in. We baked a pie today and have a huge pot of stew waiting for you. Morningstar's feeding the baby."

Teresa opened the thick wooden door, ushering the chilled men into her warm living room. "Star," she called. "They're finally here."

Sammy pushed the door shut, set Luke's bag next to it, and stood just inside the room. He shifted his weight from one foot to the other.

Morningstar rushed into the living room, baby on her hip, grinned at Luke then Sammy. "So good to see you again!" After a hug, she handed Faith to Luke's outstretched arms. "Meet Faith Brigid Colton."

"Brigid, huh?" Cradling the squirming youngster, Luke patted her back. "Like Ma?"

Teresa nodded. "Trace and I agreed that after four boys, your ma deserves to have the first girl in the family named after her!"

"And Faith?" Luke grinned at the toddler and stroked her brown hair. Hair reminding him of his own kids'— both brown and straight. He handed her back to Star.

Teresa glanced at Morningstar. "We had faith all along

that Trace and James would come home someday, safe and sound." Her eyes misted. "And we still have faith that *all* the brothers will be home soon."

Luke studied the baby while Teresa fought to compose herself. A heavy silence stung the room. Sammy squirmed by the front door, Morningstar's gaze hit the floor.

Clearing his throat, Sammy opened the door. "I best be going. Just wanted to make sure your visitor found his way." He tossed a quick nod toward Luke. "Would hate to lose you before we even met you. I'll be back later and take you over to the Corn Exchange Hotel, Mister Colton."

"Thanks, Sammy. But please, just call me Luke." He knew why Trace liked this man. Honesty and sincerity exuded from him. Probably made a helluva deputy.

Teresa pointed toward the kitchen. "Stay for coffee, at least."

"Thanks, no," Sammy said. "With Trace gone, I gotta be two men. And I'm also breaking in the new deputy. Some other time, though." Sammy tipped his hat and stepped into the afternoon.

Luke shook hands with Sammy and then shut the door. When he turned, he met Teresa's friendly gaze and wide smile.

"Can't get over how much you look like James," she said. "More than the other two. You could be twins." She pointed to the sofa. "Please make yourself at home. I'll get coffee."

Instead of sitting, Luke followed Teresa into the kitchen. He lowered his voice. "I have a question that's been on my mind for weeks."

"Sounds serious." Teresa set three coffee cups on the table.

A start then stop. Luke worked to make his voice strong. "I'm wondering...just how does that oldest brother of mine look? I know Cochise got James pretty good, but what about Trace?" He picked up a cup, then put it back down. "James says, just like him, Trace's got a couple scars. Still kinda jittery."

Teresa poured boiling brown liquid into all three cups then stared back at Luke. "He's...coping."

Morningstar, now standing in the doorway, held Faith who nestled into her shoulder.

Teresa pursed her lips then continued. "Like James, he's marked a lot more than just outside. Inside, he's scarred, too." She held out a cup to Luke. "Star can testify, they've fought day and night to put their lives back together."

Luke trailed Teresa into the living room and perched on the edge of the sofa, its wide blue stripes adding a calm dimension to the rest of the room. The three adults sipped coffee while Faith, rag doll in hand, curled up next to Teresa.

Needing to explain further, Luke spoke over his cup. "I feel left out in all this. Have for a couple years. First Cochise, then the army, and now Andy gone missing. Should've been here."

Teresa shook her head. "Be glad you missed it. At least the Apache part. It hasn't been easy. But I know Trace and James could use your help." She met his gaze.

"I'd be glad to if I can. But tell me, I'm curious." Luke hoped they would give him the answer he wanted, the answer he needed. His level-headed, responsible oldest brother had to be back to normal. "Does he talk about his capture? James said very little back there in Kansas. Left me with me more questions than answers. Will Trace tell stories or is that a taboo topic?"

"There are no secrets here, Luke. The four of us, and when Andy's around—five, talk things square." Teresa set her cup on a nearby end table. "Their captivity is not the center of conversation, but it's always there."

"From what we can tell," Morningstar glanced at Teresa, "there are stories they won't share with us."

"Or can't." Teresa's words soaked into the walls.

"I'm sure they'll tell you more than they do us." Morningstar leaned closer to Luke. "But you've talked to James. He's told you what they went through. It was absolutely unimaginable." Teresa turned brown eyes on Luke. "But, be prepared. Even though it's been this long, both still see Apache, still have nightmares, still cringe at touch sometimes. Their captivity is something they desperately try to ignore but also need to talk about."

Luke hung his head and studied the inside of his empty cup.

CHAPTER SIXTEEN

CAPTAIN JOSÉ MENDOZA RAISED HIS RIFLE HIGH above his head. "Alto!" Uniformed Mexican soldiers reined their horses to a quick stop behind him. Hooves scraping on rock and dirt, horses snorting while they rested, soldiers squirming in their saddles—the squeaking leather telling him the men needed a rest. Mendoza recognized each sound, so familiar, so reassuring. His men followed well, indeed. A rest would be soon.

Far in front, to the south and west, Indians scattered into the hills and ravines. Their bodies, like large ants, appeared to melt into the earth. Would they be so easy to find next time?

The second in command reined up next to Mendoza. "Why do we quit now? With more speed we would catch those *Indios*. Kill the rest of them." His chin pointed toward the retreating band of Chiricahuas. He glared at the Mexican Army leader. "You always stop us just before we are completely victorious. Why?"

"You question my decisions, my orders?" Mendoza snapped. "If you weren't my segundo, I'd have you shot."

"I'm sorry, *Capitán*. Of course you have your reasons. It's just that the men...well, they ask questions, too." The lieutenant tossed a quick glance over his shoulder at the other soldiers.

"Tell them when the time's right, we'll attack again." Mendoza shielded his eyes against the setting sun. The darkened figures of receding Indians brought half a smile to his face. "We killed many of the Apache at Pinos Altos. Their leader, Standing Pony, ran like a coward. Maybe he will run all the way back to his leader, tail between his legs like the mongrel he is."

The lieutenant spat.

Mendoza's gaze swept the sky. Gray clouds raced with the wind. To the west, a band of blue threatened to destroy the hint of snow in the air. "The time will come when we kill all the *Indios*. Especially their leader, the one they call Cochise." He unplugged his canteen and gulped a mouthful of cold water.

Licking his lips, Segundo reached for his canteen. "The all-powerful leader will not allow himself to be captured or killed. They say his magical powers keep him safe." After a quick sip, he replaced the cork and hung the canteen around the saddle horn.

Mendoza aimed a stocky finger at his second. "Don't be fooled for one minute thinking Cochise is not human. He bleeds and dies like the rest of us." He glanced again into the late afternoon sky. "No, we will teach him he is only a man."

* * *

ANDY LOOKED at the black man sitting across the table and then spooned more soup into his sore mouth. He spoke over the broth, meat chunks crowding the spoon. "How long you gonna stay here in Mogollon?" The words difficult to form, he took his time aligning his jaw for each syllable.

Dawson shrugged, his eyes meeting Andy's gaze. "Whilst longer, I suspect. With dem miners gone now, I got this place alst t'myself. Plenty t'do. An' the weather's cooperatin', so I'll be hangin' around."

"Indians?" Andy knew no more words would be forthcoming today, his jaw still too swollen, too out of place, too sore to continue.

Dawson's cackle split the stillness. "Indians ain't gonna bother me. See, I'm on their side." He leaned over the table, inches from Andy's face. "See, we both hate you white people. Us and them Indians. You white folk take and take, whip and whip. And why? So's you can have more—more land, more money, more...things."

Andy lowered his spoon and pushed the bowl toward the center of the table. Alarm set his nerves on edge. He shivered. He pulled both sides of his ripped shirt closer together. A glance revealed just a couple of buttons. The rest must've been torn off when Dawson sewed him up. His exposed chest made him shiver harder.

And something else didn't feel right. But what, exactly?

Dawson's lips pulled back like a rabid wolf while his eyes grew round then narrowed into slits. He swiped at Andy's empty bowl knocking the food off the table. The dish clattered to the floor. "Gotten by the sweat of our backs." Like a ribbon of smoke, Dawson snaked up to his feet.

Andy froze while Dawson leaned across the table.

"Yeah, *our* sweat and blood so you white people can go to your parties, your teas. We...we don't get no parties, no fancy doin's. We just work."

Dawson edged around the table. He grabbed a hunting knife from the shelf behind him, then threw his arm around Andy's neck. The blade poked into exposed flesh. Andy's throat burned.

"Now it's my turn to play. *You're* gonna work. Work 'til you can't stand up. Work 'til your muscles won't lift your hands. Work 'til you pass out. I wanna see sweat and blood on your back. I wanna see you work 'til you die."

Andy forced himself to swallow. Knife tip stinging, he prayed Dawson wouldn't push the blade in farther. Sticky wet inched down his neck. Mashed against Dawson's heaving chest, Andy knew in his weakened condition he was no match for this irrational man.

What seemed like endless hours dragged by. Sighing, Dawson relaxed his hold and, with the strength of ten men, yanked Andy to his feet and threw him. He sailed across the room, thudded against the cot and slid to the floor. Knife wound throbbing, arm on fire, jaw ready to explode, Andy stared at Dawson now stalking him like a hungry cougar.

The black man hovered above Andy. Their eyes locked. Dawson bent, then shoved the knife blade against Andy's bare stomach. "Now you gonna be *my* slave." He poked harder. "One wrong move, boy, and guts'll spill. Before you die, you'll mop 'em up."

Andy flinched at the burning. Any man this crazy, he thought, should be obeyed. Dawson snorted, withdrawing the knife. He shoved it under his waistband, reached into his vest pocket and pulled out rope. "Gonna tie you nice 'n tight. You struggle, this knife's the last thing you'll ever feel. Understand, boy?"

Nodding, Andy winced as Dawson tied his wrists together. Tight.

A snarl warped across Dawson's face as he wound rope around Andy's ankles. "Yeah, ol' Dawson ain't no fool. Not no more." He wagged his head. "Left first chance he got."

Andy twisted his hands, managing to regain some feeling.

"Yeah, ol' Dawson made short work of dat owner. Mas'er Johnson ain't never gonna beat 'im no more. No more whippin's." He swung his gaze to Andy. "Hell, he ain't never even gonna breathe no more."

"You a runaway?" Andy pushed out the words.

"Runaway?" Dawson's shoulders jiggled. "'Course I'm a runaway—unless Old Man Lincoln set us free. That ain't never gonna happen." He re-tightened the ropes around Andy's wrists. "I run 'cause nothin's keepin' me there. Woman, kids all sold. Friends, family died off. Nothin' left for me."

"Sorry." Andy, surprised he could speak, stared into Dawson's fiery eyes. "But not my fault."

Dawson clutched both pieces of Andy's shirtfront and hauled him up within inches of his face. "Not your fault?"

Spit hit Andy's cheek.

"Hell, you white ain't you? That's fault enough."

Heart in his throat, Andy shook his head. "Color's not important."

"What the hell you know, white boy? All your life you been free. Free t'do what you want, free t'learn numbers and letters, free t'go anywheres you want."

Without warning, Dawson shook Andy. Teeth rattled.

As if in a fog, Andy realized the sound belonged to him. Images of black and white eyes danced with each shake.

Now released and certain every joint in his body was loosened, Andy fell back against the cot. Objects spun around his head before he focused on one—a fist hurtling toward his face.

CHAPTER SEVENTEEN

STANDING PONY STOOD NEXT TO A PONDEROSA pine frowned at each of his warriors gathered around the communal fire pit. Reflecting on the most recent battle, he knew they all had fought with courage unequaled in song and legend. But, despite their best efforts and most cunning fighting skills, the Mexican Army had pushed them out of Pinos Altos, that nothing little mining village built on Indian hunting land. Stolen from the People. Cochise would be angry at the defeat. What could he do to prove his worth in the eyes of the most feared Apache leader?

Not even the aroma of roasting rabbit could shake Standing Pony's depression. Heart heavy, he gazed into the forest, dense with trees and undergrowth. He sensed his second in command at his elbow and shifted his gaze to the man he'd known since childhood.

"Standing Pony, I have just learned something you will want to know."

Facing his friend, the Apache leader nodded. "Good news?"

"It may be." Dancing Hawk cocked his head. "Remember those two Americans your brother captured before Coyuntura died?"

"The white eyed brothers." Standing Pony snorted. "The ones who cry at the whip."

Dancing Hawk pointed back at the warriors. "Tantoo tells me his brother's war party cornered those men near Fierro Mesa north of Santa Rita—two days ago."

"Did he kill them?"

Eyes plunging downward, Dancing Hawk lowered his voice. "No, the Mexican Army—"

"Always interfering!" Standing Pony spun around. Emotions under control, he turned to his friend. "Where are the brothers now?"

"Tantoo says they ride toward Pinos Altos. That is home to the younger one, the one your brother hated the most. The one almost tortured to death."

"He wasn't tortured enough. He should have been stripped of his skin for what he and the other white men do." Standing Pony tightened his jaw and fist at the same time. "Keeping the brothers captive served no purpose. They could not keep Coyuntura alive or the army from our tribe. I questioned Cochise then and question him now." Standing Pony glared at Dancing Hawk. "That young white eyes even lay with the Pima captive promised to me. My woman. He stole *my* woman."

"But Cochise himself gave—"

"Hear my words, friend. That young Colton killed my brother. Took my woman. If Cochise had allowed One Wing to do what was necessary, show the Americans this is our land, then those two white eyes would have been food for coyotes long ago."

"What you say is true." Dancing Hawk raised his eyebrows. "Do you want me to take warriors and kill these enemies? It would be an honor to finish what your brother began."

Squaring his shoulders, Standing Pony gave his head a quick shake. "Have two of our warriors follow those white eyes. But do not harm them...yet."

CHAPTER EIGHTEEN

"Nice of Sammy to introduce us, Mister Littleton. My brothers've mentioned you." Luke Colton leaned over the desk and accepted the cigar editor Thomas Littleton pushed toward him. Guilty pleasure prompted a smile from Luke. His wife never let him smoke what she called "those smelly old things" around her and the kids.

Luke raised one eyebrow. Here he was a grown man, kids of his own, worried that she might find out he smoked with the town's leading newsman. Focusing on the extended match, he grinned around the cigar.

Thomas leaned back in his chair. "Let me guess." He pointed at Luke. "Had a fight with your ball and chain, you decide to come west and find those crazy brothers of yours. A little family chat, brotherly advice is what you're needing. Right?"

Luke arranged himself in the hard chair, studying the editor-in-chief. "It shows?"

"Hell, I read you Coltons like a cheap book. Love to play poker with Trace, I know exactly what he's holding."

Thomas wagged the cigar at Luke. "But your brother, James. He's kind've a different story. Harder to read, hides everything he's thinking 'til it's time. Always on guard."

Luke removed the cigar and ran his hand across his mouth. "Didn't used to be like that. I got to know James again when he and Star came to visit earlier this year. So, it's Trace I'd like to see most of all. I do miss my brothers, we're a close family, but I worry about him. Him more than Andy."

Thomas stared out the window.

"Mr. Littleton?" Luke interrupted the silent man. "My sisters-in-law tell me Trace still isn't completely recovered from Cochise's torture. I understand why James isn't, but Trace? I find it hard to believe. I mean, it's been a year and a half now." Luke leaned forward. "Trace *is* all right, isn't he?"

The editor stared at Luke. A long drag on his cigar, smoke held, then a cloud of blue. Nodding, Thomas dropped his gaze to the desk. "Yes and no. Yeah, he's probably as right as he'll ever be. But no, he's not totally healed up. Neither of them."

"How's that?" Luke's supper sat like rocks.

"Take your baby brother, Andy, for instance. Now he's about normal as they come. Grew up mighty fast last year helping James cope with those memories. James sees things, too, like Trace. But Andy found himself on the receiving end of those memories a time or two. Even had a scrape with Cochise he lived to tell about, but Andy's still just a big pup. Curious about the world—tries everything once. Helluva nice fella."

The newspaperman stared out the window. Luke interrupted his reverie. "What about Trace?"

Thomas shook his head. "When Trace got back from

Cochise's, he was hurting. Bad. Bruises up one side and down the other, ribs busted, and his spirit..." He studied the cigar. "Broken."

"Why? He managed to get James released from Cochise."

"No, he didn't. Cochise sent Trace away to do two things and two things only. The deal was that when both were done, Cochise would free James."

"But—"

"One..." Thomas held up a finger. "Get Cochise's brother, Coyuntura, released from

the Army's grip. They'd taken five other Apache as prisoners and Cochise wanted them all back."

Luke's stomach knotted.

"Two," Thomas added a second finger, "get the Army to turn tail and get the hell outta there."

Luke clenched his cigar.

Thomas continued. "Cochise's brother was freed by an army private trying to help James' soon-to-be wife, Lila, find out about him. She thought he was dead. Hell, we all did. But since the Apache were already released, Trace couldn't do half of what Cochise had requested."

"Good God." Luke swallowed hard. "Nobody left to trade for James."

"That's right. From what I'm told, your brother came this close to dying." Thomas held up two fingers barely touching. "Hell, even on death's door, James is the one who killed that damn Apache, One Wing. The bastard who nearly tortured him to death."

"Holy Hannah."

"It gets worse."

"There's worse?"

Thomas wagged his head. "Trace couldn't help your brother because *our* Army was holding *him* prisoner." He took another drag on his cigar. "Army's just a bunch of no good—"

"If he was with the army, then why couldn't Trace just talk to them, convince the soldiers to leave?" Luke leaned closer searching for the one sane answer.

"Some sort of damn power play on the commanding officer's part. Wanted to be promoted for killing Cochise. Got promoted for killing Cochise's brother. So, even after a lot of discussion, the Army still refused to listen to Trace and went ahead and attacked." Thomas paused and shuffled papers scattered on his desk.

Luke rubbed his temples with trembling hands, cigar forgotten. "I had no idea."

"So, Trace didn't succeed. On any account. Eats at him, too. He'll never let you know, but it does. He was powerless to rescue your brother. Felt guilty, like a failure, for a long time. I don't know, maybe still does."

Luke stabbed out his cigar.

"Good thing James survived, or you would've lost two brothers."

"How's that?"

"If James had died, Trace would've killed himself. No doubt. Blamed himself. Took your brother's torture real personal. Like he was the one in charge of the Apache."

Tobacco taste coated Luke's mouth.

Thomas Littleton stood and daubed his cigar into a glass tray. "Don't worry. He's back to being bossy, stubborn, and in charge. You know, the old Trace."

Taking the editor's lead, Luke stood and pushed down anxiety. There was nothing he could do right now. Maybe this man had exaggerated the information. After all, he was a newspaper man, a storyteller. Probably only half of it true anyway. "How 'bout I buy you a drink? It's the least I can do to thank you for being friends with my brothers."

"Damn right. 'Bout time you offered." Thomas grabbed his coat and hat from the rack by the door and stepped into the crisp, afternoon air.

CHAPTER NINETEEN

"Sure is quiet out here." James perched on a flat rock and gnawed on a piece of venison jerky. Snowdrifts pushed against boulders and lodged under Ponderosa pines. Silhouetted against a raging blue sky, black arrows with wings dipped and spiraled in search of anything too slow to escape. They cawed at the world.

Trace jerked his thumb over his shoulder as he limped through powder, knee-deep. "Finally found some food for the horses. Had to dig down for grass." He grimaced at the dried meat James held out. "Think I hate this."

"We'll find him." Jerky in hand, James thumped his brother's chest. "Eat. Maybe you won't be so grumpy."

"I'm not—"

"Eat." James slapped it into Trace's hand.

The brothers ate in silence and stared into the crisp cloudless day. Chewing—his brother's, the horses, his own. Nothing but chewing and his heart beating. He prayed Andy's heart was still pumping.

A stick snapped somewhere close by. Both Coltons spun to their right. James dropped his jerky and whipped his gun from its leather. Strong-arming Trace, James pushed his brother behind a boulder, then sprinted forward. A pine tree would have to do for cover. Peering through the branches, he knelt, aimed and fired.

"What?" Trace pulled his gun and rushed to a tree close by, then squatted. He twisted right and left. "I don't see anything."

"Shhh. They're right there. Right...there." Shadowed figures darted from tree to tree. James pulled the trigger. Again and again. One shadow clutched its chest and fell backwards, silently, into the snow.

James' bullets slammed into snowdrifts and fallen tree limbs. Snow puffs and iced splinters danced.

"Who?" Trace whispered.

James furrowed his forehead, rubbing his eye with his gun-held hand. "Apache, that's who." He reloaded in seconds and stared into the white wilderness. "Can't see 'em now, ran 'em off. Killed one, I think."

Crouching, Trace hobbled over to James then knelt by his side. "Let's find the one you shot. Maybe we can tell what tribe they're from."

A nod from James. Sweat beaded down his back despite the cold. The brothers crept from tree to brush staying low and taking as much cover as possible.

James stopped in between two pines and searched the untrodden ground. "I know they're right here. I saw 'em plain as day. Those Indians, you know, they're real good at hiding." He plowed through more snow. "Maybe he's over here."

Trace followed on James's heels and scouted nearby. He stepped next to James. "Nothing here. Could've been a deer or a branch just breaking under the snow's weight."

James spun, catching his brother's worried stare. The

gun grew cold in his hand. He holstered it. "I know I saw 'em. Three, maybe four. Wounded one." He shielded his eyes against the snow's glare.

Trace shrugged and glanced around a third time. "Maybe." Slipping his gun back into its holster, he squeezed James' shoulder. "Let's get goin'. If it was Indians, we'll know soon enough." Nudging his brother toward their horses, Trace took one final check behind.

* * *

LATE AFTERNOON SUN glistened against the mounds of snow as the Colton brothers rode into the narrow valley once housing the mining camp at the base of the Mogollon rim. Muddy canvas sheets sprawled against rocks as reminders of life run amok.

Trace yanked on the reins, foot hitting the snow before James realized Trace had stopped. "Good God, James. Look here." Brushing aside crusty snow, he uncovered a man, face down. An arrow at attention in his back.

What would they find? James hoped this search would be quick, easy, successful. Was Andy's body nearby? He eased to the ground, then knelt beside his brother, the frozen specter at their knees. Trace pushed the man over. "It's not him."

"Thank God." James hung his head.

White clouds erupted from Trace. "Can't do this."

"Do what?"

"Turn over every dead man expecting to find Andy." He met James' stare. "What if we never find him?"

"We will. If he's not here, then we'll look someplace else. Hell, he's probably back in Santa Rita or even Mesilla by now having a beer and wondering where to go next." James walked back to his horse and picked up the reins hoping his own doubts didn't show. "Let's just take this one step at a time."

Trace blew out another long stream of crystals. A slow nod.

Without further words, the Coltons led their horses down the mile-long canyon, studying every body, lump, and torn tent along Silver Creek. No Andy.

Long shadows deepened as the men approached the only cabin near the end of the shattered encampment. A thin column of smoke spiraled from the rusty iron chimney. James grabbed his brother's sleeve. "Looks like someone's home."

"Good Lord, somebody survived! They gotta know something."

James tied his horse to a large bush near the front of the cabin. Trace dismounted and pointed to a lump on the other side of the bush. A leg stuck out. The brothers brushed snow off the face. Again, not Andy.

James pushed down rising nausea. "Hello the cabin!" He rapped on the door then glanced at Trace. Worry had aged his brother's drawn face. Panic dissolved into apprehension. A second knock. Noise from inside.

"Come on in, it's open."

James pushed on the door. It scrapped against the rough, wooden floor. Glancing behind him at Trace, James squared his shoulders and stepped into the one-room cabin. Warmth from the tiny stove sent waves of security radiating up and down his entire body. The aroma of stew wafting through the room rumbled James' stomach. He grinned.

Hand extended, James introduced himself and his brother.

The black man nodded. "Dawson's the name, Mr.

Colton. Good t'know ya." One hand gripped a spoon while the other shook with the brothers. "Want some stew? It's just ready."

Trace unbuttoned his coat and surveyed the sparsely furnished room. "Only if you've got enough to spare. It does smell inviting."

Dawson plucked bowls from a shelf and ladled stew into the tin containers. "Plenty where this come from. Lots of fresh meat. All kinds of game 'round here. Plenty t'pick and choose from. Still got vegetables I found back in an old mine I use for cold storage." He aimed the spoon over his shoulder.

James unbuttoned his coat and sat at the table. "Nice cabin you built."

Dawson spoke into the stew pot. "Thanks, but ain't mine, leastways official like. Belonged to a white gentleman named Treolo, but he skedaddled 'bout the time those Apache come. Ain't been back since, so figured it's mine."

"Mind if we ask you some questions?" Trace sat next to James and without waiting for an answer, continued. "You were here during the Apache attack?" He scooted his chair closer to the sawbuck table.

Dawson set steaming bowls in front of the brothers. He held out a spoon and pointed the utensil at Trace. "Eat afore it gets cold."

"Were you?" Trace picked up his spoon.

Although desperate for news of Andy, James wolfed down heaping mounds of stew.

Something in there whetted his appetite for more. Was it a special seasoning or kind of meat he'd never before tasted?

The Black man nodded. "I was here. We all was." He

pointed the spoon toward the front door. "Came on us quick like. Nobody had time ta escape."

James lowered his spoon, stew now rumbling like a beast in his guts. "You know our brother Andy? We're looking for him and last we heard he was here. He's eighteen, our height, brown eyes, straight brown hair hits the collar."

"Looks a lot like us." Trace waved his spoon between himself and James. "We're real worried."

Dawson lowered his spoon and stared at each face, then into the distance. A long silence. He shifted his gaze to Trace. "Yeah, thinkin' on it, I do remember a fella like that."

"Where's he at now? James hesitated to ask the question. "Was he here during the attack?" Voice rising, he tried not to shout. "Is Andy alive?"

Trace stood, the chair screeching against the floor. He grabbed Dawson by the shirt sleeve and leaned into the Black man. "Tell us. Tell us what you know. *Is* Andy alive?"

"Let me go." Dawson wrenched his sleeve from the frantic grasp. "Don't cotton to people pawin' at me."

"Sorry." Trace leaned farther over the table. "What'd you know?"

Dawson straightened his shirt. "Not much. Played cards with him down at Frenchy's tent awhile back. Saw him once or twice after that but ain't seen him since."

"Damn." James slumped against the back of the chair.

"Heard he moved on down toward Santa Rita." Dawson gazed from face to face.

"When?" Trace eased back down to his seat.

"Afore the attack."

"So, he's alive." James lowered his spoon and turned to Trace. "Doesn't make sense. Should've seen him or at least signs on our way here." His relief grew cold as he cocked his head at Dawson. "You sure?"

Dawson made a show of scratching his head and gazed into the cabin. Head bobbing up and down, he mumbled. "Sure, I'm sure. It snowed real good few days back, so maybe them tracks are hid. And I'm the only onest 'round here now, excepting 'ol Henry."

"Who?" Trace's eyebrows knitted.

"Henry. Real nice fella. Didn't know him too good 'fore the attack, but we've 'come real close now. We eat together regular like."

"Where's he at? Maybe he'll know where Andy is." Trace swung his gaze around the cabin.

"Just right outside. Must've passed him on the way in."

James eased to his feet and pushed back his bowl. "You mean that dead man over by the bush?" He pointed toward the door.

"Dat's the one. Don't talk much anymore, but when he do, it's mighty interestin'." Dawson scooped up the bowls and tossed them into a tub.

"I'll bet it is." Trace buttoned his coat and fingered the revolver on his hip. He cut his eyes sideways at his brother. James caught Trace's confused gaze. Pulling on his gloves, James backed toward the door. "Thanks for the grub, Dawson. We gotta get goin' before it's dark."

"You can sleep in here if'n you'd like. This floor's drier'n that forest out there." Dawson pointed at the wooden planks.

"Thanks, anyway. Best be headin' out." Trace pulled down his hat tighter.

"I'll keep my eye peeled for dat brother of yours. Ol' Henry'll sing out first, I reckon." Dawson's grin split his face. "He talks mainly at night, but if Andy comes this way durin' the day, I 'magine he'll call out then, too."

"That'd be a real help, Mr. Dawson." Trace gripped the door handle and yanked. "Thanks again for the grub."

Both Coltons bolted into the crisp evening air and shut the wooden door. They swung up onto the horses without saying a word. Setting spurs to the horses, the brothers raced up the valley.

Once out of range, James reined up then turned to Trace. "I'll bet he actually hears Henry talk to him." He shrugged. "Grub was good, though."

"Yeah." Trace met James' stare. "Real good. You know what kind of meat that was?"

Searching his brother's face for answers, then quick as a lightning strike, the answer became clear. James leaned over his horse as his stomach brought up everything.

Trace dismounted and gulped handfuls of snow. Swishing the icy water around in his mouth, he spit streams of stew onto the ground. Finally, Trace walked around to James, now kneeling on the ground.

Trace patted James' shoulder. "All right?"

A nod. James wiped his mouth with a coat sleeve, that taste still lingering. "Wonder how much of ol' Henry we ate."

CHAPTER TWENTY

LUKE WIPED HIS MOUTH WITH A COTTON NAPKIN and pushed back from the supper table. "Mighty fine cookin', ladies. Best stew I've had in a while. You put some special seasoning in there?" While he'd cooked only when forced to so he wouldn't starve, he appreciated the special care given this stew. And he enjoyed the variety of spices in the dishes his wife made. But, he admitted, he liked his ma's cooking best. Her fried chicken was always mouth-watering.

Morningstar grinned and picked up their bowls. "Yes, there's special seasoning and no, I'm not telling." After placing the dishes in the washtub, she then returned for Teresa's.

While Morningstar poured coffee into three cups, Luke leaned over and ruffled Faith's hair. "Hey, Cupcake, you want your old Uncle Luke to take you and your mom and aunt for a buggy ride tomorrow?"

Teresa gathered the spoons and napkins and pushed back her chair. "That'd be fun. You haven't seen the rest of the area, it's beautiful this time of year."

"Been doing all the heavy work this past week and we appreciate it." Morningstar handed a cup to Luke and flashed a heart-stopping grin. "It's about time we give you the day off and go sightseeing."

"Good." Luke returned the grin. "It's a date."

CHAPTER TWENTY-ONE

STABBING PAINS IN HIS LEG. ANDY'S EYES snapped open. Boot toes plowed again into his thigh. Hands flipped him from his side onto his back. He peered into the cold, inky cave then up into Dawson's glowing eyes. The runaway knelt by Andy and tugged the rope around his wrists. Horsehair fiber dug into raw flesh. A groan rattled in Andy's throat, the wide strip of material wound around his mouth stifling any productive scream, shout or sound.

"Be nice 'n quiet there, Andrew, an' I may let you live." Dawson untied Andy's ankles then pulled him to his feet. "I'll take off that gag, but one sound, an' you ain't gonna see mornin'." Dawson waited. "Got it?"

Andy nodded. Anything to save his life.

Dawson took time untying the old bandana. Freed, Andy spat lint and dirt. He worked his mouth side to side, licking his lips, the movement bringing a bit of feeling back to his face.

At a half crouch, the men navigated the abandoned mine now used for storing vegetables. Baskets of potatoes, onions and a sack of could have been rice or flour were stacked near the entrance. Darkness gave way to starlight as Andy stumbled into frigid night air.

A quick jerk on his healing arm brought a silent cry. Shivering, Andy shuffled next to Dawson, the vice-like grip on his arm reminding him of the time back home he and older brother Luke had been caught smoking behind the outhouse on the schoolyard. That old marm's clamp around his upper arm left bruises for days.

Andy stumbled through the door and into the warm cabin, which exuded a strange sort of comfort. If he could just regain feeling in his bound hands...and his body quit trembling from the cold and fright...and find a weapon, he'd be all right.

Dawson shut the door, moved in close and glared. Lips drew into a sneer.

Close enough to feel Dawson's breath on his face, Andy doubted his chances for survival. Gnarled hands pushed on Andy's chest. Powerless to stop the motion, Andy flew backwards into a corner, crashed against a chair, then sprawled over a wooden box. His head smacked into the wall, silver dots pulsating around the room.

As he lay back against the wooden wall, Andy stared into orbs, white eyes glowing like ice against black coal. Those eyes turned colder as they zeroed in on him. Like a demon, Dawson's face materialized inches from his. Lips moved before he understood the words.

"Two men rode in jest afore dark lookin' for you."

"Trace and James?" Andy worked his mouth. Even *he* couldn't understand what he'd just said.

"Sent their white asses on their way. Headed back to Santa Rita looking for a brother who's drinkin' hisself a time." Dawson chuckled, reached over the crate then yanked Andy to his feet. "Yeah, they ain't gonna be comin' back no time soon."

"No. Please, no!" Andy studied the hostile eyes of his captor. His heart sank. Was this another of Dawson's crazy games? Something he'd conjured up just to see him suffer? On the other hand, Dawson had said *two* and Andy knew his brothers would come to his rescue. Maybe they were camped just over there. Just out of sight.

Dawson grabbed Andy hands. "I'll untie you, but try to use these on me, and your family ain't never gonna find you. Won't be enough left *to* find." He stared at Andy. "Got it?"

He nodded.

"Sit." After untying Andy, Dawson pushed him into a chair and plopped a bowl of cold stew in front of him. "Eat. Need strength for tomorrow."

Andy worked a spoon into his mouth then managed to swallow the lump of food. Bits of carrots and turnips clung to meat creating a knot that sat in his throat. Several gulps of water pushed down the food.

While scraping the last half spoonful of glop then pushing it into his mouth, Andy studied the man who controlled his life. Dawson stood at the stove, back to him.

Knowing freedom was now or never, Andy searched the cabin for any type of weapon. Nothing. No time to waste. He sprung to his feet, bolted for the door, yanked it open, then raced into the night.

"Trace! James!" Andy prayed the sounds were intelligible. "Help!" He listened to animal grunts and growls echo throughout the narrow canyon. Rumbles bounced off boulders.

Somewhere behind him a door screeched across wood.

He ran.

Ice crunched. Footfalls.

He ran harder.

Hot breath on his neck. Herculean arms wrapped around his chest.

Andy screamed. The frozen ground rushed to meet him. He slammed into rocks of ice. His face plowed through a snowdrift then lodged against a boulder. The pain, the excruciating agony of a jaw broken, spiraled his world into a black void, a place filled with hurt.

Dawson flipped him over onto his back like a turtle, grabbed his feet and pulled. Rocks and sticks poked Andy's body. Numb hands couldn't fend off much. Cabin now in sight, Andy knew crazy Dawson wouldn't let him live.

Dawson yanked with the strength of ten men. Andy clawed at the door frame, but his body slid over the rough flooring then stopped near the stove. Somewhere behind and above him the wooden door shut. The bolt clicked into the frame. Andy stared up into boiling mad eyes.

* * *

JAMES TURNED on the hard ground and pulled the blanket tighter. Still, he shivered. His eyes fluttered open. What had awakened him? A noise of some kind? Trace? Still asleep, seemed to be just fine.

James sat up and reached for the rifle at his side. Running his hand down the barrel, he wondered if Indians would attack at night. Was that Apache or animal? Sounded more animal than human. Stars peeked back as James thought about the creatures in this frozen mountain valley. Mountain lion? Black bear?

Trembling, James leaned closer to the glowing embers of the fire. He blew. Small flames danced as frosted air fanned the fire. He added small sticks then nodded at the welcomed heat as orange glowed brighter. His hands, extended over the crackling flames, warmed.

Bang!

James jumped. Frowning, he cocked his head and listened. Somewhere down the valley, something like a door slamming—wood on wood—someone stirred. Probably that crazy Dawson visiting Henry.

Trace rubbed his eyes, mumbled.

"It's all right. Just noises." James glanced over his shoulder then back to his brother. "Go back to sleep."

Trace pulled his blanket closer, nodded, and within seconds snored.

CHAPTER TWENTY-TWO

THE COOL MORNING BREEZE GREETED LUKE AS he stopped at the restaurant's doorway. After breakfast at Lupe's Café, he'd decided a stroll around town would walk off some of the *frijoles* he'd enjoyed. Maybe he could even bring some gossip back to Star and Teresa. Lupe's stood next to The Corn Exchange Hotel, which faced the plaza, the center of town. From here he watched the world go about its business. People scurried past, each bundled in coats or serapes.

Another yawn and stretch, Luke then sauntered past the newspaper office, glanced in and noticed Tom Littleton arguing, rather vehemently, with a man in a black duster. The man's high crown Texas hat, pulled down low, reminded Luke of the pictures he'd seen of gunfighters, shooters.

Deciding not to interfere, Luke wandered down the wooden plank sidewalk past the old Butterfield Stage office. He peered in the window and was surprised to find a bar. He stepped back and looked up over the door. *Sam Bean's Saloon* the freshly painted sign professed. He ran his hand over his mouth, then promised himself a beer later. Or maybe something with more kick to it. Luke wandered toward the southwest corner of the plaza.

Several yards from the intersection, Luke stared at an old, gnarled cottonwood standing guard over the *acequia madre*, the main irrigation ditch. His throat tightened remembering stories James had written about his near miss of hanging. Must've been that tree right there. He pulled his coat around his body but shivered, despite the fleece lining. James sure had been through a mighty lot for being just twenty-two. Almost hanged, then captured and nearly killed by Apache, stage shotgun guard for a year, army private, and now a married saloon owner.

Luke counted his accomplishments on one hand. Two children, wife, and a farm. Sure as hell paled in comparison.

A raspy voice broke Luke's reverie. "Mornin' Mr. Colton. Beautiful day, ain't it?"

Luke spun and nearly plowed into postmaster Abe Kinnear. "Sorry, didn't see you come behind me." Luke stuck out a hand and pumped the old man's. "Yeah, it's a great day."

"Bit on the nippy side, but what'd you expect in December?"

"December?"

"Eighth." Abe pocketed his right hand and shook his head. "Time's got a mind all its own, I'm believin'."

Luke agreed. Had it already been two weeks since stepping off that stage?

Abe produced a key and stepped toward the post office. Once inside, both men unbuttoned coats and Abe hung his behind the counter. Luke pushed firewood into the potbelly stove in the corner and lit the kindling. Within seconds, the small room warmed.

Backside to the heat, Luke surveyed the office. Stacks of letters and packages sat in neat piles around the room. A narrow counter ran its width.

"How d'you like Mesilla, Mr. Colton?" Abe spoke over his shoulder.

"Like it fine. But I'd like it better if you called me Luke."

Abe disappeared as he bent over behind the counter then reappeared with a handful of mail. "Suits me. Too many of you Coltons to keep straight as it is. Your ma and pa certainly were busy. What happened? Too many cold nights out there in Kansas?" Abe's eyes sparkled and crinkled with the smile.

Luke chuckled. "Guess so. Good thing they don't live clear up in that Montana. There'd be ten of us by now."

Nodding, Abe held up a letter. "Looky here." He peered over the top of his glasses at Luke. "From Sally Colton." He snorted. "You got a wife? Cause I don't remember mention of any Colton *sister*."

Luke snatched the envelope out of Abe's tight grasp and stuck it inside his coat pocket. Silence settled in the room while Abe sorted mail and Luke held his hands over the potbelly stove, more out of something to do than wanting to warm them. He contemplated his next set of questions.

"You been around here in town a while, I reckon."

Abe nodded. "A spell."

"I been thinking of trying my luck here in Mesilla. Getting a job. Settling down." Luke eyed the man. "This a good place to live?"

Abe straightened, scratched his chest and peered out the window. "'Bout as good as any, I reckon. Fact is, we're just gettin' back on our feet since that damn old army pulled out few months back." He pointed at Luke.

"Your brother James needs to take credit for that. Hard on him, though. He was the only one around here high-spirited enough to complain to the army they were takin' all the food. People 'round here starved. He hollered and ended up in jail. His...*your* brother's jail."

Now Luke had heard about James taking on the army and losing, even spending time behind bars, but Abe's take on it was most interesting. Luke jumped in with what James had told him.

"Spent two months in there, I understand. Then ordered to leave town." Luke hated what the "good" people of Mesilla did to his brother.

Abe examined the top letter in his hand. "Guess it was 'bout that long. Then he and Mrs. Colton took off. Heard they went off to Kansas." His gaze traveled to Luke. "And now you're all back here."

Chuckling at Abe's revelation, Luke raised one eyebrow. "Yep. Don't know if I can find good, honest work, though."

Abe Kinnear set down the stack of mail and eased close to Luke. He lowered his voice. "Sheriff Trace is well liked around here. Andy, too, before he took off. You attach yourself to those two and you're liable to get employed. But just 'tween you and me...I'd keep James' name out of conversation." Abe's chest rose with a deep breath. "He still ain't too popular, I'm afraid."

"Why?"

"Still sees Apache that ain't there. Still hits for no reason. Still drinks too much." Abe ambled toward the counter and spoke over his shoulder. "Still can't be trusted not to try to kill you."

Ice cold fingers squeezed Luke's heart.

CHAPTER TWENTY-THREE

JAMES FOUGHT THE WOOL BLANKET. "PLEASE, God, no...don't make me...no!"

Trace grabbed his frantic brother's shoulders and shook them. "Dammit, wake up. You're dreaming again." He squinted into the early-morning sun. "No one here but you and me." *And half the Apache nation in your nightmares.*

James jerked against the tight grip. "Don't...I won't!"

A clenched jaw turned Trace's words hard, words he'd muttered a thousand times. "It's all right. It'll be all right."

James froze, his dreams vanquished. He blinked awake into Trace's face. Chest rising and falling like he'd just run a marathon, James pushed sweat-drenched hair off his face. He sat up, shoving Trace's hands away.

Trace's fists tightened, eyes narrowed. Damn Apache. *If I ever have the chance...*

Glowering at the world, James struggled to his feet, the blanket kicked away.

Would this be the last of their nightmares? Trace

wondered. Never. His were just as bad as his brother's. Just not as often. "Coffee?" Trace pushed aside guilt, it wouldn't do anybody any good, and stood.

Before his brother could nod, Trace poured water into the enamel pot then added spoonfuls of coffee. Snapping a few sticks in half, James pushed them into the fire and stared into growing flames. Trace perched the pot on rocks stacked inches from the center of the fire, then glanced at his brother.

"Cold stream water on your face'll make you look like my brother again. I'll watch after the coffee." Trace cocked his head to his right. "Go."

"Couldn't hurt." James dug through his saddlebag and pulled out a clean blue shirt, small towel. He held up a bar of soap, his hand trembling. "Think I'll take a look around, then wash some of the trail off while I'm at it."

"Don't get too pretty, little brother. Might shoot you for some stranger." Trace sent a silent prayer in his direction.

"The way you shoot, I'll be plenty safe." James tossed a wave over his shoulder as he ambled through towering Ponderosa pines and scrub oak.

CHAPTER TWENTY-FOUR

"YOUR CARRIAGE AWAITS, MADAM." LUKE Colton bowed at the opened door.

"Good morning." Teresa grinned, stepped back, her arm sweeping him inside. "Come in, kind sir." She followed him, closing the door.

Unbuttoning his coat, Luke sauntered into the kitchen then poured himself a cup of coffee. He glanced around. "Where's that adorable Faith?"

Teresa wiped the table and pointed her chin toward the bedroom. "Helping her aunt get ready."

Luke tested the hot coffee. "Then Morningstar's able to make it, too?"

"Of course I am, Mister Colton."

Luke jumped. He took in the shining ebony eyes of his brother's wife, her blue riding outfit accentuating her narrow waist. The hair, wound so daintily on top of her head, set off her high cheekbones. He swallowed. "You have a habit of sneaking up on people when our backs are turned?"

"Only when they're talking about me."

Teresa pointed to a small basket set on the table. "While you were getting ready, Star, I packed our lunch." She turned to Luke. "Hope you like ham sandwiches."

"My favorite." Luke gulped his coffee, then placed the cup on the table. He picked up Faith, her arms wrapped around his leg. "Shall we go?"

"Yes, let's shall!" Morningstar's face glowed. "I'll grab my bonnet."

* * *

LUKE REINED the buggy to a slow stop. Leafless cottonwoods stood like sentinels on either side of the Rio Grande providing a perfect place to sit and relax. Spotting a clearing beneath a cottonwood's bare limbs, Teresa pointed.

"How about there?" She sprung from the buggy before Luke offered his hand.

"Perfect!" Morningstar handed Faith to Luke and then scrambled out without help.

Faith darted under the blanket as the two women attempted to spread the checkered fabric. Luke chased her around a tree returning in time to help set out the food.

Ham sandwiches, dried apples, bits of molasses candy wrapped in wax paper, and tea rounded out a satisfying luncheon.

Stomach full, Luke leaned against the tree watching the women play with Faith. The only thing to make this moment perfect would be a glass of whiskey...and a cigar.

"Think I'll take Faith down to the river and we'll play with the water for a bit." Teresa held out her hand to her daughter then turned to Morningstar. "You want to come? Luke?" Her eyes darted from Luke to Star. Luke squirmed, reading his sister-in-law's questioning gaze.

Morningstar pointed to the tree, part of the blanket spread under it, the other part now occupied by Luke. "Think I'll sit right there and enjoy the sun. But Luke, you can go if you want. I'll be fine here by myself."

"I'm sure you would." Luke smiled up at Teresa. "But if you'll be all right by yourself, think I'll stay here, too." He patted his stomach. "Need to let dinner settle."

Another hard stare, those slightly narrowed eyes of Teresa's produced the warning Luke knew was intended for him. Teresa nodded. "We won't be long."

Morningstar and Luke waved as Faith toddled off with Teresa. Not knowing whether to stand or stay seated, Luke squinted at Morningstar. As if reading his thoughts, she sat next to him. "Beautiful out here, isn't it?" She leaned back, closed her eyes and sighed.

"Certainly is." His gaze strayed over the woman. His sister-in-law. His seductively beautiful sister-in-law. He looked away.

The rush of water, harsh jabs of crows crying out for food, his heart beating. Luke cleared his throat quietly. The sun only served to heat up his already-burning face. What was it about Morningstar that enchanted him? Her lightly browned skin? Her shiny black hair? Those haunting eyes? Whatever the attraction is, he thought, leave it be.

"Penny for your thoughts." Morningstar cut her eyes sideways.

Luke picked up a stick and scrambled for a topic. "Just wondering where those crazy brothers of mine scooted off to. Shouldn't they be back by now?"

"It's a ways up there and back. And if they can't find

Andy, no telling how long it'll be." Morningstar's gaze met Luke's. "Let's just hope it won't be much longer."

Nodding, Luke tossed the stick into the water.

A long silence, breathing stops and starts from Morningstar. "I hope you won't think I'm too bold, but I just can't get over how much you remind me of James. You're so easy to be around. Feel like I've known you for years."

"Months, anyway. So, how am I like my brother?"

"For one, you look just like him. The way you turn your head a certain way, your mouth curling up at one end." Morningstar looked away. "And also, your eyes..."

"Yes?"

"Same as James'. They take in the whole world at once."

Luke laughed out loud. "What else would they see?"

Growing serious, Morningstar stared at the ground. "Some people never see what's right in front of them. They never enjoy the beauty of life. They just rush around and don't stop long enough to appreciate what they've got."

Luke swallowed hard. Why was she so damn beautiful? "You always this philosophical?"

Morningstar ducked her head. "You bring it out in me."

Pushing away the awkward silence, Luke chose a neutral topic. "How do you like Pinos Altos?"

"Fine... for now." She turned to Luke. "But what I really want is to be the town doctor."

"Really?" Luke's eyebrows shot up. "I had no idea."

"I've been doing a lot of doctoring in Pinos Altos. Another lady is a midwife, but the miners don't need her services. No one else knows broken bones from bad biscuits I'm afraid." Morningstar shook her head. "But

James doesn't think I can get into medical school. And even if I could, he doesn't want me to go."

Luke picked up another stick, broke it and tossed half toward the river. "Why?"

"Guess he's afraid of losing me." She wagged her head. "I can be a good wife *and* doctor." A grin lifted a corner of her mouth. "I've written my pa in Tucson, he's the doctor there, to see if he can help get me some training. If anyone can, he can."

"You'd be great at it." Besides, if she became the town doctor, she'd be close enough to see often. Another reason to stay in Mesilla. Or maybe Pinos Altos.

The water's gurgle as it rushed past drew his attention. Torn between wanting to know more about her or more about James, Luke settled for a combination. "Tell me how you and James met. I don't think he ever said."

Her eyes softened and a tiny grin slid up one corner of her sensuous mouth. "I assisted my father in Tucson. Trace was a patient and Andy discovered he was there. Then he brought in James." Morningstar chuckled. "Andy asked me out for supper, but I was waiting for James to ask. So, I told Andy no."

"That sounds like my baby brother. He's not shy."

"No, he's not." Morningstar shook her head. "It took James a while to ask, but he finally did. And the rest..."

Luke clutched another stick and scratched in the dirt.

Morningstar squinted as she glanced at Luke. "How about you and Sally?"

He didn't want to talk about her, about them, but his silence would say more than he'd want. Star was smart. She'd figure it out. Hell, she'd probably already realized Sally didn't want him back. He'd made a terrible husband despite his half-baked overtures of reconciliation. He studied one of his crude dirt drawings. "We've known each other for years. Went to school together. Our families been friends as long as I can remember."

"So, it was meant to be." Morningstar nodded.

"I suppose." Luke raised an eyebrow. "We...Sally and me...I took her to a dance one night." His stomach knotted. "Well, we got married a couple months later. Had our son few months after that."

Cheeks reddened, Morningstar touched his arm. "That's nothing to be ashamed of. You've got a fine family now. You should be quite proud."

Luke took in her misty coal eyes. Knowing he shouldn't, but unable to stop himself, he asked anyway. "When are you and James gonna have kids?"

Morningstar picked up a pebble, examined it, picked up another. She brushed them out of her hand.

Luke chided himself for his brass. "I'm sorry. Didn't mean to pry. I apologize."

"That's all right. You're family." She met his soft gaze. "We want children, more than anything, but James...he can't..."

"Is he all right? Did those Apache—?"

"He says they didn't abuse him like that. But, Luke, something happened. Something he won't talk about." Fingers knotting the corner of the blanket, Morningstar stared into the wool material. "Something keeps him from...from..."

"Loving you like he should?"

Morningstar nodded. A tear trickled down her cheek.

Luke slid his arm around her soft shoulders pulling her against his chest. He looked up at Teresa standing yards away, arms folded, staring.

CHAPTER TWENTY-FIVE

STANDING PONY'S EYES WATERED DESPITE THE cold breeze that threatened to turn into a blustery wind. Smoke stung his eyes and warmed his lungs even though he tried not to breathe in. The screams of dying animals and terrified people curled his lips into a snarl. What did they expect? They were living on his land...land of the Apache. The People. The only answer was to run them off, kill anyone who wouldn't leave.

From atop his pinto, Standing Pony watched his warriors finish off a farmer, ax in hand. He had put up a good fight, but not good enough. Just like the rest of the white eyes. Weak white eyes.

He glanced right and spotted his second in command trotting toward him, lance sporting a black furry patch on the tip. Another weak American. Standing Pony snorted just as Dancing Hawk reined up alongside him.

"This town is burned, Standing Pony. The few people left alive have fled into the hills." Dancing Hawk spit into the dirt then rubbed his red eyes with the back of a soot-streaked hand. He let his gaze rove over the smoldering shambles of Santa Rita. "We have been victorious once more."

"I have watched them run like the cowards they are. After I speak with Cochise, we will return and reclaim our land." Standing Pony threw out his chest and sucked in more hot air. He stifled a cough. "And we lost no warriors."

"Our men were indeed brave in battle today."

Standing Pony's eyes itched, burned, and watered. His war leader's image blurred.

"We're finished here. Leave the rest of the town to the buzzards." He hoisted his lance high above his head and let out a victorious war cry. Its shrillness sailed against the wind and spun over the crackling wood.

Rising like ghosts out of fog, paint and soot-streaked warriors materialized from behind trees and burning buildings. They leapt onto the backs of their horses and sprinted into the forest.

Standing Pony nodded. Soon. Very soon this would belong to the Apache once more.

* * *

EARLY SUN BEHIND HIM, Captain Mendoza stood calmly, waiting for his soldiers to gather. They stood not in formation, but in groups, all looking at him. He strutted in front of the assemblage. Remnants of Santa Rita lay in back of him, scattered, blackened. Puffs of smoke shot into the steady breeze. The few standing timbers groaned and creaked in the cold wind.

Mendoza spread his arms wide. "As you know, men, we are finished with Santa Rita. There is nothing left for us to protect. They should have sent for us sooner." One corner of his mouth turned up. "What was still here when those Apache finished, has now collapsed or..." he chuckled, "...found its way into other hands."

Mendoza's second in command standing at his shoulder, snickered and leaned into his ear. "And those hands belong to you and me. ¿No?"

"Sí, Segundo. You and me will live well in Mexico City." Mendoza turned his back to the rest of his soldiers and spoke just above a whisper. "When we are done raiding a few more haciendas and looting a town or two, we'll buy dozens of *mujeres* and drink all the tequila we can find!"

Segundo's thick eyebrows raised while his soot-stained hands stroked his full mustache. Tortillas and bean remnants clung to black and gray hairs.

Mendoza straightened his shoulders, wiped the smirk from his lips, then turned again to face his men. "Today, we ride in search of Cochise and any other *Indios* in our way."

His men nodded and a couple smiled. One or two grunted approvals.

A spurt of smoke caught on the icy wind. Mendoza waved the scent away. "I understand a young war leader is taking control of a small band of renegade Apache. Standing Pony must be stopped. He has raided, ravaged and burned more than just this two-bit town. He laid waste to everything in his path."

Mendoza's second in command followed on his heels. "Sir, this is what our soldiers have been waiting for. The men... they are anxious for battle. When do we ride?"

"This morning we ride east toward Pinos Altos. Maybe we will find these renegades

after they burn *that* town as well." He shrugged. "It would be such a shame if we only get there in time to pick through the pieces."

Mendoza glanced into the crystalline sky, the bite of winter on his cheeks reminding him

of the warmth of Mexico City. He fought a grin. Soon. His army'd show those *Indios* what killing was all about. He'd run them off this land once and for all.

Then he would live somewhere warmer.

CHAPTER TWENTY-SIX

MOST OF THE COFFEE AND A STRIP OF BEEF jerky now consumed, Trace paced from horse to campfire and back. He'd rolled both blankets, tied them on the back of the saddles, repacked his bag, fed the horses, cleaned then loaded his gun and both rifles and waited. How long does a dunk in the creek take?

Trace spun the cylinder on his revolver again, shoved the weapon into his holster, pulled his coat tighter around his chilled body and pushed his way through the Ponderosa pines. Leg feeling better, he realized he barely limped.

A couple hundred yards down the trail, Trace spotted his brother coming toward him dodging branches and carrying his dirty brown shirt, a towel and… a well-worn hat. At this distance, the hat looked like Andy's. Could it be?

Trace plucked it from James' tight grip. "Where'd you find it?" He studied it as if it held the answers to Andy's whereabouts.

"Near the stream." James jerked his thumb over his

shoulder. "I walked down a ways and saw that poking up through snow."

Trace braced himself. "Any...body?"

He wagged his head. "Couple prospecting tools. Nothing for sure of Andy's." James stared into Trace's eyes. "He was still here when they attacked. Dammit, he was still here."

Trace gripped the hat, spun on his heels and marched back to camp. James ran to keep up.

Kicking snow, mud and dirt toward the fire, Trace tossed the remaining black coffee into the sputtering flames and spoke over his shoulder. "Gotta talk to Dawson again. He knows something."

James tightened the saddle's cinch strap. "Got a bad feelin' about this."

Trace grabbed the reins and glanced over his shoulder at his brother. "Yeah. A *real* bad feelin'."

Half a mile later, Trace flew off his horse before James could rein his in. Mud danced around the horses' hooves while Trace tied the lead lines to a bush. He stared at the log cabin in front of him. Had Dawson told the truth? Had any of it been true? He marched toward the house.

James grabbed his brother's coat sleeve and pulled him to a stop. "Easy." He lowered his voice. "We don't know anything right now. Just that he's crazy. And more 'n likely dangerous."

Trace massaged the gun holstered on his hip. "Dammit, you're right. We'll let him explain, then I'll take his head off."

The Colton brothers approached the front door from both sides. Trace knocked on the wooden door and waited for a voice to call out. Nothing but wind whispering through the tall pines. He knocked again and glanced at his brother.

James stepped back surveying the sky. "No smoke. Wonder if he's even home."

Not waiting for another sound, Trace pushed open the door and bolted inside. To his left, the sagging cot appeared to have been slept in, the blanket askew at the foot. On his right, the table contained one dirty plate and a half cup of coffee. James stuck his finger in it.

"Cold." James held his hand over the stove. "Hasn't cooked in a few hours, either."

Mouth set in a hard line, he stared down at the sticks of wood crisscrossed at haphazard angles. "That's odd." James knelt by the woodpile.

"What?" Trace swung his attention to James.

"The firewood here?" He pointed at the pile of sticks. "Knocked over. Probably fell over it in the dark." James peered out through the single window. "Suppose he's close by?"

"One thing for certain. He ain't in here." Trace sighed a long stream of frustration, then stepped out of the cabin and into the cold morning air. Behind him sat nothing but a black void of questions, in front lay nothing but frozen dead men and no answers.

Trace marched alongside the stream, its water trickling through the ravaged camp. James clenched his fists and kicked at mounds of snow.

Removing his hat, Trace ran fingers through tousled hair, then slapped his hat on his thigh. "Dammit! Where the hell is he?"

"Still lookin' for that brother of yours?"

Trace spun around, his gun clearing leather. Hammer cocked, Trace aimed it toward the voice coming from the dark mine. He squinted then recognized the former slave as he stepped into the light. "Good Lord, Dawson. You about got yourself shot!" He eased down the hammer.

James moved beside Trace and stood shoulder to shoulder, his gun also held waist high.

Dawson produced a yellow smile. "When I heard y'all talkin', I reckoned I better go see who's botherin' my peace and quiet. Never can tell when them Indians'll come back." Dawson held up carrots. "Next pot of stew."

Trace flicked his eyes toward James, a grimace crossing his face. He wanted to chuckle, but his stomach roiled instead.

Dawson shuffled toward the cabin. "If you put those pea shooters away, you're welcome t'stay. First meal'll be ready directly." He reached the door. "Yeah, ol' Henry and me get mighty lonely eatin' all t'ourselves."

Even if he was hungry, another meal with Dawson was out of the question. Trace pointed to the mine. "Our brother's around here somewhere. We're gonna look through that mine shaft."

"Suit yourself if you've a mind to. Ain't gonna stop ya." Dawson glanced over his shoulder. "Just vegetables and meat in there."

"What kinda meat?" The question escaped James' lips before he could reel it in.

Dawson shrugged. "Whatever's lucky enough to wander by." He turned his back and sauntered into the cabin, a chuckle shaking his shoulders.

Fifty feet into the mine, Trace stopped, grabbing his brother's coat sleeve. "Can't see a damn thing." He ran his hand along the chill rock wall. "Feels like they stopped drilling about here."

"Why?" James' voice pierced the dark.

Trace shrugged. "Maybe decided gold was someplace else. Colors didn't run right, or they hit water."

"Kinda creepy in here," James said. "Should've brought a torch."

Determined not to lose another brother, Trace kept a firm grip on James' sleeve and tugged him back toward the entrance. "Seems to be all there is. Let's go ask Dawson some more questions."

James balked at a second tug and called out. "Andy? Andy, you in here?"

Silence.

"Where the hell are you?"

The cabin's warmth did nothing to soothe Trace's frayed nerves as he stepped inside. He spoke to Dawson's back. "Got some questions for you." Trace struggled to keep his voice normal. What he wanted more than anything was to yell, demand answers. Instead, he jumped as James shut the door.

Dawson stoked the stove's fire while Trace and James perched on the edge of the two chairs at the sawbuck table.

"Coffee'll be ready 'bout two shakes." Dawson blew into cups and set them on the table. "What kinds a questions?"

Trace surveyed the cabin again. No sign of Andy. He pulled in a drag of warm air. "We found our brother's hat by the stream. We know he was here when those Indians attacked."

"Maybe he lost it before." Dawson hoisted a knife overhead. *Whack*. A carrot part shot off the end of the counter.

Both brothers jumped.

Recovering, Trace shook his head. "We don't think so. We've looked up and down the canyon. Nothing but the hat."

Knife still in hand, Dawson turned to the men. "You for sure it's his?"

What kind of game was crazy Dawson playing? "Our pa gave him the hat band," Trace said.

"And our other brother carved curly designs into it. He does things like that. Makes his marks here and there." James drew circles in the air. "This's one of a kind."

Trace shrugged. "Andy wouldn't be caught dead without it."

A hammer to his chest. Trace sucked in air. What the hell had he just said? He stared at James who stared back, those brown eyes wide.

A chuckle rose from Dawson's chest filling the cabin. "Looks like you mighta done spoke the truth without you even knowin' it." Another chuckle.

James smacked the table with an open hand. "He ain't dead, Dawson, just missing. We turned over every stiff body out there. Thank God Andy wasn't one of 'em."

Scratching his stubbled chin with the knife, Dawson wagged his head, shrugged, turned back to the counter, then slammed the blade through another carrot. "Stew'll be ready soon... Plenty a fresh meat in it."

Trace shot up to his feet, his chair scooting back and toppling to the floor. "We gotta go. Come on, James."

"What about the stew?" Dawson poured water into a pan.

Trace backed to the door. He jerked it open then rushed into the cool morning air.

"What's wrong?" James pulled the door closed. He held his horse's reins. "He might've told—"

"I ain't eating Andy!"

"What?"

Trace swung up into his saddle, set boot heels to the horse's sides. "That crazy devil ain't feeding me my

brother." His words trailed behind him as he trotted off.
"Gonna prove Andy's still alive. Gonna find him…"

James stuck his boot into a stirrup and swung his leg
over the saddle. He hollered at Trace's back. "That's
disgusting." He spurred his horse. "Did we? Andy?"

CHAPTER TWENTY-SEVEN

THOMAS LITTLETON TOOK A SECOND DRAG ON his cigar and puffed out blue circles. "Don't feel comfortable talking 'bout somebody I don't know real well."

Luke matched the spirals and stared at his glass of beer. The darkness of Sam Bean's Saloon soothed his soul. "Appreciate anything you can tell me about Morningstar. Just feel like I'm not part of the family—maybe if I know more about her, I'll feel connected."

"An' the fact she's a rip snortin' beauty has nothing to do with it?"

Swallowing hard, Luke shook his head. "She's James' wife." He waved his cigar in the newspaperman's face. "Don't you be getting any fancy notions, spreading gossip, Tommy."

"Don't call me Tommy." The newspaper editor sipped his beer. "And I'm not the one spreadin' anything. You're doing a pretty good job all by yourself."

"What?"

Littleton puffed. "Whether you know it, or like it or not, you Coltons are high profile people. Trace the first stagecoach driver and James almost lynched in a trial this town won't soon forget. Then both of 'em disappearing, took for dead, then reappearin' like ghosts."

"But—"

"Mesilla may be close to three thousand people, but everybody knows the Coltons." Littleton stared into Luke's eyes. "These fine citizens're watchin' you damn close, if you get my drift."

"So, they know Star and I went for a buggy ride yesterday?"

"Hell, yeah. Even that you ate ham sandwiches."

"But Teresa and Faith went, too."

Littleton spoke over the top of his beer mug, pointed his cigar at Luke's face. "I'd watch my step if I were you. James may be crazy, but people round here know him. Got a helluva lotta respect for Trace. Andy, too."

Luke banged his glass on the table. "Dammit, Tommy. I'm just tryin' to be part of the family. I spend a lot of time with Teresa and Faith, too. What's so wrong with that?"

"Not a damn thing. It's just different."

"How's that?"

Littleton leaned in close. "Morningstar's all spitfire. She ain't happy—that's plain. Just watch what you're doin' around her. You want to be part of the family?"

Luke nodded.

"Then get your sorry ass up there and find that brother of yours." Blue smoke spiraled around his head as he dropped his voice. "Leave James' wife alone."

CHAPTER TWENTY-EIGHT

Whack. THE TOP OF ANDY'S HEAD SLAMMED against the rough-hewn cabin wall. Snow filled his mouth and clogged his nose. From this position on his stomach, he struggled to breathe. Even through the blackness of closed eyes, silver stars pressed against his eyelids. Thumping. Pounding. Afraid to move, he knew his head would explode.

Dawson's grating voice struck Andy's ears. "Told you to stack 'em right, boy!" Toes of Dawson's muddy boots crashed into sore ribs.

Andy opened his mouth to scream, but instead, swallowed more snow. Boot toes pushed. Another shove rolled him over. He elbowed himself up until he could prop his exhausted body against the south wall. Firewood, like oversized toothpicks, lay scattered around him. Lightning bolts of pain hammered his shoulder despite. He massaged the arrow wound. Dawson yanked Andy to his feet, forcing his body upright, his legs to take the weight.

Dawson's sour breath pelted Andy's face. "I said pile

'em neat, slave!" He pointed at the wood. "Get it through that ugly head of yours. I want 'em stacked right. Try again!"

Andy willed his injured right arm to hold the bulky sticks. Picking them up one by one, he balanced the wood on his arms. By the ninth branch, muscles trembled, and his strength faded. He pulled in air. He bent over for the last stick, Dawson kicked the back of Andy's knees. Both Andy and the firewood crumpled like wooden blocks.

"Fool! Imbecile!" Dawson raved. "Should kill you for that!"

Boots slammed into Andy's ribs and lower back, savagely striking again and again.

Andy covered his head with his hands and rolled. Somersaulting through snow, he scrambled to his knees.

Muscles not willing to stand him upright, he crawled. *Get away. Get away.* The mantra repeated as he clawed his way through mud and snow.

Dawson snickered. "Go on, boy."

Andy clutched a thin buckbrush shrub branch and pulled himself under it.

"I see you." Dawson bent down and peered at Luke. "There's 'nother bush over there you might try ta hide under." He chuckled. "Go on whenever you get tired to huggin' that one."

Lying on his side, Andy spotted two big snow mounds in front of him. If he could just make it to that one by the stream, maybe—

"I like playin' hide 'n seek," Dawson said. "But I'll still find ya, though."

Luke curled into a trembling ball, hoping, praying for a miracle.

"I'll always find ya. Anywheres you go, I'll find ya."

"Help!" Did anything come out? "Help!" A squeak.

"Ain't nobody 'round to hear ya, but you just keep on hollerin' all ya wants." Dawson clawed at the back of Andy's coat.

Arms wrapped around the branches, the wooden lifeline, Andy used dredged up strength to hold on. "Trace—"

"Keep yellin', boy. Good for your lungs." Dawson yanked Andy out from the bush and onto his feet.

Andy wobbled, furious hands keeping him upright. Dawson lowered his voice to a venomous whisper. "So, you wanna play rough? You ain't seen nothin' yet, white boy."

Dawson released his hold and dug into his pocket bringing out rope. "What you've been through so far's a picnic."

Andy refused to whimper as the rope sawed into his tender, raw flesh. He wouldn't give this insane man the pleasure of hearing him cry.

Dawson clutched the front of Andy's coat then pulled. "Now—you're goin' to hell, boy. Straight to hell."

CHAPTER TWENTY-NINE

"MAYBE THAT *would* BE A GOOD IDEA." TERESA set a bowl of steaming potatoes on the table, then jammed a spoon into it. "We can manage for ourselves for a while. And Trace's deputy keeps a good eye on us. We'll be fine."

Luke arranged napkins and plates while Faith sat in her highchair playing with a spoon. He ruffled his niece's hair each time he passed by. "Apparently the whole town's talking. I just wanted to be part of the family, help out where I can, and now everybody's all stirred up."

Teresa glanced over at Luke. "They'll think differently when you come riding in with your three brothers."

"I hope you're right." Luke caught Teresa's stare. "I'll take off soon as I can. Let's see. It's noon now, so I've got time to buy supplies. Maybe I'll leave in the morning."

"That's best." One of Teresa's eyebrows rose as she nodded. Luke knew his perfected poker face didn't work on her. She saw through him like sheer curtains.

Luke glanced again at his niece. "Looks like Uncle

Luke's going away for a few days." He returned the child's smile. "But he'll be back."

Dainty footsteps caught Luke's attention. Morningstar, pausing in the kitchen door, looked as ravishing as ever. She cocked her head. "You're leaving?"

One shoulder shrugged as he glanced at Teresa. "Thought it's about time I go find those brothers of mine and drag 'em back. Probably holed up in some poker game and lost track of time."

Morningstar frowned. "I don't want you to go." She turned to Teresa. "*We* don't want him to go, do we?"

"He needs to." Teresa cut up a small piece of chicken for Faith. "James and Trace could use his help, I'm sure."

"But how would it look if Luke rode off leaving us to fend for ourselves?" Morningstar touched Luke's arm. "We need you here. Please stay."

Morningstar's dark eyes danced with life. But Luke noticed more. She was unhappy, just like Tommy Littleton had said, and he knew why. Luke vowed to help James any way he could. Maybe a brotherly chat or two, a few pointers about lovemaking and the problem should be solved. What if it was something else? Something he couldn't fix?

As he ate, he mulled over what exactly he'd say to James. If he couldn't fix his brother's problem, what would Morningstar do? Medical school seemed a good idea, but what about James? Would he be willing to be known as the town doctor's husband? Luke mashed his potatoes, added a spot of gravy, and ate without tasting.

Half an hour of eating and small talk, then dishes washed and dried, Luke sat in Trace's favorite chair in the living room. Faith, on his lap, fought big blinks.

Teresa wiped her damp hands on her apron and held

out her arms to Faith. "It's naptime. An hour of quiet." She smiled as Luke handed her over.

Morningstar tied her bonnet under her chin. "I've gotta mail a letter. Be right back."

Luke eased out of his chair and stretched. "Funny thing. I've got one, too. Mind if I tag along?" He glanced at Teresa as if seeking approval, but not heeding the answer if it was yes.

"Pick up any mail we've got, if you don't mind." Teresa spoke over her shoulder as she headed for the bedroom. "See you in ten minutes?"

Morningstar and Luke nodded.

* * *

LUKE HELD the door for Morningstar then followed her inside the post office. Abe Kinnear peered over his glasses perched on the end of his nose. "Afternoon."

"Hello, Mister Kinnear."

"Howdy, both you Coltons." Abe chuckled. "Nice to have half the town with the same last name. Makes it mighty handy."

Morningstar dug through her handbag then extracted a neatly addressed envelope. "I'd like to send this, please." She handed it over the counter.

Abe studied the address. "Letter to your folks again, huh? Tucson's a fur piece, that's a fact. Take a week, maybe ten days."

"That's fine. I know it takes a while."

Luke extracted a letter from his coat pocket. "While you're at it, could you send this one, too?"

Abe glanced at Luke then nodded. "Course. That's what I'm here for." He studied the address. "Kansas, huh." He tapped it. "Ah, sending a letter to the missus, I see."

Luke felt his cheeks burn. "In care of my folks. Sally and the kids are staying with them 'til I get back."

Abe locked eyes with Luke. "And when'll that be?"

Luke swallowed hard, couldn't keep the gaze. He glanced at Morningstar. "After my brothers come home. Shouldn't be much longer now."

"Uh huh." Abe shuffled around the counter, dropped the envelopes in separate piles. He turned to Luke and stuck out an upturned palm. "Three cents."

* * *

LUKE AND MORNINGSTAR stepped into the soft afternoon sun. He soaked in the warmth reflecting off the white plaster of the Corn Exchange Hotel and the peeling white of the Sheriff's office across the dusty plaza.

Morningstar held a hand to her mouth and shot her eyes back toward the post office. Luke couldn't help but chuckle. Abe Kinnear was certainly plain spoken. "What'd I do?"

Corners of Morningstar's sensuous mouth curved upwards. "Hard saying with Mister Kinnear." She held up her purse. "Listen, I need to go over to the grocer's and pick up a couple things for tonight's supper." Her grin grew to a full-fledged smile. "I'm cooking!"

"Oh, no!" Luke clutched his stomach. "Then Lupe's Café, here I come!"

Feigned outrage spun Morningstar around. She marched a few steps before Luke caught up. "All right, all right. I'm sorry." He chuckled then lowered his voice. "What're you fixing?"

"Fried chicken, Mister Colton. With green beans and biscuits."

Luke licked his lips. "Maybe I'll reconsider. These restaurants 'round here probably don't make biscuits like you do."

"I'll take that as an apology and a compliment, sir."

Luke caught a look in Morningstar's eyes reflecting the growing knot in his stomach. What exactly was it? Knowing all eyes were watching? Being so close? Guilt for his thoughts about James' wife? He pushed questions aside, determined to enjoy every minute with this little beauty.

"If you don't mind, I'd like to accompany you to this grocer. But, please let me pay. I've gotta do my share."

Morningstar nodded. "That's an offer I definitely won't turn down."

"I've got some money up in my room." Luke jerked his thumb over his shoulder at the hotel. "I'll meet you at the store. It'll only take a minute."

"The grocer's on the way. Down the block and around the corner." She pointed. "I'll show you where it is, then meet you there."

Shoulders close to touching as they strolled, Luke fought for intelligent conversation. Her nearness brought rampaging tingles to his chest. Past the plaza, they turned the corner and passed an alley. Luke stopped and peered in. Empty.

He tugged on her arm leading her into the shadowed daylight. Heart pounding and throwing caution to the wind, he faced her.

Morningstar cleared her throat. "This is crazy, Luke. Why do I feel so guilty? So wicked?"

Those eyes, rich ebony, her skin like silk, that hair... Luke ran his hands up and down her arms. "Guilty, wicked?" He moved in closer and dropped his voice. "Done anything wicked lately?"

A head shake.

Unable to resist temptation any longer, Luke pulled her into a gentle embrace. He smiled at her trembling body so close to his. She didn't try to pull away. In fact, she seemed to press against him. He breathed into her ear. "No one will know."

CHAPTER THIRTY

IT WASN'T SUPPOSED TO BE THIS HARD, THIS difficult. They were supposed to ride up into the cold Mogollon Mountains, he and Trace, locate baby brother Andy, then pluck him from the jaws of the unknown. It was supposed to be easy. Andy was supposed to be waiting for rescue. Waiting with that ready smile and hearty laugh. But he wasn't.

Where the hell was he? James shaded his eyes peering into the endless blue sky then let them sweep across the narrow canyon. Just within the few days he and Trace had been there at what was left of the mining camp, the sun had come out, shining relentlessly on the dead.

James glared into the sun, realizing he never hated heat until now. He turned his attention to Trace who was crossing the stiff arms of the last of the twenty bodies they'd lined up.

"Snow's melting way too fast." James shook his head. "These bodies gotta get buried."

Trace pried his hat off his head, then ran a forearm

across his face. "Almost wish it was back to snowing again. Leastways we'd have an excuse not to bury them."

"Dammit," James clenched his fists. "Why can't those Apache leave well enough alone? Suppose they'll ever quit killing? Suppose we'll ever just let each other be?"

Trace regarded his black plush hat, rows of stars circling the rim. Andy's was similar but the leather hatband hid his silver studs. "Need a wagon to haul these men up to softer ground. Nothing but rocks around here." From the glare of mid-morning sun, he surveyed the valley walls. Boulders revealed their size and girth as the snow melted while bushes clung to the steep sides.

James kicked at an icy patch of snow living in the shadow of scrub oak bushes. He studied the crusty white. *You're praying the sun won't move—you know you'll die otherwise. You'll melt into the earth, never to be seen again. Never to be part of life. Never to be—*

A tap on his shoulder. James flinched.

Trace's knitted eyebrows reflected James' concern. "You all right?"

No, he'd probably never be "all right." He brought his attention back to his brother. "Fine."

But what was going on in Traces' mind? James knew he still had to put his own past in order, sort out those terrifying memories and images, but big brother, sturdy Trace still called out in his sleep, still tossed and turned. They both did. Bad dreams were coming more often.

First things first. "Where're we supposed to bury them?" James asked.

A hawk circled half a mile to the northeast. It glided on warm air currents. Trace pointed. "Maybe up on top of that hill over there. You go check it out, I'll see if I can get a wagon put together enough. My horse'll take to one, I think."

"Hope so. We can't haul a loaded wagon clear up there by ourselves." James shook his head at the row of bodies. "For their sake, I hope we bury them soon. Words need saying."

James spun his revolver's cylinder. Satisfied, he snugged it into the holster on his hip and mounted his horse. What would he find on top of that hill? He shivered, certainly not from the cold.

By following a wild-animal trail, James made his way up past boulders, bushes and pines. The top of the canyon was higher than it appeared from the bottom. From up there, he had a clear view of the fractured mining camp below. And Dawson's cabin.

Up and down the valley lay tent remnants, gray canvases strewn around like a patchwork quilt sewn by blind women. James let his shoulders sag while he knelt and sent a short prayer upward. Those men shouldn't have died. Not like that. Not at the end of Indians' lances and sneers.

He took his time scouting the area, even riding across the top of the ridge and back into a clearing ringed by trees. No signs of Indians or miners, alive or dead. He spotted a flat quarter acre without boulders, which would serve well as a cemetery. Sharp pine scents, brought along on a soft breeze, tickled his nose. He knew he shouldn't smile, but with the turquoise sky, birds twittering and looking for seeds, and that soothing smell... he thought of Pinos Altos and how much he enjoyed living there. With Morningstar by his side, he knew he'd found Heaven.

Pulling thoughts into the here and now, he mounted his horse, reined her around and took another good look at the cabin. Dawson slammed the door as he stepped out, now aiming toward the mine behind it. Crazy man. James gigged his horse.

It took longer to get to the bottom than he'd anticipated, letting his horse pick her way through rocks and snowdrifts. He reined up next to Trace, who mopped his forehead.

"'Bout damn time you showed up. Got that wagon mended and Sophie hitched. Had to talk sweet nothin's in her ear just to get her to cooperate." Trace rubbed a sore shoulder. "She's not too keen on wagons. Find anything?"

James pointed toward the ridge. "There's soft enough ground, not too many boulders, up about three quarters of a mile. Should suit them just fine."

Trace rubbed the other shoulder while both men studied the hilltop. "Not too worried about suiting *them*." He glanced at the bodies. "I'm worried about *me*."

Low whistling, a tune sounding like "Camptown Races" pierced the canyon's silence. Dawson walked toward them, the whistling now louder.

"What d'you think he wants?" Trace asked.

"He's not carrying a stew bucket or such. Looks like he doesn't want to feed us, at least." James nodded as Dawson stopped. Trace edged over closer to his brother.

Dawson cocked his chin toward the row of miners. "Gonna plant 'em?"

Of course, they were. "Can't imagine riding off leaving the bodies to every jackal and fortune-seeker who came near." James pointed toward the top of the hill. "Found a good place. It's the least we can do."

Trace stared into the distance. "Still can't find Andy anywhere."

Dawson stuck his bottom lip out, more of a habit than a pout. "You try the lake?"

"Lake? What lake?" Trace faced Dawson.

"Oh, 'bout ten miles up that trail." He pointed due east. "Follow close to the stream. You'll find that lake sooner or later."

"Good Lord!" James swung his gaze from Trace to Dawson and back again. "I thought the trail ended 'bout a mile from here. We followed it but with the snow and such, figured that was as far as it went."

Trace peered into the cloudless blue, a breeze pushing a hint of welcome cold. "Gotta get to buryin' these men, but first thing in the morning we'll take off."

Dawson stared at the line of dead miners then knelt beside a man about his size. "Shame to waste them clothes. Could use a new shirt or two, a pair of britches."

Trace stepped between Dawson and the body. "We're buryin' 'em just like we found 'em. Need to respect the dead."

"The dead? Hells bells! What about the *livin'*, Mister Colton?" Dawson stood nose to nose with Trace. "Or ain't you ever been hungry enough, dirty enough, cold enough to steal? Ever know what it's like to do without? *Really* do without? So hungry the only thing you feel is your stomach pressed against your backbone? So desperate you'd do anything? So tired you couldn't lift your head 'cause there's no food in your body, no shirt on your back, no..." Dawson dropped his voice. "No hope?"

James chewed on the inside of his cheek and thought about Dawson's questions. "We've been through some of that, Mr. Dawson. Yeah, I see what you're gettin' at."

Terrifying images, horrific anguish, unrelenting memories charged across James' mind. He cringed, now powerless to stop them. He forced open his eyes. Rapid shallow breaths brought a graying world.

"James." Trace's voice. "James."

Trace's face inches from his. James blew out a long breath. His world colored again. Jaw clenched, he forced words over it. "Take only what you need, Dawson."

CHAPTER THIRTY-ONE

STANDING PONY RACED HIS PINTO LEADING HIS Apache warriors. Mud splattered up from frenzied hooves as they galloped toward the purple mountain looming to the east. Calculating his next move, Standing Pony felt the blood lust in each of his warriors, the anger and determination of men whose land and lives were lost.

He knew the mining camp of Walker sat between them and the Mogollon Mountains. Standing Pony turned his entourage north-northeast and aimed for their first victory of the day. The miners and prospectors there were aware of the destruction of Santa Rita, but he banked on the town thinking the enemy was long gone— lulled into believing they were safe from the likes of this fearsome warrior and his ruthless Apache.

As he rode, Standing Pony recalled Cochise's final instructions. *Take back what is rightfully ours. Leave no survivors. Then maybe, the mighty Washington will notice us and return our land.*

A couple miles west of tiny Walker, Standing Pony

raised his hand and slowed his pinto to a walk then stopped. Stands of mountain ash provided perfect shelter from prying eyes riding past.

Standing Pony's chest swelled, and his shoulders straightened as he watched his men gather around, waiting for his orders. In minutes, he would allow Cochise's... no, *his* best warriors to begin the killing, raiding, looting.

"My warriors. Listen to my words. Today is only the beginning of our victory. We have harassed the settlers around here, killed a few, but now—now we ride to take back what is ours. To call Mother Earth ours, once again." Standing Pony spread his arms and surveyed the swelling hills, the piñons, birds calling to each other.

Standing Pony studied the face of each man who rode with him. These were friends and relatives he'd known his entire life, people who would die for what they believed in. In fact, all of Cochise's tribe felt that way.

Cochise. Standing Pony thought of the most powerful leader of the entire Apache nation. Cochise was a man of integrity and loyalty. Something about him inspired people to follow. A true leader.

Standing Pony grunted. Why couldn't he be like that? He'd learned to rule by killing the weaker person. His brother, One Wing, had taught him torture and brutality were the only way to control others, to get what you wanted.

He thought back to the days when his brother, One Wing, had brought in those two White Eyes as prisoners.

Standing Pony sat on the chest of the White Eyes called James, pinning his body to the ground while another warrior perched behind him on the White Eye's legs. The man squirmed under Standing Pony's weight, wriggling like the snared worm he knew he was.

One Wing scooped a handful of sand, pebbles and small cactus needles while Standing Pony pried open the captive's mouth. It took yet another Apache to hold the head still. Even though weakened from much torture, this white man remained strong. Sand poured into his open, ugly mouth. The man bucked hard. But not hard enough.

More handfuls until the mouth was full. Sand and tears ran down his face, pooling in the dirt. The other prisoner screamed, struggling against Apache arms holding him.

Standing Pony imagined the terror of sucking in only sand, the lungs screaming for air. No wonder this captive thrashed. Taking life. The power! Standing Pony's chest swelled, his lips curled as he felt life drain from the White Eyes. Another enemy slain!

Then Cochise stopped the game. A sharp command, a wave of his hand and the man lived. Barely.

Standing Pony blinked, pushed memories aside. Renewing his hatred for the White Eyes, James in particular, Standing Pony watched the faces of his followers.

Raising his feathered lance, he lifted his face to the winter sun, closed his eyes, breathed in the pine-scented air and prayed.

Silence hung over the group while each man followed his lead and prayed for strength in battle—victory in life.

A deep breath, Standing Pony then released a blood-curdling war whoop, kicked his pinto, then raced toward the unsuspecting mining camp.

CHAPTER THIRTY-TWO

"YOU'RE AWFULLY QUIET. SOMETHING WRONG?" Teresa washed the final plate and handed it to Morningstar.

She wiped the dish and shook her head. No way she'd tell her thoughts were with the distraction seated right now in the living room. "A little tired, I guess." She glanced at Teresa. "Those men of ours should've been back by now. Suppose something's happened?"

"Don't even think that. It's a long way up there and back, and you know Andy. He probably wandered way off in the hills. The men are just having a hard time tracking him down." Teresa picked up the dishpan and tossed the dirty water out the back door. "It'll go faster when Luke joins them."

Morningstar arranged the plate on the shelf then folded the dishtowel. "I'm sure you're right. No need to worry quite yet." She met Teresa's gaze. "They're fine."

"Uh huh." Teresa lowered the wick in the lantern. Gray filled the kitchen. She touched Morningstar's arm. "What else?"

What could she say? Or admit? Morningstar looked at a spot above Teresa's shoulder. "Just keep thinking how lucky you are to have Faith and then another one coming. Wish it was me, too."

"It will be. Just isn't your time, yet." Teresa touched Morningstar's arm.

Morningstar looked down at her hands. "Can't have kids or medical school." A glance at Teresa. "Is that asking too much?"

"You'll have to choose one or the other. I don't think you could be a doctor *and* a mother at the same time. Besides, what does James want you to do?"

"Why is it always a man's decision? Always *his* choice?" Morningstar's voice dropped to whisper. "When's it *my* turn?" With that, she turned and marched into the living room.

The women joined Luke playing peek-a-boo with Faith. He held her on his lap, and both giggled revealing similar grins. Teresa settled into her rocking chair and picked up a shirt, needle and thread.

"Talked to Sammy today." Luke crossed his right leg over his left knee and ran his finger down a scratch in his boot. "Seems his replacement deputy got kicked by a horse and can't work. He needs some help and says this town's too big for just one deputy sheriff."

Was there a chance Luke would stay? Morningstar held her breath, then let it out.

Teresa stopped rocking. "He offered you a job?"

"Temporarily." Luke raised an eyebrow. "I know we agreed that I should go, but he says he needs me here. So, told him I'd help out as deputy-deputy only until my brothers get back." He paused, setting Faith on the floor. "If that's all right with you two."

Morningstar beamed. "So, you're staying?"

Luke nodded again and glanced at Teresa.

She sat up straighter, cocked her head. "You don't have to ask our permission. Of course, you do what you think is best." A quick smile ran across her face. "You'll be mighty busy. Guess we won't be seeing much of you now, will we?"

Luke studied his hands then stared up at Morningstar. "I'm curious. Why wasn't James a deputy? Didn't he want to?"

She shook her head while a knot twisted her stomach. "He was certainly interested. Especially since Trace is such a good sheriff. He's real popular."

"So I've noticed."

Teresa cradled her daughter rubbing her eyes. She lowered her voice. "With James still seeing Indians and fighting them...the town council didn't want someone like that. They were afraid... afraid James would—"

"That's not right. Just because an Indian decides to take out his hostility on my brother, the town says he's crazy? Is that what they say?" Luke clenched his fist.

Morningstar hung her head. "I'm afraid so, Luke." She met his stare. "But you've seen him. He's much better now."

Teresa set her sewing aside. "Better, but not healed."

Morningstar stood and touched his arm. "The town council has the right to decide who protects their city, Luke. They're just doing what—"

"Not the town." Luke spun, his eyes landing first on Teresa then shifting to Morningstar. "I understand that. But it's just not right James has to keep paying for his captivity." He stared at the door. "When will it end for him?"

Those same questions plagued Morningstar every

time James shook at night, every time he cried out. Every time...

Morningstar lowered her voice. "There's something else."

"Something else? How can there possibly be *anything* else?" Luke sprung to his feet. "Isn't that bad enough?"

Morningstar nodded. "As you know, James sees Indians where there aren't any."

"And?"

"And..." Morningstar looked away. "Luke, he's almost killed four people."

"Good God!" Luke rubbed his forehead. "I had no idea."

"There's a little more than that."

"More? There's *more*?" Luke shouted, turned his back on the women, took a deep breath, then turned around.

How much could she tell him? Morningstar considered, then decided. "He stabbed the former sheriff. Alberto Fuente died a few months later."

"He killed a sheriff?" Luke paced the room. "A Goddamn Sheriff? Why the hell didn't anybody tell me? Why'd I have to find it out like this? That's a helluva thing." He slid to a quick stop. "My apologies for the language, ladies."

Luke scrubbed his face like it was on fire. "Gotta get some air." He yanked his coat off the back of the chair. "Thanks again for supper. Night."

The door opened and closed in a matter of seconds. Like a banshee, he disappeared into the cold December night.

CHAPTER THIRTY-THREE

ANDREW JACKSON COLTON HUDDLED IN THE back of the frigid mine shaft and prayed he would see another day. He shook his head. Dawson and his blusterations! Obviously a man besotted with hatred. What had he said about his life? The landowner and Dawson's wife... then a baby. She sold off to another plantation. And then the baby's sudden death. Dawson's face curved into a half-crazed, half grief-stricken mask when he mentioned the baby.

Like a lightning strike, it all became clear. Dawson killed that baby! And the landowner! It all made perfect sense. Wife sold, infant reminding him of his wife's assault. No wonder he ran away.

Pulling his coat tighter around his trembling body, Andy held his bound hands in front of his face. Or so he thought. Way too dark to be sure. He pulled his knees up under his chin and leaned back against a solid rock wall. His stomach rumbled. How long had he lay in this cave, jammed between rocks, before regaining consciousness?

This morning he had scooped up his last mouthful of

breakfast stew when Dawson yanked him into the mine-shaft. Fear gripped Andy's stomach at the cat-eating-the-mouse arrogance on Dawson's face. The face changing on a whim. Tugged down the mineshaft behind the cabin, a sudden turn in the far reaches of the cave surprised Andy. With a spur at a sharp right angle, only torches lighting the area would reveal its secret turn.

The last thing he remembered—asking Dawson what was going on.

Andy focused on the present. Besides his body being stiff and sore, blood caked on his face. To pass the endless hours, he made a game of smiling, then frowning, listening to the various crusted crunches.

Ankles wrapped with wire, Andy jerked and kicked. Flexing stiff fingers, he ran them around the metal until he jammed his ring finger on a sharp end.

Andy tried to soothe the stinging by putting his finger in his mouth, but between the cloth gagging him and the tight binding around his wrists, he achieved a grunt and a twisted arm.

"Hmmmpp." His word echoed off cold rock. Again locating the end of the wire, Andy forced his fingers to wedge, curl and tug.

Figuring he'd be fingerless within a matter of minutes, the cold so severe he knew they'd break off, Andy quit.

A scraping noise somewhere in the distance jolted him out of self-pity. Peering into the ebony, he spotted a faint glow of orange. Torch or lantern? Rescuers?

Within minutes, he squinted up into the towering figure of his captor, lantern in hand. The runaway knelt by Andy, dropped what looked like a heavy coat, then set the lantern on the ground. He unwrapped the dirty bandana from around Andy's mouth.

Jaw stiff and aching, he moved it back and forth and eyed the man at his feet. Golden light haloed Dawson's entire body.

"Cold." Andy hoped the word made sense. He eyed the pile of material on the ground, then swung his gaze to his captor's coat. Different from his other one, this coat was of deer or calf. It sported deep pockets and a high collar, which could stand up against wind and rain.

Dawson's breath clouded as he spoke. "I'll get these ankles free if you promise you ain't runnin'."

Andy nodded.

Dawson unwrapped the wire, coiled and then shoved it into his pocket before looking at Andy. A slow sneer curled both lips as he slid his fingers down Andy's cheek tracing the blood ribbon. "Good thing 'bout freezin'. Dries fast."

Andy jerked at the touch but held his hands out in hopes of release. They trembled, shaking with the damnable mixture of cold and fright. How could he get that coat?

Dawson's changing face. Andy suddenly understood. The man kneeling beside him would keep him. Keep him forever. Death would be the only release.

Binding around his ankles now gone, he flexed his legs, knees screaming while his hips grated against the frigid ground.

Dawson gripped Andy's coat sleeve and tugged. "You move slow, 'bout like molasses in winter." He chuckled. "You ain't as sweet, though." He yanked harder. "Come on. Gotta get you outta here 'fore you freeze to death."

Andy recoiled from his captor's rank breath. He anticipated pain, waiting for the slap, for his cheek to burn. At least his cheek would be warm.

Black eyes shining, reflected in the lantern's glow,

Dawson gripped Andy's bound hands and, with bull strength, yanked him to his feet. Andy's rigid legs refused to bend, to move. He willed them to keep his weight.

"Brought ya somethin'." Dawson wrapped the coat around Andy. It's wool lining rubbed soft against his own coat. A faint smell of tobacco wafted with each movement. No way would he ask where he got this coat, or why Dawson gave it to him. No, Andy would just be grateful.

"Thanks." Between the cold and his broken jaw, Andy produced grunts and groans. Hopefully the meaning came through.

"Let's go." Dawson shoved Andy.

Moving like a wooden soldier he'd played with as a child, Andy plodded down the tunnel, pushed by a man who would kill without much provocation.

Andy stumbled into the fresh air and squinted at banks of clouds covering a setting sun. They opened, revealing a steel sky. Shivers again bolted through his body.

A push. A strong one, but not what Andy expected from this lunatic. But he was still on his feet. Still alive.

Dawson pushed again. "Gotta get a move on or we'll stick freeze to da ground."

Skirting frozen bushes and slogging through snow mounds, Andy picked his way across the field toward the cabin. Near the door, he hit a patch of ice. Andy slid into the cabin, his face slamming against the rough planking. Dawson grabbed the back of Andy's coat.

"Watch where you're goin', Andrew. You wanna be in one piece to see them brothers of yours, don't ya?" Dawson cackled, pulling Andy out of the way, and then opened the cabin door. Andy stepped in.

He fought to make words. "My brothers...here?"

Dawson's yellowed teeth showed under the snarl. "Already told ya. Them ol' boys stayed 'round three, four days." He pushed his face closer to Andy's. "'Parently decided to head on home." He shrugged. "Guess dey tired of lookin' for you."

As if reading Andy's thoughts, Dawson cackled. "Even if they do come back here, you ain't gonna be 'round for that tearful family reunion."

"You're leaving?" Andy prayed for the right answer.

"Leavin'. Yessiree, we is. You and me. Together." Nodding, Dawson plucked the new coat from Andy's shoulders, then pushed him into a chair at the table. He poured water into the coffeepot, shoved kindling into the stove and used flint and steel to light it.

"Why?"

Dawson centered the pot on a burner, lifted the top and spooned coffee into it. He took care measuring and then setting the pot just so. Finally, he turned to Andy. "Why? Seems plain 'nuff to me. Those Apach' is done gone, but seein' as it's dead a winter, ain't much game around."

Andy swept his gaze across the room as if expecting a chicken or rabbit to pop out of a pot. No meat hanging or sizzling in a pan.

"All we gots is vegetables, and those're runnin' low." Dawson scratched his chest. "No, 'bout time to find someplace else to live. 'Specially since your brothers done took all the fresh meat around here."

Meat? Brothers? None of it made sense. Maybe the lunatic would listen to reason. Maybe there was hope yet. Andy worked his jaw back and forth. Would the words be clear enough?

"I can help. Doesn't have to be like this." Andy

waited for strong hands to grip his throat, squeeze. Instead, Dawson blew into two mugs and set them on the table.

Obviously, he wasn't listening. Andy raised his voice. "There's people in town... who can help. Good people. Even a few colored folk—"

"I could kill you tonight."

Ignoring the threat, Andy leaned forward, gaze riveted on Dawson. "We could ride back together." Nothing left to lose. "I'll get you a job. Livery stable's always looking for good hands. I'll tell 'im you're a friend of mine." He prayed Dawson listened. "They'll hire you for sure. You'll earn money and can—"

"But I ain't gonna kill you. No siree. Not tonight." Dawson measured Andy with his eyes. "Havin' you ride upright's easiest."

Jaw on fire, Andy's shoulders sagged. He'd tried running, he'd tried reasoning. Now he'd have to find another way.

Dawson poured coffee in a cup and plopped it in front of Andy. "Drink up. Get ya nice an' toasty warm." He pointed toward the cot. "You gonna sleep in here tonight. Floor's warm 'nuff for ya. Got that extra coat. You'll sleep good 'nuff."

Dawson's nearness set Andy's nerves on edge. He looked up into the man's coal eyes.

Andy shivered.

CHAPTER THIRTY-FOUR

JAMES BREATHED OUT A STREAM OF ICE crystals and poked another stick into the fire. The end bursting into flame, he pushed it closer toward the center. Images of his youngest brother rushed through his mind. The day Andy was born. Pa had let him and Luke come into Ma's room shortly after the birth. Standing at Ma's side, he watched the swaddled bundle wiggle. Little hands waved.

That jubilant look on Trace's face. Being the oldest at almost eight, he'd been allowed to assist by carrying water and towels back and forth.

Ma's eyes sparkled with pride and love while Pa just looked relieved. Was that what having a baby felt like? Relief? Shaking his head, James remembered how much work a new baby was and yet, Andy'd been so much fun. At the age of barely four, James helped as much as he could with the care of the baby, but Luke was only two and needed a lot of looking-after. That was James' main job—taking care of Luke.

Trace's job as a child was looking after James. Being

the oldest brought a lot of responsibility and that didn't give a great deal of time to being a kid. A grin split James' face. Being a kid. What about the time he and Trace, about eight and twelve, waved goodbye to Ma one spring day and never made it to school. That stream and fish were calling. Must've been noon when Pa showed up at the fishing hole.

The three men spent the entire afternoon swapping stories and dangling their lines in the water. James remembered catching more than supper when he got home.

"What're you grinning at, little brother?"

"That time we skipped school and went fishing." James pushed the well-burned stick into the fire then dusted his hands.

Trace chuckled. "Ma sure was mad. I think she lectured Pa more than us."

Safety and security of home, its memories, drew a cocoon around James. He picked up another stick, then etched a picture in the mud. "She did, for a fact. But I remember... the whole time, Pa tried to hide that grin."

Trace nodded. "Kinda miss those days."

He did, too. James stared again into pulsating embers covered with blackened sticks, capped with popping orange flames. A snowflake glided onto his nose and melted. He pulled his blanket around his shoulders and lay near the fire.

Tossing and turning, watching the stars move across the sky, James huddled under his wool blanket. Snow dusted the ground creating a thin white cover for the men.

Sleep finally captured him and sent dreams.

I stare at the young Pima woman trembling in front of me. Her
beauty is in the way she looks at me—those ebony eyes. They
trust me. I reach out and pull her in. Ignore the Apache faces
around us, I tell her. Their white teeth glint in the late afternoon
light. Dark Cloud presses against my bare chest, her naked body
melting into mine.

My hands slide down her soft back. I pull her closer…closer
to my anxious body. I kiss the nape of her neck, nibble at—

"Damn! Look at this!"

A firm grip on James' shoulder startled him awake.
"Huh?"

"Six, seven inches."

"What?"

"Snow. Last night." Trace stood and pulled his
blanket tighter around his shoulders. Clouded early
morning light bathed him in gray.

Running his hand through his matted hair, James
allowed crisp air to fill his lungs. Eyes squeezed tight, he
sucked in a sharp lungful. Unwilling and definitely not
ready to open his eyes and face the new day, he lay still.
Would that vision, that dream return? Did he want it to?
And was it not a dream, but a nightmare?

Knees crunched against the hard ground. Trace
touched James' shoulder. "Another dream?"

Pushing out a stream of air, James peeked out from
under reluctant eyelids. He nodded.

Trace raised both eyebrows. "Dark Cloud?"

Again, James nodded.

Trace stood. "Better get a fire started and that coffee
perking. I'm cold."

James knew he should be cold, too. But the feel of
Dark Cloud's body against his warmed the entire forest.

Trace tossed the remainder of his coffee into the fire

and scooped up snow with his cup. Sloshing it in the tin, he dumped the water on the fire. From his perch on a fallen log, James refocused on his brother now dousing the fire with the few brown drops left in the coffeepot.

Easing to his feet, James yawned and stretched. Trees, rocks and bushes emerged from under white crystals, reflecting the early morning sunlight. James glanced into the rising ball of orange and shook his head. Depression gripped his soul as tight as Cochise's hand had squeezed his throat. Even after all this time, he still felt those fingers' power. He swallowed.

Trace shoved the coffeepot into his saddlebag and tied the leather strings. He glanced over his shoulder as he slung the brown bag across his horse's rump. "You gonna stare at the trees all day?"

James picked up his saddle and slogged through the snow toward his horse. Saddle cinched and blanket rolled then tied behind the cantle, James propped his forehead against his horse's side and closed his eyes. Could he go on today? What was the point?

"What's eating you?" Trace's hand on his shoulder.

His gloved hand tightened into a fist. "Nothing. Everything." He took a deep breath choking on frozen air. "Hell, I don't know."

Trace's impatient breathing behind him. James turned around. Trace tapped James' forehead. "Whatever's goin' on in there, put it away. I need you right now. I need you to be strong and believe we'll find Andy." His eyes met James'. "I've got enough doubts for the both of us, so you've got to help here. I can count on you?"

Of course he could. James stared over Trace's shoulders to the Ponderosa pines, now grayed silhouettes against the blue sky. He nodded.

Trace patted James' shoulder then turned around.

"Trace?" James gripped his brother's sleeve and waited until his brown eyes looked at him. "Tell me. How do I 'put away' these dreams? Quit seeing Indians?" He studied his snow-covered boots. "Make love to my wife?"

CHAPTER THIRTY-FIVE

Deputies Luke Colton and Sammy Estrada hurried toward the crowd gathering in front of the Mercantile. In just the past few minutes, from the time Luke had peeked out the office door until now, twenty, perhaps thirty, people had collected. While Saturday crowds were known to congregate around the store's bench facing the plaza, there was something ominous about this group.

"What's all the fuss here?" Sammy spoke to a man on the crowd's fringe.

"Indian attack. Again."

Sammy and Luke pushed in toward the man who seemed to be the center of attention. A few of the women and all of the men muttered but moved aside as the two deputies shoved past. Luke recognized the postmaster.

"What's goin' on, Mr. Kinnear?" Sammy wrestled a blackened envelope from the old man's grip.

"Indians is what's goin' on. Lots of Indians. Mean,

fearsome killers. On the warpath, slicin' up innocent people."

The crowd drew a collective breath and women clutched children to their skirts. Men muttered as the crowd's crescendo built.

"Kill them stinkin' Indians."

"Only good Apache's a dead Apache."

"Shootin' em's too good. Hang 'em!"

Sammy held up his hands and the letter. "Now just simmer down, all of you. I'll find out what happened. No need to get all lathered up over something that might not be." He turned to Luke. "Get this broke up right now or it'll get ugly."

Luke's badge burned against his chest while his Colt cleared leather. "You heard him. Just go on about your business." No one moved, a few even turned their backs.

"Hey!" Luke shouted above the crowd. "Time to get on home. Now go!" One woman, two young boys in tow, tsked at the new deputy and dragged her reluctant children down the rough boardwalk.

"Mr. Kinnear." Sammy shouted to be heard. "Let's step into my office." He slid his hand under the man's elbow and guided him through the crowd and out into the plaza.

Passing Luke, Sammy dropped his voice. "I said get this crowd broke up."

His face heating, Luke coughed, then shouted. "Get on home. Nothin' to see here. We'll let you know if anything's really happened."

One man grumbled and wandered away.

More threats from Luke. Two men muttered, threw a disgusted look his way, then wandered off. With the most vocal of the group gone, Luke trotted to catch up with the other deputy. He wound his way through growling ranchers and businessmen, past worried women and around curious children. If dresses rustling and low chatter was any indication, the throng had followed him.

Reaching the office door just as Sammy and Abe slammed it, Luke's empty hand curled into a fist. Bringing it up to smack the closed door, he thought better of his action. Instead, he turned to a renewed, growing crowd, his back against the door.

"Best go on about your business, just like Deputy Estrada asked." A rush of power simmered in Luke's brain. He was the man in charge. He had the gun. And the badge.

Shoulders squared and standing just that much taller, he pointed his revolver at the center of the crowd, cocked the weapon, then barked a final order. "I said go on home. Don't rile me. I'd hate to have to shoot you."

People turned and ambled across the plaza. Murmurs of "Crazy like his brother," and "Indian lover," drifted behind them.

Hoping his disdain didn't show too much, Luke let down the hammer and eased the cold metal back into its warm holster. One corner of his mouth drew up as his heart rate returned to normal.

"What the hell's goin' on, Colton?"

Luke jumped at the voice in his ear. He spun around. Thomas Littleton loomed bigger than life. Luke rushed his words.

"Kinnear thinks Apache attacked again is all. He's got a letter that's all burned up." Luke stared at the newspaperman's stubbled face, a shave would have been in order yesterday.

"Gawd dammit, boy. What the hell you standin' out here for? Get inside and find out what's happenin'."

Littleton pushed open the door and stepped in. Luke wedged his foot in before the rest of his body was crushed by the slamming wood.

"I still don't see how you made the connection, Abe." Sammy's voice echoed doubt tinged with impatience. "Yes, this letter is from Walker. But it had to go through Santa Rita before it got here. Right? That's where it got burned."

Abe smacked the desk. "Sure. But that's ain't what happened. Walker's been hoorawed and that's that!" Abe snatched the singed envelope from Sammy.

Littleton rested his rear on the sheriff's desk and gazed upward. "Both towns've been attacked, boys. 'Member Mogollon got it just before Trace and James left? Apache were heading on down to Santa Rita."

The three men nodded.

"A smart leader," Littleton continued, "such as Cochise, or his pathetic bootlicker, Standing Pony, would come back and attack again. The town wouldn't be expecting to be hit twice, so soon."

Luke pulled up a wooden chair, planted his right foot on the seat and leaned into the conversation. "But what would that prove, Tommy?"

"Good Lord, boy, what the hell've you been usin' for brains all these years? Damnation, you're as dense as that hardheaded brother of yours. Hell, even James would've figured it out by now." He took a deep breath and glared at Luke. "And don't call me Tommy."

Luke clenched his jaw and studied the wanted posters on the wall behind Sammy.

Thomas Littleton took a deep breath. "It proves they can do it, Luke. Those Apache now control the entire Mogollon basin." Littleton pointed north. "It means... everyone up there's in a helluva lot of danger."

CHAPTER THIRTY-SIX

JAMES JERKED AWAKE AT SHAFTS OF SUN piercing his eyes. He rolled to his left and plowed into his brother's knees.

"Just gonna wake you." Trace stood and pointed toward the campfire. "Coffee's 'bout ready."

"Right." James located his boots next to his head and tugged them on. Freezing, stiff fingers made the process difficult, but finally his feet occupied cold boots.

Navigating around the icy lake had taken the better part of yesterday and most of the men's energy. With the snow softening then melting under the winter sun, evidence of a few abandoned camps had pushed through the crust. However, both Coltons knew that what they were looking for was hidden. Well hidden.

And yesterday's slow ride had given James time to think, really think about his life. His and Morningstar's. And whatever it was he was doing wrong. At one point, a trout had broken through the thin ice covering the lake. Sticking its head barely out of the surface, the mouth flapped open and closed, desperate for a fly or bug to happen by. Obviously needing something, the fish wasn't getting it from the lake. That's when the answer hit him. Star needed something he wasn't providing. And he knew what that was. Maybe a change of scenery would change him.

Hands hovering over the fire, James stared into the flames. "'Bout decided that when we get back, I'm gonna sell my saloon."

Trace's cup stopped halfway to his lips. "What? Sell the Buckhorn?"

"Yeah. I'm not really a businessman. And I'm thinking I'll use the money to take Star to California. San Francisco. See the ocean. Neither of us've seen it. Maybe, just maybe..." James pointed his cup west. "Yeah, that way's the answer."

"Just could be." Trace sipped the hot liquid. "What d'you think Morningstar's gonna say? Would she want to go?"

James stared into the black liquid. "I've been thinkin' on that very question, and she'd probably be willing to. For a while anyway. May have to do some fancy talking, but she might."

"Instead of selling, maybe Andy would run your saloon for you while you're gone. Then you wouldn't have to start over when you get back." Trace eyed his brother.

James studied the fire then turned to Trace. "But that's just what I intend to do. Start all over."

CHAPTER THIRTY-SEVEN

"ENOUGH'S ENOUGH. LET'S HEAD ON BACK TO Mogollon. Nothin' here worth bothering with." James pried off his wide-brimmed hat and ran his other hand across his face, smearing a mud glop from ear to chin. Besides, two trips around the entire lake and nothing to show for it. Time to look elsewhere.

Reining to a stop, Trace squinted, the noon sun rays, like spears, stabbed through the trees. "Got a feelin' he's never been here."

"We can make it back tonight if we hurry." James tugged his hat around his ears and kicked his horse into a fast trot.

Full dark ushered the two exhausted men and horses into Mogollon. The stillness and nerve-biting cold bought immediate shivers to James. "Don't see hide nor hair of Dawson. Smoke ain't even comin' from the chimney." He pointed toward the shape of the singular cabin just coming into view and glanced at his brother riding next to him. "What d'ya suppose that means?"

Trace flipped his coat lapels up around the back of his neck. "It means we'll stop and find out."

Tying their mounts to a nearby tree, the Colton brothers stretched their lanky bodies and then pulled their revolvers from the holsters. A quick spin of the cylinders revealed full loads.

Trace reholstered his .44 Colt, but James kept his aimed toward the cabin. Just in case. Besides, he'd built a reputation for being a good shot. Butterfield Stage Lines had hired him as shotgun guard for that reason. That and the fact Trace drove for them. Now, maybe he'd put his skill and hours of practice to good use.

Lowering his voice to a whisper, Trace gazed at the dark cabin, moonlight reflecting off the single windowpane. "Don't know what kind of game Dawson's playing but be damn careful." He swung his attention to James. "Don't want you all shot up. One brother in danger's enough."

"Don't worry." James flashed a wide grin. "I'm the expert marksman of the family, remember?"

Trace wagged his head. "Just... watch yourself."

Nodding, James rushed the door and slammed his shoulder against the wood. It held tight. Clutching his arm, James reared back and kicked. He fell into the dark room as Trace also rushed the door. Both men stumbled into the cabin and slid to a stop.

James crouched. His own wheezing and Trace's breathing broke the deafening silence. Moonlight threw a tenuous beam on the table managing to illuminate shapes within the cabin.

Pacing side to side, James checked under the cot and table while Trace stepped back outside and circled the cabin. They met inside.

Trace let out a long sigh. "Dammit. Been gone a while, I'm reckoning."

"Why'd the hell he leave?" James holstered his revolver and pushed his hat up off his forehead. Trace fired up a lantern and its warm, golden glow flooded the room. He set it on the sawbuck table.

James opened the side of the stove. Curled bark shaving made perfect kindling. After lighting those, he pushed in two sticks. Flames licked the dry wood. He glanced around the cabin now warming and spotted no single clue to explain crazy Dawson's departure. Judging by the cold and dishes in disarray, Dawson left two days ago, maybe three.

A knot in James' stomach leaped to his throat. Why'd he leave? He'd seemed content to stay here forever. Something nagged at his thoughts. Something wasn't right. Cabin now toasty, James removed his coat and tossed it over the back of a chair.

Trace perched on the edge of the sagging cot, pulled off his gloves and unbuttoned his coat. "Where the hell is he?" He wrenched it off and threw it on the cot. "Andy's here. I just know it. I can feel him."

"Something hot'll taste good tonight." Dented coffee pot in hand, James gripped the door handle. "I'll get some water." His brother sat, running his hands through his hair. After a pause, enough time for Trace to respond, James opened the door, allowing a rush of icy air inside. "Be back in a minute."

James located a bank of snow near the mineshaft entrance, scooped and filled the pot to the brim, then turned back to the cabin. The mouth of the tunnel caught his attention. Setting the pot down, James peered into the dark, the moon casting enough light to tantalize his curiosity.

"Hello?" Cocking his head toward the entrance, he stepped closer. "Anyone in here?" He waited. Silence. Shaking his head, he picked up the pot and trudged through the snow back into the cabin's sanctuary.

Snow immediately melting, James added the coffee grounds, pushed the tin lid on and set it over the stove's burner. James thudded into the wooden chair, studied his hands and then the chips and scratches in the table. His eyes closed while allowing the boiling coffee's aroma to push panic from his mind. James' shoulders rose and fell with every breath.

Images of curlicues, Andy's hatband, curious markings marched across his dreams. As if a hand slapped him, he jerked awake. James whipped around to his brother stretched out on the cot. "Where's a lantern?" He stood so quickly the chair scooted out from under his weight and clattered to the floor.

Trace lifted his head. "Why? There's plenty of light in here."

"Mine shaft. Think I saw something."

"What?" Trace sat up.

James held up the extra lantern from the corner and shook the bottom. Nodding at the distinctive slosh of fuel, he struck a match and lit the wick. "Come on."

"What'd you see?" Trace grabbed his coat and followed into the cold dark.

Both men stopped at the shaft's entrance and stared. James held the lantern shoulder high and edged in. Stepping into the golden-lit tunnel, James knew instinctively to search for clues. Somewhere, somehow Andy had been here. Or *is* here.

Woven baskets lining the cave's sides held scant vegetables, tin containers most likely empty of flour and coffee, James guessed. Rifling through the foodstuff, they searched for a sign, something to point them in the right direction.

It came as James wandered to the end of the shaft. A sharp turn revealed another tunnel. "Trace." He held the lantern above his head and pointed. "There's more back here. Damn! We missed it the first time."

James waited for Trace to stand next to him, then both crept down the narrow abyss. Twenty yards brought the brothers to a dead end. Turning around twice, James let out a stream of frost. "Dammit, I was sure this was it. Felt it in my bones." He thumped his chest. "Right here."

Trace nodded. "Me, too." Glancing behind his brother, Trace then squatted and studied the dirt. "Look here." He held up a kinked strand of wire.

"So?" James knelt next to Trace.

With a shake of his head, Trace tossed the wire against the rock wall. It sprung back.

Tracking the wire's path, James peered into the edge of the light. He held the lantern closer. Definite marking in the dirt.

Trace leaned over his shoulder. "What is it?"

"Andy."

CHAPTER THIRTY-EIGHT

ANDY STUDIED THE MAN RIDING TO HIS LEFT
and a few feet in front. Dawson's hand, callused and
gnarled, gripped the leather reins of both horses as they
rode, plowing across cold ground.

The unbroken crystal blue sky created a canopy of
calm. A bird or two soared above the distant trees, below
a wispy cloud pushed by winter wind. But despite the
easy feel to the day, Andy rode tense, wound up like a
spring. What lay ahead?

They crossed the open plain then into a boulder-
strewn valley. Andy kept both eyes wide open sweeping
the terrain for any sign of movement. Apache could pick
off both him and Dawson in a heartbeat. No one would
find their bodies for months, if not years. Andy slumped
in his saddle and itched for a gun.

He stared straight ahead and tried not to think about
his future. What gnawed on him was Dawson. Crazy-as-
a-bedbug Dawson. Where were they heading? And why
was Dawson so nice all of a sudden? Other than keeping

Andy's hands tied, he'd made sure Andy was warm, his stomach full from a long mid-day break. That lunatic mentioned stopping early so they could catch a rabbit or two and cook a real feast.

They rode out of the valley and up into the hills, always heading west. Ponderosa pines trembled with a breeze that caused Andy to button his coat. Out in the flats with the sun beating down, he'd been warm. But now the shade brought a shiver to his body.

"Best be findin' us a good stoppin' place." Dawson pulled on his reins and turned around to Andy. "How 'bout here?"

Andy shrugged. One place looked a lot like the others. "Fine. There's a place for a campfire over there." He used his chin to point left. Besides, a get down would feel good. His legs would enjoy supporting his weight for a while and his back needed a good popping. His kidneys urged him to find a bush. Soon.

Campfire blazing, rabbit turning crispy brown over the flames, Andy sat near the warmth and thought about his brothers. Were they doing the same thing? Most likely. Were they still looking for him? Most likely on that account, too. Would they find him, or would he find them? No answer.

Stomach now full of rabbit and turnips Dawson had brought along, Andy's eyes threatened to close. He fought the urge. He needed to be awake until Dawson fell asleep. Then he could escape. Run deep into the forest. Run until he found help. He peered across the fire at the madman. Wide awake, humming *Camptown Races*.

A twig crunched behind him. Andy sat bolt upright and spun. A hand grabbed his throat, lifting him to his feet. Dark eyes, wide bronzed face glared at him. All air blocked, Andy's world turned gray. He clawed at the hand killing him. Out of the corner of his eye, he spotted Dawson, held by an Indian.

Before blackness took him down, the hand released its hold. Andy doubled over, sucking in delicious air and his world colored again. Strong Apache hands clamped around each arm. They yanked him upright.

He jerked at the grips, but to no avail. No way they would let him go. Faces, streaked with red and white paint, surrounded him.

Dawson and an Apache, more than likely the leader, stood nose to nose. Two bulls about to charge.

"You are either very brave or very foolish, Gray Man." The Indian brought his face inches from Dawson's. "My warriors could slice your throat then hand you your head before your body hits the ground."

"I ain't the enemy here, Standing Pony. You know that. Remember Mogollon? You came by my cabin?" Dawson pointed over his shoulder and squirmed against the hold on his arm.

The Apache leader nodded.

Dawson stared up into Standing Pony's face. "Let's do some business. Brought somethin' t'sell you. Something I know you'll like." He wrenched loose from the grip.

Although trembling, Andy's legs were strong enough to run. Give him one chance to escape. One. With the cover of darkness, he could get away. He studied the faces of at least five Apache and Dawson. He couldn't get away—yet.

Standing Pony raised an eyebrow then frowned. "What could you have that I want?"

"Just wait." Dawson held up a hand and swung his gaze to Andy.

Bravado in place, Andy jutted out his chin, threw

back his shoulders, and stared straight ahead. He prayed he masked the terror and uncertainty raging across his heart.

Dawson chuckled while his eyes tracked sideways toward Andy. "I know just how you feel, White Boy." A deeper chuckle. "Yeah, I do. But now it's your turn to beg for mercy, be separated from your family. Be sold." He cocked his head. "'Ceptin' we ain't got no big ol' river to sell you down to!"

Then, as if presenting royalty, Dawson swept his arm toward Andy. "Standing Pony, you gonna be wantin' him." All eyes turned on Andy who sucked air.

He tried to stand straighter, to push his chest out, to look unafraid. Dawson poked Andy's chest. "This here's prime stock." He stepped back allowing the Apache room to inspect.

Standing Pony cradled Andy's face in his hands and turned it side to side. A sneer curled his lips. "You have been in Cochise's camp. I know your face—and that of your brothers."

Andy jerked his head from the grip and stared straight ahead.

Standing Pony stepped back, studied Andy boots to hat, then swung his gaze to Dawson. "How did you come into possession of this boy?"

"Don't matter. I have him and that's all you needs t'know." Dawson cocked his head toward Andy. "You wanna barter or do I go t'the Pima?"

Andy fidgeted with the thick ropes around his wrists. Get out of here! Get away! Somehow, if he worked free, then he'd get away.

Standing Pony frowned into Andy's face. The warriors raised shotguns and arrows, all aimed at Andy's heart. Using both hands, the Apache leader gripped the front of Andy's jacket and shirt, then yanked. Buttons flew. In one fluid motion, both coat and shirt ripped off of Andy's shoulders. Standing Pony pulled the material down around his elbows.

Andy shook so hard his teeth chattered. He prayed he'd stay on his feet before the Apache killed him.

The Indian punched Andy's bandaged, healing upper arm. Nausea boiled to the surface. He leaned over ready to vomit. The tight grip on his arms kept him on his feet.

"Careful with my property!" Dawson elbowed Standing Pony out of the way. He glared at the Indians. "I takes proper care of my things." He dropped his voice. "You buy 'im, then I don't care how you treat 'im."

"What's this?" The Apache poked Andy's stitched arm again, yanked off the bandage, then spun around to Dawson. "You try to sell me damaged property?"

"Well, hell, Standing Pony. He ain't hurt for good. Day or two, he'll heal up. After all, it was *your* arrow what damaged him." Dawson ran his hand down Andy's other arm. "He's strong, but if you don't want him—"

"How much?" Standing Pony held up his hand.

Dawson's gaze ran up and down Andy who followed the stare. A sigh, then Dawson turned to the Indian. "Gold. A thousand."

Standing Pony let loose a whoop and threw his head back. "You're a thief, Gray Man." He circled Andy, running his hand across his bare chest and back. "Strong. Young." He pried open Andy's mouth and peered inside. The Indian leader stepped back and nodded. "Make fine slave. Five hundred."

Dawson pulled Andy's shirt up around his shoulders, slipped his coat over his arms. He yanked Andy toward his horse. "Let's go."

"Seven."

"Eight hundred."

"Done."

CHAPTER THIRTY-NINE

HE SHOULD SCREAM. OR FIGHT. OR RUN. BUT nothing would change his situation. Nothing. A slave? For the Apache? The Apache who held and tortured his brothers? The same damn Apache who wiped out an entire mining camp?

This was a dream. Of course! Surely that explained the insanity of it all. He closed his eyes, tight. If he took a deep breath and opened them, he would find himself back at camp, the miners preparing for another day of backbreaking work. The sun shining at the prospect of today being *the* day? The day they'd become rich. Their good-natured chatter over campfires of coffee and biscuits soared across Andy's mind. Veiled locations of the Mother Lode whispered around camp. A tug on his arm opened his eyes.

Scowling faces glared. Not a dream, a nightmare come true. Captured and sold like castoff livestock. Only his life wouldn't be as easy as a horse's. No, his would be... whippings every day, just like brother James'. Work before sunrise, arms loaded with cut wood, killed game, tanned hides. One bowl of rabbit stew at sunset. Kicks, beatings, ropes digging into flesh, tethered tight at night like a wild animal. All of it rose in his throat.

He raised his bound hands and swiped at a strand of hair plastered to his tender, swollen face. His eyes darted from Dawson to Standing Pony. Could he stay calm? After all, what could be worse than being an Apache slave? He considered, but nothing came to mind. Whatever the outcome, he'd do anything to stay alive.

Dawson's lips curled as he accepted the bag of coins. He jingled it against his ear. "Since I now got me some money to buy my supper, don't have to cart him along no more." He nodded at Andy. "Was gonna eat you but looks like you're one lucky sumabitch."

Andy leaned away from Dawson. What was worse than being an Apache captive? Eaten by a crazy man. Visions of the frozen miners, then Dawson's stew roiled in Andy's stomach. Maybe being sold as a slave saved his life.

Dawson threw his shoulders back and pointed the jingling bag at Standing Pony. "You got more of this coinage, I got more boys look just like him."

Standing Pony's grip tightened around Andy's arm, but his expression didn't change. "Explain."

An icy cold shiver raced down Andy's spine. Before Dawson opened his mouth, Andy feared what Crazy Man would propose.

Dawson jerked his thumb over his shoulder. "His brothers be chasin' his ghost up around d'lake." He glanced at Andy. "'Bout now they should've figured he ain't there."

Standing Pony's grip tightened. He studied Andy. "Cochise's white-eyed prisoners." He nodded. "The younger one cut me. Now I cut his throat!"

"Ain't revenge sweet?" Dawson cocked his head at Andy.

"No!" Andy tugged against the strong grip on his arms. "Leave my brothers alone." He turned to Standing Pony. "Keep me. I'll work for you... hell, kill me if you want." He forced words over the aching jaw. "But don't touch them. They've been through—"

"Ain't up to you, boy." Moving within inches of Andy, Dawson's rancid breath blew in his face. "Nothin' up to you now." He chortled. "Got a feelin' you'll be seein' those brothers of yours soon."

Rage. Uncontrollable rage surged over Andy. Using his head as a battering ram, he smashed into Dawson's nose. Blood splattered both shirts. The men hit the ground, Dawson *whumping* onto his back. Andy landed on top.

Dawson flipped over, taking Andy with him. Again and again, Dawson's fists pummeled Andy, his broken jaw taking the impact. Pinned against the hard ground, Andy's head snapped side to side with each punch. His world shrunk. Stay alert, he repeated over and over to himself. Kill this man.

"Not...my...brothers." Andy hissed.

If he couldn't escape the Indians, by damn he'd take down Dawson. More punches. His. Dawson's. Andy's bound fists found shoulders, an occasional ebony cheek. Strength dredged up, Andy bucked, toppling Dawson who rolled like a top-heavy toy. Now on top, Andy straddled him and, using his bound hands as a club, struck.

Groans. Grunts. Moans. Blood ran into his eyes.

When his arms hurt too much to strike again, Andy grabbed both sides of Dawson's face and slammed his head over and over into dirt and rocks. Andy's arm muscles shook.

Andy raised his bound hands for a tighter grip, but Dawson flopped like a rag doll. Blood spread like red fingers from beneath Crazy Man's skull.

Dawson lay still.

"You sonuvabitch!" He yelled at Dawson. "You hear me?" Andy stared into the slave's bloodied face, the eyes swollen, lips split.

Sweat, mixed with blood, dripped into Andy's eyes. He gulped air and ran a sleeve across his face. His stomach churned and he fought back the rising gorge in his throat. Using his last bit of energy, he spit at Dawson.

Hands jerked at Andy's arm. He'd almost forgotten about the Indians. Why had they not intervened? Andy allowed hands to jerk him to his feet. He kicked Dawson. Definitely dead.

Behind Andy, one of the Indians plucked the bag of coins from Dawson's lifeless hands. He held it up and nodded.

* * *

"SEVENTY, eighty miles we have ridden, Capitán. All we do is chase those *Indios*. And for what? The towns... Santa Rita, Walker, Pinos Altos, Mogollon... destroyed. Nothing left." Segundo pointed his filled coffee tin southward. He lowered his voice, glancing side to side. "We, you and me, have enough to live well in Mexico. We should leave now, tonight, under darkness, before those *Indios* take our scalps, too."

"Not yet." Captain José Mendoza gripped his cup and stared into its half-filled contents. Black liquid sloshed as he nodded. "These men have served us well. One more village and *then* we'll have plenty for Mexico." He fought fatigue—deep down, chest-ripping fatigue. And frustration. Where was the gold he'd heard about? The promise of wealth beyond his imagination.

As Segundo stood by his side, Mendoza surveyed his camp. Bedrolls lay splayed around several campfires. Men sat on them preparing for a night's rest; others sat near the fire, warming hands and passing bottles. A few others sat alone.

Tomorrow, he decided. Tomorrow he'd lead his men toward Pinos Altos for the last time.

His lieutenant's face. Firelight danced on it, highlighting pockmarks like so many other men carried. Under those marks lay frustration. Did his own face reflect Segundo's thoughts? Those brown eyes, once fierce with determination to gain land, now dulled with defeat. Those damn Apache refuse to leave their hunting grounds. Land they considered their God-given right to use.

But what about the Mexicans? They had forayed north and taken Apache land. It once belonged to us. Shouldn't it still? Of course. And the Americans? Mendoza spit. The newcomers who think this land is theirs. What did signatures on paper mean? To hell with "treaties" and "purchases." Such words meant nothing to him. He'd decided some time ago the people to fight were the Apache. After they were defeated, then the Americans.

"Segundo, think this." Mendoza swept his arm across the darkening valley spread beneath them. "True, we follow the Apache. True, we pick up the pieces of broken towns. But also true, the Americans are glad to see us. They sing our praises when we chase out those demon *Indios*. Once their villages are put back together, we will be welcomed."

"But—"

"Then, Segundo, then... we move in and reclaim our land. Just wait. The Apache will not claim victory much longer." Mendoza nodded at his compatriot. "Not much longer."

CHAPTER FORTY

TRACE PEERED OVER JAMES' SHOULDER. "I DON'T see anything. Just scratchings."

"Look. Right here." James squatted, his finger following zigzags in the dirt. "See this? Feather of an eagle." He let out chilled breath. "Andy's alive."

"What?" Trace held the lantern closer.

"Yeah, and look here. Part of the letter A." James traced the angles. "He wrote most of the letter then looks like it got smudged, or that's all he could write."

"So, how do you know?" Trace cocked his head at the marks. "You sure he's alive?"

Rocking back on his heels, James glanced up at his brother. "Remember back last year when Andy and me were in the army, we went out looking for Apache and got lost?"

Trace nodded.

"Well, we promised each other that if we got separated, we'd draw the feather of an eagle—"

"Apache sign for life." Trace ran his hand through the line. "I remember."

"Right. We agreed so we'd know where we were, and we were all right." Frost blew from James' nose. "Dammit, I knew it. He *was* here."

"But the question is—where's he at now?" Trace stood, taking a final glance around the tiny cave. "He's not here, that's for sure. Let's go, this place is—"

"Creepy." James followed Trace to the entrance and stepped into night, illuminated by starlight and the lantern's glow. The brothers picked their way back to the cabin.

Pouring two cups of coffee, Trace handed one to James then eased into a wooden chair. He pried off his hat then scratched the top of his head. "So." A long pause, hesitant sip of coffee. "Where is he?"

Both brothers stared into their cups.

A full minute passed. James lowered his cup, held it mid-air, then plunked it on the table. "Dawson."

"What?" Trace frowned.

"Andy's with Dawson. That sonuvabitch took him." He shifted his attention to his brother's drawn face. Seething anger knotted in his chest. "That's what happened. Probably gonna sell him some place. Dawson's crazy enough to think he can get away with it."

"But who'd buy—" Trace jerked up his head and met his brother's stare. "Good God. The Apache."

A fist plowing into James's face couldn't hurt as much as this revelation. He forced a swallow and stared at his brother. "Dammit! I've heard Negroes and Apache trade and barter with each other." The knot closing his throat, he struggled to speak over it. "You and I both know a white slave would be quite a feather in any Apache's hat."

"Especially Standing Pony's"

"Dammit! Should've known." James pounded the table. His cup shook. "Dammit, I should've known." He glared into a dark corner. "I didn't listen."

"To what?"

"Remember I told you about the fight in the Buckhorn right before I came to Mesilla?"

Trace nodded and finished his coffee.

"Big Dan said an Indian...Sitting Horse, was around." James clenched his fist, ready to pound again. "Dan never gets names right." He met Trace's steady gaze. "He meant *Standing Pony*. I just didn't put two and two together."

Trace ran a hand across his forehead.

"For God's sake...not *him*." Memories swam around James.

Trace shut his eyes then rubbed them. "Probably *his* war party that raided Mogollon."

"Dammit!" James slid back his chair, stood gazing out the single window. Stars twinkled like eyes taunting him. Every star was an Indian's eye—staring at him. He shoved his hands in his pockets and frowned. "Sonuvabitch! Why him and why Andy?"

"Standing Pony's always hated you, especially after you killed his brother." Trace's voice turned sharp. "I remember in camp how he treated you—he and One Wing. So many times I wanted to kill them. Too bad you didn't kill Standing Pony when you had the chance."

"I know." James drew a quick breath. "When me and him fought last year over the cavalry's freedom...and even though I won, I figured sparing his life would impress Cochise. At least enough to let the soldiers go."

"It was," Trace said.

Awkward silence filled the small room. James stared out the window. The moon rose over the Mogollon rim, spreading the mountain tops with icy silver. Standing Pony. Could he tell Trace the whole story? What he didn't know? Up til now, James had hidden his ultimate humiliation. Whored by Apache! What Standing Pony and the other warriors did every time they'd take him out hunting was unspeakable. How much the assault hurt, not just the physical pain, but the degrading tauntings, the knowing looks every time they sauntered past. It was all there, etched in his memory. He held his breath and cringed, remembering the beatings he received when he'd throw up afterwards. Damn Standing Pony! Damn the Apache!

"James?" Trace's voice pulled him out of memories. "You're shaking." He slid his chair back. "What're you not telling me?"

"Nothing." If he turned around to look at Trace, he knew he'd spill the story. Even as close as they were, he couldn't face the telling. Not yet. James held up a hand. Trace was right. It shook. He returned his attention to the window.

Heartbeats, heavy breathing and skittering night critters broke the heavy stillness. James focused again on the stars. They weren't diamonds in the sky like Ma had told him; they were glimmers of hope lost—too far away to touch.

Trace's voice behind James grew flat. "I'll get him back. Rescue him before... before they hurt him anymore. No more whips, no more pain. Couldn't get James out... save him. But I'll save Andy. I'll—"

"Trace?" James turned, stunned at his brother sitting on the cot's edge, rocking back and forth. Head gripped with both hands, Trace's eyes squeezed tight. He mumbled into his chest.

"Rode fast as the wind...couldn't save James...God, I

tried." A tear hit the table. "He hurt so bad. God help me, I tried."

James had rarely seen his brother this distraught. The first time, five days after James' rescue, was at the doctor's office in Mesilla, when he and Trace and their two friends had ridden in... what he remembered of it. Just like then, Trace was now on the edge of collapse. James pushed aside his own demons and knelt beside his brother. "Look at me." He paused, waiting for those brown eyes to meet his. "Look at me, I said."

Trace's fists tightened. "If I'd been quicker, if I'd stayed, James wouldn't have been whipped, suffered like he did. He wouldn't have—"

"Dammit, Trace. Look at me!" James gripped his brother's shoulders. "I'm right here. Still in one piece." He fought the urge to scream. "Hell yeah, it hurt. But I survived. I'm here. Right. Here."

A pulled in breath. Trace's eyes raised to James'. "I tried...protect you...take your pain...get you out." His words quivered. "Couldn't do it. God, I couldn't do it." He sat up gripping James' vest. "I'm sorry. So damn sorry."

James patted his brother's hands. "It's all right. I know."

Trace's shoulders heaved.

James waited for the sobs to quiet. "We'll get Andy." He hoped his words were stronger than he felt. "He'll be all right. You'll see."

CHAPTER FORTY-ONE

STANDING AT TERESA'S FRONT DOOR, HAT IN hand, Luke smoothed his hair. His fingers hit that damn upright sprig on top, the prickle familiar as his hand struck it. Cowlick, Sally called it. Licking his palm, he ran it over the offending spike. Maybe if he didn't part his hair down the middle, and maybe if he'd used a handful of pomade this morning, it wouldn't stick up like a hedgehog's. He knocked. Waiting, he used the time for another quick lick and swipe. Morningstar opened the door.

"Good morning, Mr. Colton. What a pleasant surprise."

Lovely this morning. As usual.

"Luke?"

Mouth refusing to make words, he smiled, stomped dust from his boots and stepped into the warm house.

"Teresa, look who's here." Morningstar took Luke's coat and draped it over the back of the sofa. "The new law in town!" She turned to him with schoolgirl innocence. "Is there a problem, officer?"

"No, ma'am." Luke dropped his voice to a bass timber and hooked his thumbs into his pants waistband. "Just makin' the rounds, checkin' on the fine citizens of Mesilla." He whispered, "Especially the beautiful ones." He winked.

Morningstar, standing less than a foot away, wiped her soft hands on her apron, smoothed her raven hair, and batted her eyes.

Luke caught Teresa's stare from the kitchen door. "Breakfast dishes're already done, Luke. Not close to mealtime, I'm afraid." Teresa thumbed over her shoulder. "But I could put on a fresh pot of coffee, if you're gonna stay a while."

No doubt where she stood about him. Despite the luke-warm hostility, he marched across the room to hug her. "Didn't come for your delicious food, Teresa. Not this time." Behind him, a squeal and giggle and then two little arms wrapped around his leg. He looked down into big, brown eyes. Faith.

Picking her up, he tossed her into the air, which produced more squeals. He cuddled her, his own son and daughter's images bumping into his memory. "Hey, Buttercup. How's Uncle Luke's favorite niece?" He ruffled her light brown hair.

She returned his hug with a grin and then wiggled out of his grip. He looked at Morningstar. Just the nearness of this woman sent fire throughout his body.

Why exactly was he here? Plenty of town matters to keep him busy. To occupy his thoughts. Thoughts that kept reverting to forbidden territory.

Teresa interrupted his thinking. "So, Luke, I understand Abe Kinnear stirred the town up the other day." She pointed to the sofa. "Please sit."

Luke sat at the end of the medallion back couch, its

needlework fabric soft. "Yeah. Lucky no one got hurt. Town turned a bit ugly." He leaned on an elbow, glad his sister-in-law spoke civilly to him. "But I kept things under control."

Morningstar sat across from him in the rocker and leaned forward. Her sparkling eyes narrowed. "Any truth to the rumor the Apache control that entire area? I mean, my home's up there. Our friends in Pinos Altos, James' saloon... everything. What'll happen if we can't go back?"

Luke refrained from grabbing Morningstar's hand, holding this sensuous woman in his arms and telling her everything would be all right. Instead, he raised both eyebrows at Teresa. "This Indian trouble, from what I understand, is a last-ditch effort on their part." He shrugged. "I don't think it'll last long."

"Why's that?" Teresa sat at the other end of the sofa.

Luke stumbled on his reasoning. He hadn't spent much time thinking this through, just formulated ideas from rumors around town. But he wanted to sound thoughtful and intelligent. "The tribes aren't united, like our states before this fighting started. If they banded together against the settlers and miners, they'd be unstoppable. But they fight among themselves."

"Quite a soapbox speech, Mr. Colton." Teresa picked up Faith.

Something dark, a thought, maybe a memory, changed Morningstar's face. Her eyes shifted downward and her lips did, too.

Did he speak out of turn? Maybe he insulted her because of her Apache background? Luke eased to his feet, both women's eyes on him.

If neither woman wanted him around now, maybe he should quit being a deputy and head out to find his brothers. Teresa would welcome his absence. And Star? He'd miss her. Threading his arms through his coat sleeves he considered: what kept him in town? He stared back at the two sets of eyes watching him. The answer— simple. They depended on him to keep them safe—safe, so James and Trace would have wives to come home to.

Their wives. *His* wife. The permanent knot in his stomach gripped his heart then worked its way to his throat. Dammit anyway.

Remembering the excuse he'd used for stopping by, he reached into his coat pocket. He looked at Morningstar. "I apologize. Nearly forgot. Mr. Kinnear asked me to bring this to you." He handed her an envelope.

Furrows creased Morningstar's forehead then a smile erased the lines. "It's from my folks in Tucson." She glanced at Teresa, then Luke, and ripped open the envelope. Unfolding the letter, she scanned it, then read again.

Teresa stood, setting Faith on the floor. "By the look on your face, I'd say it's good news?"

Morningstar's eyes sparkled. A tear in one corner? Joy? Had to be. Luke stepped closer. "I hate to sound like Mister Kinnear, but... I'm dying of curiosity." He peered over her shoulder.

Morningstar beamed. "My pa says a doctor in California, San Diego to be exact, will take me as a medical student. And since he's a friend of my pa's, he'll teach me for free. All I have to do is get out there!" She clutched the letter to her chest. "I wish James was here. He'd be so excited for me."

"California? That's...far." No, no, no! Might as well be the moon! Could he stop her? He swallowed. "James won't go."

His words had no effect on Star. She hugged her

sister-in-law, dancing Teresa around the room. After a turn or two, a few giggles, she released Teresa and turned to Luke. "James? Why not?"

Because I'll miss you! Luke's heart pounded in his throat. You can't leave! Not now! Not ever! He stammered and hated himself for it. He spread his arms wide. "It'll take too long. California's too far. James owns a saloon." Luke whispered, "Stay here."

Teresa ignored Luke's concerns. "Just think. We'll have a doctor in the family. A sheriff, a businessman and now a doctor. The Coltons are on their way!"

And I'm on my way to nothing. Luke struggled to rein in his bad mood. No need to spoil Morningstar's glorious news. He forced a grin. "Congratulations. We're all proud of you. You'll be great!"

Morningstar hugged Luke and beamed. "Thank you. I'll work real hard."

He released the reason to get up in the mornings. "I best be going. I'll stop by later."

Luke busied himself dusting his hat. Anything to avoid Morningstar's eyes. Those black diamonds seemed to follow his every thought, his every move. They pierced his soul and spun his world into possibilities, then ripped his heart apart with reality. He could never have Morningstar.

She belonged to his brother.

"I'll see you out." Morningstar's sweet voice followed him.

A thought hit him as he opened the door. As he stepped into the chilled air, she closed the door. Her presence behind him...intoxicating. He twisted back, leaning into her warmth. "Meet me at Big Swede's Livery in an hour."

CHAPTER FORTY-TWO

MORNINGSTAR WRAPPED THE GRAY SHAWL around her shoulders and smoothed her hair in the front room mirror. She called over her shoulder. "I'm going out for a while, Teresa. Want anything while I'm in town?" Guilty words soaked into the adobe walls.

Teresa stood in the kitchen door. "You know what you're doing?"

Eyebrows raised in feigned innocence, Morningstar stood straighter. "I'm simply going into town. I need to pick up a few things."

"Like your brother-in-law?"

Morningstar licked her dry lips and stared into Teresa's brown eyes. Would she explain? Could she? Door handle in hand, she forced a tight grin. "I'll be back after a while. Probably eat in town." After a quick glance back, Morningstar Martelli Colton opened the door and stepped into winter air.

They're looking at me. All of them. A few people she recognized as she made her way down the street then across the plaza. She nodded to their *"Buenos Dias"* or

"*Señora*" greetings. They know. Everyone knows where I'm going. What I might do.

She cut across the dirt street and entered the alley leading to Big Swede's stable. Buildings towering on both sides shaded the livery. Boxes and crates, some stacked, some jammed against a wall, made the narrow passageway more like an obstacle course than a shortcut. Navigating well, Morningstar held her skirt out of the dirt. More than halfway in, she stepped around a barrel and glanced up. Directly in front stood a man, his shoulder-length hair sticking out like a frightened spider. An oily, frightened spider. His dusty black hat pulled down low, and the stained long coat added no pounds to his skeletal body. He leaned against a wall. Cruel lips warped into a sneer.

"Howdy there, missy."

"Good morning, sir." Morningstar sidestepped to the left. He mirrored her move. "Excuse me, sir. I need to pass." She stepped right.

"Yeah? Where ya goin'?" He sashayed with her movements while his narrowed eyes roved up and down her body.

"My husband, the sheriff, is expecting me." She emphasized *sheriff*, praying the slight lie wasn't noticeable. She spun around heading back the way she'd come.

"Sheriff, huh?" He scrambled over a crate, blocking her path. He grabbed her arm. "Law dog's wife." His gaze undressed her. "This day just gets better."

"Let go. You're hurting me."

"Wouldn't want bruises on a fetching little thing like you." He gripped both arms, pulled her close and nuzzled her neck.

"Stop!" She wriggled against the ironclad grip. Rancid breath turned her stomach. His thin lips grated on hers, then moved to her cheek and down her neck. A tongue scraped up and down her skin. Ensnared like a fly in a spider's web, her fists pounded his back.

"Keep fightin', missy," he said. "I love feisty women. Just that much more excitin' when I take 'em.'"

"Let go!" Morningstar pounded harder. His mouth slammed against hers, his droopy mustache muffling her screams. His hand slid down her back and grabbed her rear. He fondled the skirt material and whatever flesh his skinny hand could seize. Like an awkward waltz, the man danced her back against a wall. Hands groped.

"Leave her the hell alone!"

Morningstar spun sideways as the man released her. As if in a dream, Luke Colton appeared out of nowhere. Two right punches from Luke and the assailant staggered back giving Luke enough time to whip out his Colt .36. The men squared off. A few townspeople stopped, gasped, then moved back. Morningstar held her breath. Her world thundered with every beat of her heart. Luke's eyes glowed.

The stranger's hand hovered over his holstered revolver. Each finger twitched.

"Saw you around town earlier." Luke stared at the man. "You need to be leaving."

"Nope. Like it here. Pretty scenery."

Morningstar plastered herself against a wall. Could she melt into it?

The man shifted his gaze to her. "Real pretty." His eyes scanned her body—up, down, up, down. Luke raised his weapon, drawing the hammer back. "I said get outta town." He aimed dead center. "Now."

In a heartbeat, the man whipped out his weapon and fired. Luke pulled the trigger. Tendrils of flames erupted from both guns. White smoke filled the passageway.

Both men crumpled.

Morningstar stifled a cry as townspeople rushed to Luke now lying in a pool of blood. Several others crowded around the stranger. She knelt next to Luke and wiped blood from his eyes.

She scanned the crowd. "I'm a nurse, but he needs a doctor." She cradled Luke's head in her lap. "Someone get the doctor! And a blanket."

Ripping part of her skirt, Morningstar wadded it into a compress and pressed it against Luke's forehead. She prayed he would survive; prayed his wound wasn't life threatening.

"What...?" Luke flopped his hand toward his head.

"Hush now. You've been shot. Doctor's on his way."

* * *

"HELL AND DAMNATION, Luke. About got yourself killed." *Mesilla Times* editor, Thomas Littleton, stood at the side of Luke's bed at Dr. Morgan's office, and scribbled on a pad of paper. "This's gonna to be one helluva story. Maybe even make it to the big newspapers like the *San Francisco Examiner*. Better yet, how about New York? Those people in the East eat up anything Western. Yeah, I'll send this article the tonight."

"For Pete's sake, Tom." Dr. Morgan straightened up as he rolled white gauze then set it on the bedside table. "Can't you see he needs rest right now? Ask him questions later."

"Paper won't wait 'til later, Doc. Few more facts then I can go to press." Littleton nodded to Morningstar who sat next to Luke holding his hand. He dragged a chair over to Luke. Plunking his body in it, the newspaperman licked the end of his pencil. "Now. How'd you come to shoot this sonofabitch?"

Luke ran his tongue over his dry lips. "He was harassing Star. Afraid he'd hurt her."

"He told him to stop," Morningstar said.

Luke interrupted. "But he drew down on me."

"Yeah, I can see that." Littleton glanced again at Morningstar, then scribbled on the paper. Were Luke and Morningstar having a tryst? He'd heard rumors. Newspaperman's instincts keen, he wanted to ask, but chose discretion. At least for a while.

Littleton frowned at the doctor. "Know who that shooter is? Rather—was?" A quick glance at Luke, whose eyes glazed from the laudanum's power. Wouldn't be much more coming from Luke. No, he'd be asleep within moments, or he'd start seeing things that weren't there.

Dr. Morgan sighed loud enough for Morningstar to turn in her chair. He wiped his hands on a towel. "All right, we're curious, Tom. Who *is* the gunman?"

Littleton paused, enjoying the drama. "What does the name Waco Kid mean to you?"

The doctor shrugged.

Morningstar shook her head. "Sounds mean."

"Out of Texas?" Littleton leaned in.

Luke massaged his temples.

Littleton spread his arms. "Hell, gentlemen. He's only the fastest gun this side of the Rio Grande! Reports say he's plugged nine men." He lowered his voice. "And one woman."

"Good Lord!" Luke peered around his shaking fingers. "Damnation!"

The doctor rearranged the white gauze wrapped around Luke's forehead. "Couldn't of said it better myself, Luke.

You're lucky." He turned to Littleton and cocked his head toward the door. "Enough for today. He needs rest." Then to Morningstar. "I'm sorry, ma'am. You can come back later."

Satisfied he had enough to create the story of the century, Thomas Littleton stood, pocketed his pencil then smacked the bottom of Luke's feet with his paper pad. "This story'll be front page. Hell, you'll be a *real* hero!"

CHAPTER FORTY-THREE

ANDY RAISED HIS BOUND HANDS HOPING TO deflect the stick whipping his face. *Whack!* One side of his head caught fire, a streak throbbed from his forehead to his chin. Another whack. This one across his right eye, already swollen from last night's fists.

Besides the knots throbbing on his head and now face, thick welts burned under his sleeve. One final smack and the stick splintered. The Apache hurled the two broken pieces across the makeshift camp and turned his furious black eyes on him. A second Indian appeared behind the other one. Black Hawk, if Andy remembered correctly.

Bronzed hands grabbed the front of Andy's shirt. He stared into eyes blazing like a million fires. This would be his life. From now on. Unless...

Black Hawk's rancid breath blew into Andy's face, turning his stomach. The Indian's spit hit Andy's cheek, the warm glob sliding downward, dripping off his chin. He glared at his captor. He would *not* be weak. Would *not* be a victim.

The Apache who'd beat him, spun Andy around and, in one quick move, planted a moccasined foot in his backside. Andy flew forward, tasted dirt before his face slammed into rocks.

Black Hawk rolled Andy over and sat on his chest. He pressed a hunting knife against Andy's throat. The cold blade dug into his skin, the weight of the Indian's anger pinning Andy to the ground. He squinted at the Chiricahua, his full weight squashing Andy. He lifted his chin. "Slice it, Indian. Kill me," hoping the man understood English. "Standing Pony will be proud when he finds out *you* destroyed his property...behind his back."

When Standing Pony had ridden out this morning, Andy hoped they'd let him go. But the leader's absence served only as a chance for others to abuse him. Andy pulled out all the stops.

"Will he sing around the campfire? Sing of you killing *his* captive?" Stomach flip-flopping, Andy hoped the meager breakfast he'd had would stay down.

The blade's fire sliced his skin. Burning streaks ran up his entire body while something sticky wet ran down his neck.

Black Hawk held up the glinting blade as a sign of victory. The smirk on the Apache's face bunched the corners of his eyes as his lips curved upward. Leathered skin pulled taut over high cheekbones reminded Andy of old mummies. At least the pictures he'd seen in books.

Andy stared into those fiery eyes and waited for the man to get off, or at least change his position so he could breathe. Neck and throat throbbing, Andy knew he'd had a close call.

After what seemed like days, Black Hawk shifted his weight and stood. Anger and bloodlust crowded the

Apache's face. Andy shouldn't push this Indian ever again. This was his one wordless warning.

Strong hands yanked Andy to his feet. Why had he been assaulted? Even though he tried to do everything asked, maybe he hadn't tried hard enough. Then one event came to mind—dropping that skinned rabbit in the dirt. But a quick swipe through a snowbank had it clean again. Whatever the crime was, he sure didn't want to repeat it.

More strong hands tugged him through the temporary camp, past glaring, spitting warriors. They stopped at a pine. Thrust back into the tree, branches scratched Andy's face, tugged at his clothes.

"Here." Black Hawk produced a length of rope and mashed Andy's body against the trunk. Looping the rope through the tight bindings around Andy's wrists, the Apache ratcheted him against the tree.

Andy peered through thin branches. Several jabbed his side and back. He realized—again—Standing Pony and the other Apache had nothing to lose if he died. True, the leader had given Dawson eight hundred dollars, but also true, Andy had killed Crazy Man. And they had retrieved their money.

Andy wagged his head. What an idiot! Standing Pony not only had *him*, but the money, too. And by killing Dawson, *Andy* had been the one who destroyed any leverage, any bargaining power he might have had. Mistake number one.

* * *

MID AFTERNOON SUN warmed Andy's face as he stood against that tree...waiting. His leg muscles quivered. It'd been at least half a day since Black Hawk had cut his throat. In that time, no one had come by with water or to make sure he hadn't bled to death. He licked his split lips and turned his head side to side. The crackle of dried blood reminded him of what he already knew— he was the luckiest man alive.

Alive. The important word. But, had his brothers found his drawings in the cave? What would happen if they never came? Or if he couldn't escape?

The sun's final rays bathed the entire camp in golden light by the time Standing Pony and three of his warriors rode in. They slid off their pintos and strutted toward Black Hawk. One of the returning warriors gripped a lance with something brown and hairy poked through the end.

Andy peered through his swollen eyelids and wondered whose scalp. Would he be next?

He eyed the furry token and the strutting Indians and fought down rage. He couldn't help that victim now and any backtalk to Standing Pony or his band would undoubtedly result in his own scalp being paraded around camp.

As if reading his thoughts, Standing Pony turned to Andy and signaled his warriors to bring the fresh scalp. Like a pack of snarling wolves, the Apache marched toward him, faces, reflecting the setting sun, glowed red. Andy squirmed, fighting the bindings.

They stopped, now circling him.

Standing Pony pushed aside branches, breaking several. He ran his hand down Andy's neck, poking at the recent knife wound.

Andy jerked back, slamming his head against the tree trunk.

"Black Hawk wanted to kill you, White Eyes. He almost succeeded." Standing Pony yanked the scalp off the lance tip then shoved the hairy specter into Andy's face.

The stench of fresh blood... the raw, feral odor of sliced meat. Andy swallowed hard. Greasy hair pressing against his cheek. He forced down disgust, stood straighter and squared his shoulders.

Standing Pony cradled the scalp and stroked the hair like he would a pet dog.

Andy raised an eyebrow. "You take more like this?"

"Many more." One last stroke of the hair then Standing Pony handed the scalp to a warrior. He grabbed a handful of Andy's hair and yanked hard. "Yours will be next if you anger Black Hawk again." The Apache leader tugged Andy's shoulder-length hair until his chin rested on his chest. His entire body strained against the ropes.

Andy squeezed his eyes shut and winced at the pain, the ropes cutting across his chest. Standing Pony shoved Andy back against the tree. His head slammed into bark again. Stars throbbed white and silver.

The Chiricahua leader pushed his face inches from Andy's. "I see your spirit, White Eyes. Stronger than your brothers'. In Cochise's camp, my own brother, One Wing, broke their spirit—like I will break you." His voice lowered to a whisper. "Or maybe...I kill you."

CHAPTER FORTY-FOUR

ALTHOUGH THE SMELL OF ALCOHOL MADE HER cough, she knew here in Dr. Morgan's office, the odor was a good thing. Meant the instruments were sterilized and his patients' wounds were clean. Morningstar tucked the blanket under Luke's chin, then perched in a chair at the side of his bed. "You'll be fine. A day or two, you'll be right as rain." Then what? Would she want to continue where they'd left off? Could she? A much better question—*should* she?

These past two days, she'd done a mountain of thinking. She loved her husband. That was a fact. But this brother-in-law... a crazy magnetic attraction, the unsolicited feelings. Butterflies, schoolgirl giddiness, endless smiles. Best of all, he could give her children. How would she explain it to James? But now, she had a chance at medical school. Did she want children? On the other hand, Luke was a sure thing. Or was he? As soon as he was well enough, they could...

"Thought I died and an angel talked to me." Luke's

mouth curved on one end. He reached for her hand. "I was half right. You're the angel."

"Silver tongued just like your brothers. That part of the Colton family charm?" He *was* charming. Maybe even a bit more than James.

"You mean you've heard that before?" Luke pursed his lips into a pretend pout. "Thought I was original."

"Oh, you're original all right." Morningstar stroked his outstretched hand, the contact raising tiny bumps on her skin.

Luke's mouth twisted into a full grin. "Now who's got the silver tongue?" He chuckled then winced, clutching his head.

She moved over to the edge of the bed, waiting for Luke to open his eyes. Luke, this man who'd fought for her, this man who'd laid his life on the line for her. He groaned.

"Want more laudanum? It helps." Morningstar patted his arm.

"Please." Luke's chest rose and fell twice before he opened his eyes. "Might be more like *three* days before I'm up dancing. What'd he shoot me with? A buffalo gun?"

"Shhh." Morningstar sprinkled white powder into the water glass at his bedside and stirred it. "Drink." She supported his head while he sipped. When he finished, she set the glass on the table and stared at her trembling hands.

"What?" Luke grasped one.

Should she pull away? Of course, but she needed his touch. His velvet touch, so strong yet, so gentle. Avoiding his eyes, Morningstar glanced out the window. "Just wondering if I should send an express letter to your wife, tell her you got shot. Wondering if she'd rush here to take care of you. Just wondering—"

"I'll write her tomorrow, just to let her know so she won't kill me when I get back." His eyes fluttered open then shut. "I don't need her. I need you."

I need you, too. Her hand easing from his, Morningstar leaned over and kissed the top of his head. She swept strands of hair off his sweaty forehead. "I'll be here when you wake up. Rest now."

CHAPTER FORTY-FIVE

JAMES POINTED TO TWO SETS OF TRACKS IN THE thawing mud. "More over here, Trace. They're not moving fast, but they sure as hell never stop." Reining up, he swung his leg over the saddle. The leather creaked as if sighing, relieved to have weight off. Both feet on the ground now, he twisted his back, enjoying the release. For the past couple of days, all he'd done was stop and inspect tracks, stop and inspect, stop...

Chilled top to bottom, James shook his legs then squatted by the hoof prints. Two horses, one shoe missing a nail. Dawson's. Very distinctive, very trackable. Both had riders, the prints' depression in the ground staying consistent. Good news—based on the depth of the indention, Andy was still in the saddle and still, hopefully alive.

James pried off his hat, scratched the top of his head. "Where the hell are they?" He glanced over his shoulder at his brother unplugging his canteen. "Don't they ever stop and rest?" James stared into the distance. The setting sun bounced light off rocks and trees, igniting the entire forest into flames of orange and red.

Trace waited beside his brother and tapped the canteen against his shoulder. James shook his head and knelt. He ran his hand through the hoof prints, somehow, this simple movement connecting him with Andy. He shut his eyes. Blue jays squawking overhead synchronized with the wind whistling through the Ponderosa pines. If he hadn't been so tired, so frustrated, the sounds would have induced sleep. Instead, they taunted him, whispering *failure. You're a failure.* He rubbed his eyes.

"I'd say still a day or two ahead, but we're closing in." Trace pointed toward the valley floor below, the plains spreading in all directions. "Sun'll be down in about an hour. Want to camp here or get another mile under us?"

Opening his exhausted eyes, James mumbled into his chest. "What if we're too late?"

"What?"

James stared into the muddy hoof prints. "What if we're too late? What if he already sold Andy?"

"Don't even think like that."

"Why the hell not?" James jumped to his feet and spread his arms wide. "Why not think he's already dead? Hell, that way we'll be surprised if we find him alive."

"He'll be alive."

"You sure?"

"We gotta keep the faith."

"Why?" James moved in close. "Pray he survives so he can end up like me? Like us? Scars and demons? Nightmares? Ghosts lurking around every corner, behind every bush? No, thank you." James turned his back on his brother and dropped his voice. "I'd rather he dies."

A clawlike grip on his shoulders stopped James, his brother's hot breath in his ear.

"Don't *ever* say that. *Ever*. We're gonna get him back, and he's gonna be fine." Trace shook James' shoulders. "Believe it. You gotta *believe*."

James wrenched out of the hold, so tight it hurt, and then faced him. Those brown eyes glowed with what? Anger? Panic? No. James felt it, too. Experience.

Trace clenched his fists. "Dammit, James. You just gotta."

Realizing his brother was on the verge of another breakdown, James reeled in doubts. "Alright, Trace. I'm sorry."

"He'll be fine." Trace nodded. "All three of us will be. Just wait and see." He paused, then nodded toward his horse. "Let's give it one more hour."

* * *

WOOL BLANKET CLUTCHED in his gloved hand, James rolled onto his side then wadded the material under his chin. He opened one sleepy eye. The campfire, several feet away, smoldered gray-orange and cold. Wrestling the fabric, a sudden draft on his back chilled him. He twisted the blanket around to drape over the exposed shirt and skin. His coat covered part of him, but a frigid breeze bit into his entire body. The overhang they'd holed up under afforded only mild protection from the wind and cold. At least it kept the snow off.

Like a landed trout, James flopped side to side, tugging and pulling his blanket. He rearranged his saddle under his head and shivered. Eyes threatening to shut, James managed to keep them open long enough to stare at his brother's dark form, Trace's back to him. Silver starlight outlined the rise and fall of Trace's chest. Soft snores disturbed the night.

James grumbled. Even though his brother was closer to the overhang opening, he didn't seem to be cold—no shivering or tossing and turning. What was his secret? James jerked his blanket again. At long last, he fell into sleep, full of Indians and pain.

Something interrupted his rest—a noise, movement, dream. Before opening his eyes, warm sun on his face and the rustle of birds flitting from branch to branch quieted his nerves. Today would be a good day, a day to locate and rescue Andy, head back to Mesilla, and then into his wife's loving arms. He couldn't wait to see the look on Star's face when he told her they'd be going to California. He couldn't give her children or medical school, but he *could* give her the ocean.

Legs stretching under the blanket, he rubbed his eyes and thought of his wife. Morningstar was the perfect mate—hard-working, considerate, understanding when it came to his past, and very, very beautiful. Her Apache ancestry shone at just the right moments. The fire in her eyes ignited any room she entered. A sudden longing, a sharp pain pierced his gut. Why couldn't he give her children? He cursed his body and then the Indians for taking that pleasure from him. Time to get home. Time to be with the only woman who mattered. Time to be the man he dreamed of becoming.

Flinging off his blanket, James rolled to his knees then crawled out from under the granite overhang. Trace's blanket lay crumpled a few feet away. He ran his hands through his tangled hair, brought his six-one frame to its full height and stretched. Vertebrae popped. Yawning, he glanced right and left. "Trace?"

Silence. He hollered louder. "Trace? Where you at?"

More silence. Birds stopped chirping. James frowned. He pushed away confusion.

His brother was either out looking for dry firewood or relieving himself behind some tree too far away to hear his shouts. Trace would return any minute.

James squatted by the dead campfire and pushed twigs into the center. Where was his brother? This wasn't like him. He always started the fire, put on the coffee. It was a ritual.

"Trace?" He stood. Shielding his eyes against the rising sun, he squinted into the forest. Nothing but trees and snow. He retrieved his brother's saddlebag from under the overhang. Locating lucifers in the front pocket, he started a small fire. Warmth hit his face. No need to panic. Trace wandered farther than he'd intended. He'd be back soon.

Spooning the coffee grounds, James started a short pot. While waiting, he rolled up his blanket, then his brother's, knowing he'd be pleasantly surprised when he returned. One less chore to do. James grinned at the promise today held. A twig snapped behind him. "Hey, Trace. 'Bout gave you up. Where've you been?"

Silence.

"Trace?" James turned and peered into nothing but forest, snow and the crackling fire. Another stick snapped, flames doing their job.

By the time coffee was ready, James had saddled his horse and Trace's. An empty knot in his stomach enveloped his body. He searched in a widening circle for any hint of his brother. Any sign of his whereabouts.

Thirty feet from the campfire, between two trees, James found it. An unmistakable dragging boot print.

Fresh. Looked like Trace had been lifted that far, then somehow, he managed to get a boot in the ground.

Questions jumbling in his head, James ran forward, stopped, turned, ran back. A couple of circles then he stopped. He slowed his breathing.

Under control now, James followed the direction of the print and found a moccasin track. One. He clenched his jaw. Those Indians were good! They marched into camp bold as the Roman army, he thought. Kidnapped Trace right from under his nose, and almost succeeded in hiding their tracks.

A quarter of a mile from camp, indicated by the tracks, the Apache turned south, heading toward the trail to Pinos Altos. James considered. Had Trace resisted or had they hurt him? How had they managed to get him this far without his calling out? And why did they take his brother? Why not him? Why not both of us?

Dodging trees and underbrush, James rushed back to camp. He dumped coffee on the fire, pushed snow over the sticks, and left the pot laying on its side. Any appetite or thirst for coffee evaporated. Nothing would get past the knot in his throat.

James lashed his brother's horse behind his and gigged Sophie into a fast trot. Partially frozen mud created hazardous footing. He knew not to push her too hard. What he didn't need right now was a broken horse. James fought the urge to gallop, instead keeping the pace slow and easy. That's what Trace would do, what he would insist on.

Trace. Always the level-headed oldest of four rowdy brothers. As James rode, he thought about all the scrapes he'd had, how they could've been much worse if his brother hadn't been there—to pick him up, brush him off—to set him on his feet again.

He mumbled a childhood prayer as he rode. Maybe now was his turn to help his brother. Now he'd be able to repay a little bit of the years of help. *Please, God, don't let me be too late.*

James spurred his horse into a gallop.

CHAPTER FORTY-SIX

ANDY TILTED THE WOODEN BOWL AGAINST HIS swollen, split lips, and swallowed hot chunks of rabbit stew. The warmth slid into his stomach bringing immediate comfort, temporary relief from the cold. A glance right and left. The Indians on either side of him he recognized. Both had contributed to the throbbing lumps on his face.

He remembered back to mistake number two, yesterday, a day he knew he'd never forget. Evening shadows had grown long, and he'd been on his horse since before sunup. Although they'd stopped once for food, the Indians hadn't bothered to feed or water him. Head still tender from hitting it twice on the tree the day before, Andy's world had grayed and then whitened with each passing mile.

The rhythm of a slow gallop, combined with fatigue and a numbed head, lulled Andy into semi-consciousness. He recalled looking over his shoulder to see how many Apache were behind him. Spinning his head like that was all it took for blackness to overtake him. With only rope reins to grip, his horse slipped out from under him, and Andy crashed to the ground—directly in the middle of the Chiricahua warriors.

As if in a dream...rather, nightmare, the horses bucked to avoid stomping him. Three Apache riders flew into the air, then smacked into the ground. Pounding hooves. Bucking horses. Furious words as he lay in the middle of the raiding party. Rage on Standing Pony and Black Hawk's faces. Andy sank into blackness.

Last night after coming to, he received the beating of his life.

Shuddering, glad that incident was behind him, Andy adjusted his weight on the rock near the fire and grinned inwardly at the freedom of unbound hands. He scooped another helping of breakfast stew from the bowl and licked his fingers clean before attempting another scoop.

His right eye remained swollen shut, but his left sported only a lump. Breathing was difficult over cracked ribs, but otherwise, he was lucky to be alive. The bruises and eyes would heal, and his jaw felt better, even though it'd been punched. He'd have stories to tell his brothers if...*when* they were reunited. A soft groan as he moved. How in the world would he be able to ride all day like this?

Standing Pony swaggered into the center of the group and caught the eye of every man.

"We ride into Pinos Altos, my warriors. They will not be expecting us, since we have already raided that town. But today, we destroy the White Eye settlement, kill the people, run off the cattle, burn the houses." Standing Pony glared at Andy. "Today, we take back what the white man has stolen!"

The entire raiding party leaped to their feet, makeshift bowls clattering to the ground. Chanting, whooping, hollering set his nerves on edge. A few lifted their lances, shaking them to the awakening sky. Their prayers drowned out Andy's thoughts.

Celebration of imminent victory stretched into stomach-clenching minutes. Andy wolfed his stew figuring it may be the last food he'd see today... maybe ever. This brief time gave him a chance to think, plan how to save his brother's house and maybe the town. He came up with little.

Still perched on the rock, Andy lowered his bowl as Standing Pony's stare across the campfire brought shivers. Andy sat upright as the leader marched toward him. The Apache grabbed Andy's arm, jerking him to his feet.

"Your brother, James, lives in Pinos Altos."

"How'd you know that?" Andy swallowed the last bit of stew.

Snorting, Standing Pony glared. "This warrior knows many things." He pulled Andy closer. "Many more than you."

Andy felt more than heard Black Hawk hovering over his shoulder. The Indian's hot breath raced down Andy's neck as the brave's barrel-chested body pressed against his back. Black Hawk pinned Andy's arms behind him, the strength impressive. Standing Pony held up an eight-inch hunting knife, glinting in the early morning glow.

Vowing not to be afraid, to make his family proud, Andy pushed his chest out.

Quick as lightning, searing fire tore across Andy's left cheek. He gasped, jerking back into Black Hawk's chest. Knees threatening to buckle, Andy swung his head back and forth desperate to shake off pain.

Sticky liquid streamed down his face. Angry hands yanked his pinned arms back harder; his sore ribs screaming as he sucked in air. Face burning, he knew to keep his head, to make these Apache think he was tough. Real tough.

Andy brought his leg up to kick the leader but reconsidered. He was in no position to attack. Instead, Andy forced air into his lungs. Blood dripped onto his coat.

Standing Pony's thin lips curled on one end revealing a gap where two teeth used to stand. The knife waved inches from Andy's left eye while the Apache's tight grip on the handle turned his browned knuckles white.

The leader jammed the tip against Andy's "good" eye. "I could make your life much more painful, more difficult, White Eyed soldier."

"Not a soldier now," Andy whispered.

Instead of stabbing Andy's eye, Standing Pony sliced the buttons from Andy's coat, ripped his shirt open and, in one smooth motion, jerked the sleeves over his shoulders. Andy sucked in a quick breath but lifted his chin to the Indian who snorted and slid the knife tip down to Andy's lower rib cage. The Apache rested the tip there. He brought his eyes up to Andy's, then pushed.

The point poking his bare skin, Andy met the Indian's stare. What had his ma always said? *Be brave.* He sure as hell was trying now.

Sneering, the Apache huffed in Andy's face and ran the knife down his trousers, stopping at his crotch. The blade stabbed through the heavy cotton material while Standing Pony grabbed his open shirt with the other hand. Andy stood still, breath captured in his lungs.

Sharp metal piercing his most sensitive area, Andy prayed this Indian wouldn't press any harder.

"You ever want to have a woman again, you'll do exactly what I say." Standing Pony shoved the blade in farther. The knife tip hit skin.

Andy winced then nodded.

"The fire on your face is nothing compared to what you'll feel here." The Apache leader pushed another half inch.

Groaning, Andy knew another inch and he'd pass out. He couldn't let them see him afraid. Forcing down bile, he murmured, "What do you want?"

Standing Pony pulled the blade out and released Andy's shirt. "You ride in front today, lead this raiding party into Pinos Altos. You, brother of James, will burn, raid and rape."

Mouth open, Andy shook his head.

Standing Pony's powerful fingers clutched the front of Andy's pants and squeezed.

Andy held his breath, clenched his jaw and fought to stay upright.

Savagely twisting the handful of man, Standing Pony spit as he hissed. "I make this clear. You *will* lead the warriors. You *will* burn. You *will* kill." He pulled Andy within an inch of his face. "Just like your brother, you *will* rape."

Tears welling behind his swollen eyelids, Andy sucked in air as the entire lower part of his body burned, then grew numb. Stew surging upwards, he struggled to keep it down, not to pass out.

"Today." The Indian's eyes narrowed into cruel slits.

Andy nodded.

Finally releasing Andy, Standing Pony rocked back. "I see by your face, you did not know James raped women, many women."

Crazy. This Indian was crazy. James would never in a hundred years do something like that. Andy eyed the Indian leader and cringed every time Black Hawk moved. Arms still pinned behind him, but pains subsiding, escape would have to come later. Better play along with this insane Indian. Andy shook his head.

Standing Pony snarled as he spoke. "James took a woman promised to me. A Pima girl we captured. He forced himself on her as Cochise ordered. At first James protested, but he liked it. She fought him, but after many days, he broke her spirit." Standing Pony lowered his voice. "When he wasn't working, he was on her."

"He wouldn't do that. Not James."

Standing Pony cocked his head. "To survive, men do whatever is needed. Ask your brother." He paused. "Will he say the truth?"

He stared into the Indian's face, wondering how much, if any, was true. He knew James and Trace had done things they struggled to forget, things continuing to haunt their dreams, stealing their sleep. But James hadn't mentioned this woman more than in passing. He said he'd married her. That was different from raping... but how different?

Standing Pony nodded to Black Hawk who released Andy's arms. He clutched the front of Andy's coat and led him toward a horse. "You lead, we follow."

CHAPTER FORTY-SEVEN

THE PLAN: WALK FROM THE DOCTOR'S OFFICE TO the hotel. Simple. But what Morningstar hadn't counted on was Luke's weakness. He'd seemed much stronger at the doctor's.

Now, halfway to the hotel, she regretted the decision. The trek across the plaza turned into an endurance test. Morningstar gripped Luke's arm as they walked. True, he was healing, and true, he stood unaided, but his gait had taken on the appearance of a drunken man navigating a slippery riverbed. He stumbled, slid off the boardwalk, and lurched sideways into the front of the *Mesilla Times* office.

It was a miracle the editor hadn't rushed out to berate Luke for bumping into his building. Thomas Littleton was too brash and bold for Morningstar's tastes.

Ten minutes and hundreds of steps later, they paused at the hotel door. Morningstar held it wide open while he gripped the doorjamb, leaning against one side. She pointed her chin toward the narrow staircase. "Think you can make it?"

"Do I look helpless?" Luke's red cheeks, bloodshot eyes and gauze-wrapped head turned to her. "Sorry. Didn't mean to sound ungrateful."

This must be hard for him, Morningstar thought. Strange town, no brothers around.

Luke pushed off from the doorway and whispered. "Don't baby me. It's embarrassing."

Morningstar smiled despite knowing she shouldn't. Men liked to be babied, but not so much as they knew it.

The desk clerk stepped out from around the counter. "Heard what happened. He all right?"

"Rest and quiet," Morningstar said. "He'll be fine in a day or two."

Nodding to the clerk, Luke aimed for the stairs across the lobby. "I'm fine." He lurched forward. Long steps then he grasped the stair railing. Swaying, he sank to the bottom step.

"I'll get the doctor. Stay right here." Morningstar turned toward the door just as the clerk handed a nickel to a child.

"Kid's gonna fetch him." The clerk shut the door and then ambled to Luke. His gaze trailed from Luke to Morningstar, resting on her. "When I saw you two come in like you did and Mr. Colton, here, not looking too good, well I figured the doc'd be needed sooner or later. Didn't think it'd be quite this soon, though." His stare ran up and down Morningstar. "Gonna need lots of close attention."

Morningstar's face burned. "His other sister-in-law and I will be taking turns seeing to his injury." Probably not Teresa, but it sounded better. "He'll be up and around in no time, I'm sure."

The clerk raised both eyebrows and glanced up the stairs. "I keep a respectable hotel here. I'll get this fella up to *his* bed, get him out of the way, here. Got too many guests for one to be hoggin' the stairs." He slipped an arm around Luke's chest and hauled him to his feet.

He muscled Luke up the narrow stairway to his room. In the hall, the clerk fought for breath. "If you need... extra blanket...my housekeeper...can get you one."

Opening Luke's door, the clerk walked Luke in then turned to Morningstar. He took a deep breath, his reddened cheeks beginning to lighten. He twisted his face into a one-eyed squint. "*Very* respectable hotel." He then stepped through the door, leaving it wide open.

Luke sat on the bed's edge and sighed long. "If my head didn't hurt so bad, I'd tell you I'm glad we're finally alone." He cut a sideways glance at Morningstar. "You gonna stay for a while?"

"I shouldn't. People are starting to talk." Her gaze trailed from the open door to her brother-in-law's face. She pulled off the boots of this man who so closely resembled her husband that she sometimes forgot he was Luke, not James. They certainly spoke alike, moved alike, looked alike, but they didn't think alike. Similarities stopped at the physical. But still, something about this man compelled her, drew her toward him.

"I feel better already." He patted the bed. "Please, sit here. I won't bite."

Morningstar chuckled. "I know you won't." She set his boots at the end of the bed. "I'll bring supper over later. Need anything before I go?"

"It's just that...well, it'll sound childish."

"What?" She eased down on the corner while he lay back and stretched out.

"When I was a kid," Luke said. "Ma would rub my head when it hurt, when I'd get sick. I'd go to sleep with her singing to me." He gazed up into her brown eyes. "Would you... rub my head? Please? It's thumping and pounding."

She hesitated. Stay or leave? Those sad eyes...

"Please?" Luke's voice turned velvety soft. "Close the door, first."

Unable to resist, she eased the door shut. Returning, she sat close to Luke and placed her hand over the bandage. "I'll rub, but I won't sing."

He swung his arm around her shoulders and pulled her into him. His warm body against hers. She smelled his excitement, tasted the temptation.

Their lips met. The soft kiss grew red-hot.

World spinning, fire racing over her body, she relaxed into Luke's embrace. Her mouth caressing his, she nibbled his lower lip while he pulled her closer against him.

Luke slid his hand around to the front of her blouse, ran trembling fingers over the material, fumbled with a button. Morningstar took a breath and gazed into his eyes. He was tempting. She shook her head.

Luke whispered over heavy breaths. "James wants you to be happy, doesn't he?"

Morningstar nodded.

"So do I." He nuzzled her ear lobe. "Let me make you happy. I'll teach you things James doesn't know." He breathed in her ear and ran his hand along her arm. "Let me love you."

"Doctor'll be here soon."

"I'll send him away." Luke kissed her hand. "I'll show you how to love James when he's ready." His hand strayed to her skirt button. He undid one.

"This isn't right." She sat up and straightened her hair.

Gripping both shoulders, Luke then eased one hand down the front of her blouse. "It is. Trust me, it is." He pulled her back into his warm chest and cooed. "It's time. Time you became the woman James needs."

Morningstar kissed him long and hard. Stirrings in her stomach and even lower pressed her body into his. Her mouth searched his. Somehow, it was so familiar, so warm, caring. She buried her face in his neck and kissed the soft skin.

He whispered, "Let me love you. James would want me to. *You* want me to." Luke unbuttoned her blouse and ran his hand over the soft camisole underneath. "*I* want to."

Shaking her head, she sat up again. "No, this simply isn't right. Not fair to James."

Shallow wrinkles cascaded across Luke's forehead as his lips pouted. "He's not fair to you. You're very desirable. Warm, sensitive. You deserve to be happy. You deserve...someone who's *all* man."

Hanging her head, she noticed her shirt undone and buttoned the bottom. Was she glad she'd hadn't bothered with a corset today?

Luke propped himself up on one elbow and ran his hand through her hair. "Look at me." He turned her head toward him. "If I hadn't come by when I did, that Waco Kid would've...well, he was ready to..."

Tears welled as Morningstar remembered the fear yesterday, knowing what that killer intended.

"I saved your life. Doesn't that count for something?"

Morningstar nodded.

Luke breathed in her ear. "Then show me."

CHAPTER FORTY-EIGHT

JAMES REINED HIS TIRED MOUNT TO A STOP AND surveyed the plains stretching before him. Where the hell was Trace? Who exactly took him? Late afternoon sun spread its warming fingers over the valley and James knew if he pushed a little harder, he could ride out of the mountains and down into that wide valley before nightfall.

Sucking in cold mountain air, James gigged his horse and reflected on his life as he rode, ducking brush and low limbs. He'd always had one of his brothers at his side. Before Trace left home, all four boys had played and worked together. A close family. Even after he followed Trace to Mesilla, big brother had been there, right by his side the whole time. Except for the two weeks in Cochise's camp... His stranglehold on the reins turned his knuckles white. Push it away, he repeated. Memories won't do any good.

As he picked his way through heavy oak under-growth, a broken branch here, a footprint there—scattered signs of Trace's capture—tempted him to hurry.

They'd left just enough evidence to follow, to lure James on, into some sort of trap. But why?

James turned his options over. If he rushed back to Mesilla for reinforcements, it would be at least a week before he'd return. And the Mexican Army, well, they were nowhere around. He hadn't seen hide nor hair of them since before the Indian attack on Santa Rita. More than likely, they were already in Mexico enjoying tequila and señoritas.

So, no help to count on. Only he could save Trace. Once they were reunited, they would continue their search for Andy. James pushed down guilty thoughts. Should he have continued the search for Andy, called off once Trace disappeared, or was he right trailing Trace?

Two brothers lost. At least he knew with certainty where younger brother Luke was—safe at home with Sally in Kansas.

Where the hell was Andy? Of course, there was the good chance Dawson had indeed sold Andy to the Apache. James' chest tightened. While he wanted his youngest brother to still be alive, he sure as hell didn't want him alive as an Indian captive.

Without Trace, he'd have to go in alone, into the jaws of Cochise's band or one of those other Apache. Maybe Standing Pony. Were they the ones holding Trace? And why would they want to lure James in? He was just another White Eyes, an American encroaching on Indian land. Why hadn't they simply killed Trace and him when they'd had the chance? What could James do that Trace couldn't?

What kind of game were they playing?

A crow squawked overhead. James stared at the circling silhouette as it glided toward safety or possibly a snack in a towering pine. Movement out of the corner of his eye caught his attention. Deer? Puma? Indian? James jerked on the reins and let his gaze trail over the forest floor. Straining to hear feet rustling, birds calling or frightened squirrels chattering, he heard only silence. His beating heart echoed in his ears.

Swallowing down panic, James leaned over his horse and peered into the forest. Nothing moved, spoke or attacked.

Another long look then James urged his horse forward.

CHAPTER FORTY-NINE

ON HIS LEFT RODE STANDING PONY. ON HIS right, Black Hawk. As they barreled toward Pinos Altos, Andy mumbled low, "Gotta stop 'em. Stop 'em. Gotta stop..."

James. Morningstar. Trace, too. Directly in the Apache's path. Could he warn them in time? No.

White tents glared against the greens of pines as the horses galloped through the outskirts of the growing mining community. The few men in the fields picked up rifles and fired. A bullet splintered the bark off a nearby tree. Andy ducked.

Leaning far forward, Andy glanced behind, cringing as a warrior jumped off his horse and bludgeoned the man who'd shot at him.

Screams.

War whoops.

Panic.

Andy gripped the rope reins and prayed he could stop this senseless killing. Somehow.

They galloped into Pinos Altos, the wooden buildings

representing back-breaking work and dreams. The townspeople and miners had come from all over the world in search of that elusive gold or silver, and with it, the life such metal brings. The happiness everyone deserved. It was all about to go up in smoke, and the damnable thing was, he couldn't stop it.

Charging into the center of town, Andy spotted James' pride and joy, The Buckhorn Saloon. Was he inside? Defending it? Or did he even realize Apache were about to change lives. He could be killed before Andy could say goodbye.

He remembered helping James set up the saloon after he bought it last year. There'd even been a ribbon-cutting ceremony Trace had attended. The party lasted a full day.

Standing Pony raised his lance and let loose a war cry. Half of the warriors veered off to the left while Andy and the others aimed straight for the saloon. Shots fired from behind buildings echoed off the surrounding hills. Men scrambled for cover.

Before Andy could rein to a full stop, an Indian yanked him off his horse. Andy hit the ground and bolted toward the saloon. "Run, James! Get away!"

Bullets lodged into the wooden post holding the roof as he ran past. He hit the door. Stuck tight.

"Apache! Run!" He pounded on the door. Shoulder against it, he shoved. Before he could pry it open, two Apache rammed into it. The wood creaked and then flew open. Andy and the Apache fell into the saloon just as five men appeared from behind the bar.

Andy hit the floor and rolled under a table. White smoke erupted from shotguns. An Apache clutched his chest and slumped against the wall. Bullets flew, smoke clouded the room. Without warning, more Indians swarmed in. Using the tables as cover, Andy crawled to the corner, hoping no one paid him particular attention. Without a weapon of any kind, he was a sitting duck. No, he thought, more like a dead duck.

But where was James? Surely his brother would be in the middle of this, defending his beloved bar. A careful look at the men. No one he recognized. Maybe James was with Morningstar, back at the house. Or if Dawson was right, James and Trace were still out looking for him.

As if answering his prayers, a Colt .38 skidded across the floor, landing not ten feet away. Glancing left and right, he crawled toward it hoping everyone else was too busy to notice. Grunts, moans and curses filled the air. On hands and knees, Andy rushed forward, dodging a blood-covered miner who lay unconscious near him. Andy focused on his quest, knowing the only way out was to capture that gun and defend himself. With extra luck, he could take down Standing Pony.

Then he'd go find Trace, James and Morningstar.

Arm outstretched, Andy's fingertips reached forward and brushed against the warm gun. A boot plowed into his still-healing arm. Blinding pain raced up and down his body. Was that a bone crunching? The pounding in his head blotted out shouts and gunfire around him.

Strong hands yanked him to his feet. Grabbing his shoulder, he fought agony. A groan escaped his lips.

Black Hawk pressed Andy against his chest, using him as a human shield. Fighting nausea and stepping in rhythm with the Indian, Andy navigated through the melee and into the back storage room. Rows of whiskey bottles sat on shelves and more in boxes. It hit him. He knew what the future held for James' coveted saloon. It would soon lie in ashes.

"No. Won't help." Andy shook his head as Black

Hawk released him. He backed toward the crates and glared at the Apache. "Won't."

Using his good arm, Andy hefted a small wooden crate over his head and threw it at the Indian. Mistake number three. Black Hawk ducked then barreled toward Andy. Taking the full force of the Indian, Andy flew backwards plowing into the shelves and stacked supplies. An old table stopped Andy's movement.

Andy lay on the table and the Apache thudded on top of him. Andy saw it all.

Furious Indian eyes. A fist hurtling toward his cheek. Blackness.

CHAPTER FIFTY

RIDING ANOTHER HALF HOUR, JAMES TOPPED A rise and froze. South, toward Pinos Altos, billows of smoke rose on the wind, boiling clouds of brown blotting out the afternoon sun.

Galloping his horse this hard would surely wear her out, but he had to get to town. Had to. Less than a mile out, he reined up, tied his horse to a pine and listened.

Rifle fire. Screams.

Women. Children.

Running. Horses snorting.

Smoke.

Death stench.

Memories. Always the memories. He gritted his teeth, pushing down memories. *Not again, One Wing. No more, Cochise.* In his mind, he watched Cochise lead the frenzied raiding party against a helpless ranch in southern Arizona. That woman screamed, begged for mercy as James sliced her scalp—

Focus on now, James. Focus on helping these people. You're no longer bound, not a captive anymore. You can do this. James rubbed his eyes and bit his lower lip.

Tying his horse to the tree, he checked his revolver. Both barrels loaded. Before jumping into the middle of things, James surveyed the town. From this vantage point, he had a clear view of downtown, such as it was.

On fire.

Flames licked the top of his beloved saloon, burning wood groaned and crackled. Another building, Norton's General Mercantile, groaned then caved in. Black wood splinters flew in all directions as another structure erupted into flames. Smoke, thick enough to cut, enveloped James.

Coughing, he swiped at watering eyes, then staggered closer into town, away from the wind carrying the brown cloud. Skirting the main street, James used chokecherry brush and boulders for cover. A block from his saloon, he eased around trees and peered toward his house. The door stood wide open, furniture, dishes and clothing scattered in the yard.

He circled around behind his house and peered through the bedroom window. One curtain hung lopsided, but he could make out enough to know his house was ransacked beyond repair. Holes in the walls, scorched clothing and bedding strewn throughout. Had he ever lived here? This wasn't his house. He was a stranger in town. He'd never been the saloon owner, the occupant of this ramshackle house. What the hell was he doing here?

James shook his head desperate to clear the confusion. Gun shots. Apache war cries. Thundering hooves. Women screaming. He squeezed his eyes shut. Always the women screaming.

Revolver in hand, James crouched low and raced to

the cabin next to his. He peeked around front and spotted an arm lying halfway out the door. James recognized the shirt on the extended arm. Big Dan Baker. His wife expected their second child in a few months. What had happened to her? Their four-year-old son?

James squared his shoulders. Gruesome images, gut-wrenching memories ignored, he rushed from cabin to house using more trees and debris as cover.

Around the corner from Main Street, he dodged behind the blacksmith's shop and edged around the side. Three Apache swooped past, their pintos kicking up muddy ice chunks. James turned his attention to his saloon. From this hiding place, he had a clear view. The building teetered on smoking pine beams and swayed with the heat. His saloon would collapse within moments. No doubt.

Two Apache, red paint smudged across their faces, emerged from the smoke-filled door dragging a man, his face streaked with blood and soot. James squinted. Not an Indian.

Something about him looked familiar. James stepped into the open and froze. Andy. James moved in closer. A bullet whizzed past his arm and slammed into the blacksmith's door. He scrambled for cover.

Four Apache staggered from the saloon, whiskey bottles in hand. James prayed they were drunk and therefore made easy targets. Maybe with his help the tide would turn. The towns-people didn't seem to be winning this fight.

He sighted his Colt, finger pressed against the trigger. He stopped. The bottles were full. Those men weren't drunk or even close to it. He relaxed his grip. He couldn't hope to pick off all four if they were sober.

Thundering hooves. James spun around. More

Indians galloping into town. As they passed, he recognized one. A vicious man who had participated in James' torture and gloated each time he cried at the pain. This was Cochise's band and Standing Pony the leader!

Why did it have to be him? James envisioned the brutality his brother had undoubtedly endured. What more would they do to him? Did they know Andy was another Colton brother? Probably. The family resemblance was too strong to ignore. And he'd been in their camp last year. James knuckled his smoke-stung eyes.

He rushed around to the other side of the blacksmith's and, using a forge as cover, stared at Standing Pony. The war party stopped in the middle of the street where Andy lay. An Apache kicked Andy's ribs. Once. Twice. The others jeered, shouted curses. James mustered every ounce of restraint he possessed not to interfere. If he attacked now, Andy would be killed in seconds. And James would be next.

Where was Trace? He listed possibilities. Then it hit him. Of course, it was these Apache who had captured him. But where *was* his brother? Probably somewhere close. The Indians wouldn't spread themselves too thinly. If James remembered right, Cochise sent no more than twenty men as a raiding party. Enough to accomplish the mission, but not too many in case everyone was killed. The tribe would be decreased, but not destroyed.

James crouched low and raced for an overturned wagon. He slid to a silent stop behind it and prayed the Indians hadn't noticed. Now he waited only a few yards from his brother. Andy's eyes fluttered open, his mouth forming words. James offered a silent prayer.

Two Apache yanked Andy to his feet. The youngest Colton sagged in their grip, but still, he was upright. Ma's words in James' head rang. *Be thankful for small favors.* One corner of his mouth flitted up. He was damn thankful.

Andy turned and stared straight toward the wagon. James' hiding place.

Did his brother recognize him? *Please no!* James shook his head. *Don't draw any attention over here. I can't save your life if I'm running for my own.*

As if somehow connecting, Andy nodded and swung his gaze in the direction of Indians stumbling from the Buckhorn. Smoke and flames engulfed the building. One Apache brandished a burning chair leg while whooping threats to the enemy. The entire war party erupted into fits of chanting and shot their arrows and rifles into anything that moved—horses, burning timbers, people.

Pop! James ducked. A bullet zipped past his face and lodged in a wall not ten feet away.

He swallowed fear and peered around the wagon. Standing Pony stood talking, pointing at Andy.

James caught a few words.

"...to the church." The Apache leader grabbed a handful of Andy's hair and yanked his head back until their eyes met. "You will... until all these White Eyes die." He jammed his face inches from Andy's. "Then *you* die."

Two barrel-chested Apache clamped rough hands around Andy's arms and marched him up the center of Main Street, toward the new Catholic Church. Following behind, James thought back to last year, before he and Morningstar moved to this town. The first grave was dug and filled. A former military man named Marston had been killed by Apache, slain by none other than Mangas Colorado, a distant relative of Cochise's.

James wagged his head. Mangas Colorado ended up

being killed himself, just this past spring, close to where Marston was buried.

James refocused on the present. How was he going to rescue Andy? James dodged behind buildings and over-turned wagons—anything for cover as they proceeded up the street.

Any sound his movement made was drowned out by the cacophony of chaos. Chanting Apache...collapsing buildings...ear-shattering gunfire—all resonating off the surrounding hills.

The whitewashed pine church sat half a mile north of town. The single steeple, complete with bell, stood in stark contrast to the brown cloud billowing behind it. Two tall, imposing doors faced the dirt road and, on the side, stained glass windows presided over the beginnings of the cemetery. The war party stopped in front. James slid behind a Ponderosa pine and hoped he blended in with the undergrowth.

Standing Pony clutched Andy's shirt and addressed the gathered Apache. "The time has come, my warriors, to finish our business here in Pinos Altos. To destroy the White Ones. To regain what is rightfully ours." He grabbed Andy's hand and held it up like a conquering hero. "Our captive will lead us to victory!"

"Death to the White Man!" Lances and arrows held high overhead. Standing Pony thrust his lance skyward. "We will be victorious!"

After a couple of deafening minutes, the raves died. Standing Pony jerked his head toward the church. "Women were hiding in there. But we found them." He glared at Andy. "It is time you become an animal."

"No!"

"My warriors have already selected the women." With the confidence of a Roman emperor, Standing Pony lifted his chin. "One is like Dark Cloud—young—too young to be a wife. But your brother took her for a wife anyway." The Apache cheered. The leader turned back to Andy. "The women wait."

"No!" Andy wrenched out of an Apache's grasp. James raised his gun and aimed.

Standing Pony clutched Andy's other arm and pointed towards the church. "One is James' wife. You will take her first."

"Sonovabitch! I won't!"

"Then I give her to Black Hawk." Standing Pony twisted Andy's arm behind him and yanked up hard.

"No!" Andy's flushed cheeks paled as he fell to his knees. He twisted.

The Apache leader yanked him back up to his feet. "You'll watch Black Hawk then others take her. Then you die."

"Sonovabitch! You'll burn in hell for this! You sonovabitch!" Andy's words rushed past bloody lips. "I won't. Sonova—" He spun and reeled back into the arms of an Apache. His cheek glowed from the red handprint.

Instincts overriding reason, James leaped up and stepped forward. He had to tell Andy that Morningstar was safe in Mesilla, not here. *What the hell'm I doing? Out in the open like a sitting duck.* He jumped back behind the tree.

Andy drooped in the Indian's grip. After a breath, he straightened his knees and stood. "Kill me." Andy turned his head exposing his neck. "Slice my throat like my brothers. Whip me until I scream, 'til I pass out." Like you did with my brothers. "Do what you want, but I won't help."

Standing Pony jerked Andy against his chest and whispered. James leaned as close as he dared but heard nothing. Andy leaped back and shook his head. "Liar!" The shout retorted like a cannon blast. He stared at the church.

James didn't hear Standing Pony's reply. He strained to hear anything else. His brother shook his head then nodded. Shoulders slumped. Andy limped toward the church.

Indian warriors on both sides, Andy hobbled up the steps to the front doors, their white wooden planks reflecting the late afternoon sun.

James watched and considered. What the hell was he doing? Andy sure as hell wouldn't hurt a woman. Ever.

Andy rubbed his shoulder then gripped the door handles. "It's me! Andy Colton. James' brother. I'm coming in."

James waited for bullets to fly through the door, knock his brother back—kill him.

Andy pounded on the door. "Don't shoot. I'm unarmed." Andy swung his head side to side. Standing Pony nodded.

Deathly silence. Andy took a second grasp and pulled. One door inched open. He tugged again.

Andy pulled. One door inched open. He tugged again.

Then James remembered. Barred from inside. The parishioners told him about safety measures they'd put in place. Just for this reason.

And then... wood scraped against wood.

Andy pulled on the heavy wood.

Both doors creaked open.

James held his breath.

Doors swinging wide.

In the middle of the church, strung up by his arms from the rafters, hung Trace Joseph Colton.

CHAPTER FIFTY-ONE

LUKE COLTON SAUNTERED INTO THE *Mesilla Times* office and plopped his body into the chair in front of Thomas Littleton's desk. Reaching across the desktop with the finesse of a man with no cares, Luke handed the editor a cigar. Using a silver tip cutter retrieved from his pocket, Luke ceremoniously loped off the end of his own cigar and planted the oblong roll between his teeth. He stared at the editor.

Littleton regarded the cigar then stared back. He huffed through his mustache and retrieved a match from his desk, striking it against the wood. The sulfur tip exploded then settled into a gold-yellow flame. He held it up. Luke leaned over the desk, eyes on Littleton.

Luke puffed, waiting for the fire to ignite the tobacco. He pulled in a drag then blew a cloud of gray-blue smoke. The haze drifted toward the newspaper editor.

Cigar clamped between two fingers, Luke turned it side to side. "Nothing like a good smoke, eh, Tommy? Unless it's a beautiful woman." He crossed one leg over the other and leaned way back in the chair. Gazing at the ceiling, he puffed, gray o's forming and then expanding into wagon wheels.

Luke spoke to no one in particular. "Yep, expensive whiskey, good lookin' women and imported cigars." He cocked an eyebrow at Littleton. "Don't get much better."

The editor propped one elbow on his desk, tossed his unlit cigar into a cluttered desk drawer. "What the hell you want? And don't call me Tommy. Only your brother's allowed to do that."

"Which one? Law Dog or Bar Man?"

"Law D—? Bar—?" Littleton slammed the desk drawer. "Either. Both are good men. I'm proud to count them as friends." Littleton shuffled papers. "Now, what d'ya want? I'm busy."

Luke blew smoke toward the newsman. "Wanted to compliment you—great front-page article 'bout me. Hell, since you ran that, I haven't had to buy even my own meals or drinks!" He leaned closer. "Just wondering when you're going to report how much that reward money was."

"Appears more than your head got sideswiped, Luke. Your good sense and manners got shot to hell besides." Thomas Littleton stood. "Nobody cares how much you got for shootin' that man. Five hundred's a lot of money, but that ain't the important part. In the eyes of the town, you're quite the hero."

"And yours?"

Littleton huffed. "A hero's somebody who doesn't go around parading his reward. Just knowing they did right is all they want." He turned his back to Luke and stared at the framed picture behind his desk. A mountain stood alone, strong. "Now Trace, there's a hero. James all hurt, real bad, and only thing Trace wants is for his brother to live. Did everything he could to save him, gladly give his life if he could. Did he want a reward? No. Did he go parading around? No."

Luke shrugged.

Thomas Littleton spun around, jerking a pointed finger at Luke. "If you grow up to be half the man your brothers are, you'll be a helluva man." He marched around the desk and towered over Luke. "But you ain't grown yet, boy."

Luke bolted to his feet. "What d'you know? You hide behind your desk all day, go out and wander around, then come back and just write stories. How many lives *you* saved? How many gunmen *you* faced down? What makes *you* an expert on life?"

Littleton straightened his shoulders and took a deep breath. "You know, if you weren't James' and Trace's brother, I'd wallop you right here, right now, boy. I'd toss you over my knee and beat your backside 'til it bled." He pointed toward the sheriff's office. "But, 'cause I respect those boys, especially Trace, I won't tan your hide —today."

"You threatening me?"

"Nope. Just reminding you who you are."

CHAPTER FIFTY-TWO

JAMES FROZE. WAS TRACE ALIVE?

James loped toward the church.

"Death to the white man!"

"Burn him!"

He dove for cover under a scrub mesquite.

Moving as one, the Chiricahua Apache swarmed into the church, rushing past Trace and sweeping Andy along with their frenzy.

A piñon tree near the church would have to do as cover. Gun in hand, James sent up a quick prayer and aimed for the next bush.

War cries. Gunpowder stench. Heart in his throat. He fought the urge to rush the warriors. When would they kill Andy? Trace?

Three Apache swaggered out of the church, one a calico dress wrapped around his shoulders. The other two Indians pointed, laughing. One James didn't recognize, grabbed the dress and tied the material over his own head like a scarf. He swished, parading in front of the church as his friends whooped and hollered.

Bang!

Thundering hooves. Rifle shots. The one Apache, still bedecked in the woman's dress, clutched his chest and hit the ground.

Green-brown uniformed men rode down on them. Twenty, perhaps thirty Mexican army horses topped with armed soldiers thundered over the hill.

Hunched behind the largest piñon in the churchyard, James aimed at the closest Apache and fired. The Indian whipped around, spotting James through the branches. He bolted toward him. The knife, gripped in the Apache's hand, reflected the afternoon sun and glinted into James' eyes.

Momentarily blinded, James lost track of the charging Apache. Eyes squeezed tight, he shook his head, then opened them. He focused on the man close enough to smell and bearing down fast. Gun chest high, James squeezed the trigger.

Nothing.

Cursing his forgetfulness to reload as soon as he'd fired, James bolted for the next tree, praying the Apache would fall dead of his own accord.

Rounding a boulder behind the church, James stumbled over a small pile of rocks hidden under a snowbank. A grave. Plowing into mud, he somersaulted, scrambled to his knees and searched for his gun, somewhere outside his reach. Sliding on icy rocks, James failed to gain footing before the Apache jumped him.

Determined to beat this enemy perched on his back, James twisted, turned, bucked. Pushing up with his arms, James rolled over, taking his attacker with him. The Indian lost his grip but stayed on top of his stomach. James glared into the Apache's paint-streaked face. "Not again. Not this time."

The knife swung toward James' face. Grabbing the hand, he wrestled the knife free. It slid away. Still on his back, James stretched out his arm, managing to grab a rock. He swung. *Thwack!* Blood splattered his shirt. The Indian sagged off James's chest and lay still.

Scrambling up to his feet, James wiped his face then scanned the area for his weapon. Bullets flew, pinging into the church, ricocheting off rocks. Apache whooped, their cries echoing off surrounding hills. Soldiers' screams muffled by gunfire.

He sure as hell couldn't defend himself without a gun. Searching, he spotted the weapon under a mesquite. James scooped it up and checked the chambers. All six empty.

"James Colton."

The deep, Apache-accented voice brought memories. On the church steps stood Standing Pony, Andy pressed against his chest, a knife at his throat.

James glared at the Indian. James' and Trace's living nightmare.

He glanced side to side. The Mexican army aimed rifles, waiting for... something. The Apache stopped. The world grew quiet.

James stood tall and stepped from behind the mesquite into the open. "Standing Pony. We meet again."

Using Andy as a human shield, the Apache war leader marched down the church steps stopping several yards from James. The Indian pressed the knife against Andy's throat. Blood trickled down his neck, his tanned face paling.

"Let my brothers go. I'll do whatever you want." James eased closer to Andy whose eyes squeezed shut. He lowered his voice, hoping it took on the hard edge he felt. "Trade them for me."

Standing Pony gripped Andy tighter. "Call off your army friends, Colton. They are not wanted here." He yanked the knife from Andy's throat, then lowered it to his ribcage. Andy's legs buckled as he slumped against the Indian.

Turning to Captain Mendoza, James waved, hollering, "You heard him. Back off."

But they didn't back off. They moved closer, making a show of aiming their rifles, cocking them.

Beyond frustrated, James flapped his arms as if herding unruly stock. "Back off! Lower your weapons. Captain, he'll kill my brother if you don't."

Mendoza sneered. "He'll kill us all if he gets the chance. I won't let him."

Bang! A rifle shot zipped past Standing Pony's shoulder and planted itself into an Apache. The man crumpled to the ground.

"Now your brother dies!" Standing Pony shoved the knife tip through Andy's shirt and into his side. Blood soaked the cotton material. Andy moaned and coughed. The Apache pulled out the knife.

"Not my brother! Not..." James bolted toward them, hands held high. "Wait! Please. This is between you and me. Let him go. It's me you want." He shouted over his shoulder. "Dammit, Mendoza! Call 'em off now!"

Captain Mendoza shrugged then turned to his men. "You heard him. *Alejarse.*"

Attention riveted on Andy, James moved in as close as he dared. "It's all right, Andy. You'll be safe."

Getting no response, James glanced around. To his right stood war-ready Indians. To his left, the Mexican army.

James hollered at Standing Pony, "My other brother?" Breath caught in his chest. "Alive?"

Lips curling into a snarl, the Indian jerked his head in a quick nod. "Not much longer."

Another prayer sent upward, James focused on Andy's sagging body and wondered how much longer he would remain upright. "Let him go. It's me you want."

"You speak truthfully, James Colton. We knew your older brother would lead you here." Standing Pony snorted. "The game. You played well. Gave my young warriors time to learn."

"Learn?"

The leader sneered. "To torment before killing. Two kinds of torment." A smile flitted and then like lightning, disappeared. "His and yours."

Not truly understanding and hoping he could figure it out later, James pointed to Andy. "And my brother you hold in your arms? How did you get him?" James glanced side to side. So far, no one had moved.

Standing Pony smirked and strengthened his grip. "Sold by Buffalo Man."

Just as he'd suspected. Dawson. A closer look at Andy. Hurt bad. "Release my brothers. Take me. Kill me if you must. But let them go."

Standing Pony wiped the bloody knife on Andy's face, smearing the red mess from forehead to chin. Finished, he shoved Andy to the ground. He crumpled to his knees and clutched his side. The youngest Colton brother peered up at James and nodded.

Knife shoulder high, Standing Pony crouched, eyes locked on James. "I have waited long, James Colton. Now I kill you...like you killed my brother."

"Your brother died a warrior." James crouched also, scanning the ground for a rock. Anything to use as a weapon. "There's no shame in that."

"You took my woman. Dark Cloud was promised to me." The Apache inched forward.

James stepped right. "How's that?"

"Cochise promised the Pima captive to me. She was mine. After your marriage ceremony," Standing Pony moved left, "I stayed by your wickiup all night. Should have been me." He lunged.

James jumped back. "I didn't know." The woman's flesh. Her trembling body. "Remember, Cochise...forced me to—"

"Three dark moons of rutting." The Apache circled James. "I listened, ear against wickiup, heard her moans, your—"

James charged, tackling the Apache at the knees. Both men slammed into the ground, somersaulted across icy rocks and then plowed into the church wall.

Crushed by Standing Pony's weight on top, James dredged up Indian fighting tactics he hoped he'd never have to use again.

Thrusting his legs upwards, he pushed the Indian's body over his head. Twisting his torso and finding his feet, James spotted the knife on the ground to his right.

James dove for the blade, grabbed and rolled. Springing to his feet, he crouched, waiting for his adversary to attack. Before James took a second breath, Standing Pony plowed into him, both men splatting against the ground.

Tumbling over and over, the men crashed into a mesquite bush. The sudden stop gave James the advantage. He straddled the Indian, jamming the knife into his side. The blade struck flesh and muscle before stopping at bone.

Jerking it out, James strengthened his grip and plunged the knife in again. The man under him shivered.

Frantic hands grabbed James' face, fingernails raking down his cheek. Death throes shook Standing Pony as he clutched James' knife-held hand.

Standing Pony's body relaxed.

James squeezed his eyes tight, curled forward, then slid off the Apache. He sunk to the ground as Standing Pony's last breath struck his face.

CHAPTER FIFTY-THREE

JAMES RAPPED ON THE DOOR AND TIPTOED across the sun-filled room. Trace lay still, as if dead. But James knew better. His brother was alive. Although barely. He scooped a feather pillow from the chair by the bed and shook his brother's shoulder.

"Good thing you've got such a hard head." James pushed the pillow under his brother's head. "Those Apache nearly took it off. But Mrs. Durris says you'll be up and running in no time."

Trace whispered garbled words. James eased down to the bed's edge, praying his older brother would recover. By the time the Mexican army had cut him down, Trace had quit breathing. Apparently, hitting the ground jarred his lungs and heart enough to bring him back. James shuddered for the hundredth time. Damn close. Too damn close.

Trace plopped an arm toward James. He winced.

"What's wrong? In pain? All Mrs. Durris got is whiskey." James cocked his head at the bottle on the bedside table. "From my broken saloon."

Locating a glass on the bedside table, James poured an inch into it. He held it up, morning light turning the whiskey a liquid gold. He stared at the elixir. "There was a time this was my only answer to pain. This Essence of the Gods numbed the world." He held it to Trace's lips. "You need this much more than I ever did."

Whiskey dribbling down his chin, Trace coughed and pushed the glass aside. His right eye, ringed in black and purple, closed. A crimson fist print glowed on his left cheek.

Trace's mouth opened, mumbling words James struggled to understand. Making out a few, he grinned. "Andy. Yeah, I found him. Alive—here in Pinos Altos. In fact, he's right here in Mrs. Durris' home." James pointed toward the door. "Just down the hall."

Pulling the blanket off his body, Trace pushed up on his elbow.

"You're not going anywhere." James pressed his brother's chest back to the bed. "Andy's sleepin' now. Got banged up pretty good, took an arrow in the upper arm during that raid in Mogollon, broken jaw, couple knife wounds, but she says he should be able to come see you tomorrow." James patted Trace's arm. "Andy's going to be fine."

Trace nodded.

"Neither of you're gonna run any races soon." Bringing the whiskey to his lips, James

stopped and stared at the soothing liquor. Shaking his head, he set the glass back on the table.

CHAPTER FIFTY-FOUR

"Mornin', Mrs. Colton." Abe Kinnear looked over his rimless glasses perched on his nose and nodded to Teresa. She closed the post office door. "Not too cold today."

"Hello, Mr. Kinnear. It's going to be very pleasant." She stepped up to the counter. "Just wondering if we got any mail."

Kinnear's eyebrows shot up. "Holy smoke, Mrs. Colton. My Lord, I plumb forgot. You got a letter from that crazy brother-in-law of yours."

"James?"

"Yup." He nodded. "Came express delivery early this morning."

Hand automatically flying to her constricting throat, Teresa's stomach knotted. "Not Trace?"

Disappearing behind the counter then straightening up, Kinnear handed her the white envelope. Surprised at her shaking hands, she accepted the mail and glanced at the postmark. Pinos Altos. James and Morningstar's home. Her gaze riveted on the envelope.

"You gonna open it or just keep it warm?" He ambled around the counter and stood next to her. "Want me to?"

Nodding, Teresa handed over the letter praying the news was good. Maybe James had intended to address this to Morningstar and sent it to her, instead. Then, why hadn't Trace written?

Carefully sliding his hand under the envelope flap, Kinnear pulled the folded paper out and presented it to Teresa. Staring at the bad news, or was it good news, she touched the paper then brought her eyes up to meet his.

"Want I should read?" Abe Kinnear unfolded the note while Teresa nodded.

"I'm strong, Mr. Kinnear. I can handle anything. But...what if...?"

"'Fore you get all fret up, let me read this quick and I'll tell you if it's bad." Kinnear lip

read the message then nodded at Teresa. Handing it to her, he patted her shoulder. "Better fire up that cook stove, Mrs. Colton. Your men're comin' home."

* * *

LUKE SAT in Sam Bean's Saloon, his thoughts keeping him company. Dark. It was dark in here and he liked it that way. Nobody recognized him back here in the corner. Since saving Morningstar, not only was it impossible to have privacy, but with his fame came a lack of focus. Should be head back home to Sally, now that Morningstar turned cold, or stay around until his brothers came back? If they did.

He chilled at that thought. Another beer would chase away worries. He looked up at Thomas Littleton who plopped down a full beer glass, directly in front of Luke. The editor then pulled out a wooden chair and eased into it, managing not to spill a drop of his own beer. Pushing his hat up on his forehead, Littleton pointed his chin at the beer. "On me. Sort of an early homecoming cele-bration."

Luke's gaze shot over to the newspaper editor. "Whose homecoming?"

"Don't tell me you ain't heard." Littleton leaned closer. "All three of your brothers."

"What? All three? How'd you know?" Luke studied the man's face, searching for any hint of a lie, a ruse to get him to leave Mesilla.

"Sorry. Thought those sisters-in-law of yours would've told you. About an hour ago, Mrs. Colton—Trace's missus—got word from your brother James, all three of them are safe. Right now recovering up in Pinos Altos. Guess there was some Apache trouble, but like a Phoenix rising from the proverbial ashes, those Colton boys survived."

Stare shifting from the journalist to the saloon door, Luke scrambled to his feet and threaded his way through the bar. Skidding to a stop at the batwing doors, he turned back and nodded to Littleton.

Sprinting down the street toward Trace's house, Luke mulled over the information. Thank God they're safe, but why did Teresa announce this turn of events to the world before telling him? By the time the house was in sight, Luke knew what he would do next.

Knocking, then pushing his way through the wooden door, Luke removed his hat. "Teresa? Star? It's me, Luke." He shut it harder than usual.

"In here." Teresa appeared at the kitchen door, wooden spoon in hand. "Have you heard?"

Luke crossed the room, tossing his hat on the couch.

"Yeah. Wishing it didn't have to be from the town gossip."

Teresa shrugged, tossing him a rare smile. "Star's out looking for you now. Abe Kinnear read the letter and I'm sure within ten minutes most of Mesilla knew what it said." She flashed another grin. "Coffee?"

"Please." Luke followed her into the kitchen, pulled out a chair, sinking into it. Steam escaped the cup she set in front of him. Luke frowned. "Well? What'd the letter say?"

"James is fine, but Trace is hurt. Not as bad as...well, when he came back from Cochise's, but James wanted to prepare me. Apparently, Andy's hurt worse. They're both with Mrs. Durris, the town's midwife." Teresa chuckled.

"Midwife, huh?" Luke sipped his coffee and stared out the window.

Teresa stirred the bread dough. "What's wrong? Thought you'd be happy. Finally get to see your brothers again. And in one piece. It'll be wonderful having you all together."

"Sure will." Luke set his cup on the table. "Been waiting a long time. But guess I'm scared."

Teresa spun around. "Of what?"

Luke ran a hand through his hair. "They won't like me. I know I've changed. Maybe I won't like them. Afraid of Trace's scars. James' visions, his crazy head. How do I talk to him, especially after Star and..."

Teresa clutched the mixing bowl and leaned close. "What about you two? She won't talk about you since the day after you got shot. What does James need to know that she's not telling?"

Rubbing his eyes, Luke shook his head. "It was all innocent fun. Guess it just got out of hand." He paused. "We—"

The front door opened.

"Hi, Teresa," Morningstar called from the living room. "Can't find Luke anywhere. Suppose he—" Jerking to a stop in the kitchen door, her eyes widened at Luke.

Silence saturated the room. Luke's gaze darted from Morningstar to his coffee.

"Luke was just having a cup. Want one?" Teresa asked.

Nodding, Morningstar blinked a few times then eased into a chair across from Luke. "I'm guessing you've heard about your brothers."

"Thank God they're all right."

Teresa set a cup in front of Morningstar. "Have something warm. Then, we need to talk about our men coming home. Think they'll feel up to a party?"

Dragging his eyes from Morningstar, Luke turned to Teresa busy now needing dough. He weighed his words. "If what you tell me about James', even Trace's reactions to Apache is right, I'd think they'll need time to put it in place. They might have those nightmares and visions all over again." He glanced at Morningstar. "I don't think a party is what they'll want."

"But..." Cup untouched, Morningstar stared at Luke.

"Look," Luke shrugged. "Everyone'll be asking me, congratulating me about saving you. Might take the spotlight away from my brothers."

Morningstar glanced up at Teresa. "Maybe he's right. Not about Luke being the center of attention, but they might have those nightmares again."

Teresa stopped kneading and wiped her hands on a towel. "You're both probably right. Guess we'll just wait 'til they get back to plan a party. Plenty of time."

Luke finished his coffee and plunked the cup on the table. "If you'll point me in the right direction, think I'll ride out to meet those brothers of mine. Might just surprise them."

"Oh, you'll surprise them all right." Teresa poured more brown liquid into Luke's cup. "When're you planning on leaving?"

Luke shrugged. "I'm not really needed around here. Sammy says he can handle things in town and you two women seem to have everything under control. Suppose I'll leave as soon as I rent a horse and buy supplies. How far *is* Pinos Altos?"

CHAPTER FIFTY-FIVE

LUKE TIED HIS HORSE TO THE HITCHIN' RAIL
down the street from Mrs. Durris' house and stretched.
Riding three straight days created kinks and sore spots
he'd only imagined earlier. Where were his brothers
now? At the midwife's or James'? A sign across the street
decided his dilemma. *Red Horse Saloon*. Wiping the dust
from his lips, Luke sauntered toward procrastination.

Across the rutted road, burned buildings lay scattered
like charred toothpicks. Indian attack had been apparent
from five miles south of town. Arrows remained stuck in
dirt and trees, burned, overturned wagons littered the
ice-encrusted mud and the creaks and groans of buildings being torn down pounded his ears. Acrid fumes of
ashes assaulted his nose as he'd ridden past.

Stepping into the saloon, Luke coughed at cigar
smoke spiraling around his head. Shafts of sunlight
filtered through the boarded-up window, while gas
lanterns threw pools of yellow light around the six-table
establishment.

Luke leaned against the wooden plank serving as the

bar, ordered a beer then turned his back to the barkeep. One cowboy, two men clothed in miner's garb, and one apathetic saloon girl lazed in the smoke. The woman glanced over her shoulder at Luke then disregarded him.

Luke half turned to the bartender who pushed the beer across the bar. "Kinda dead in here," Luke said.

"Yeah. Everybody's either run off or out workin'." The barkeep selected a glass from behind him and used his apron to polish the glass.

"Heard about the raid," Luke said. "Many die?"

"Too damn many, mister. 'Bout twenty of us Americans and ten or so of those red devils." He shook his head. "'Course none of them Mexican Army got shot. They stood and watched as James Colton and that Apache fought it out."

The skin on the back of Luke's neck burned. "You see it?"

The barkeep shook his head. "Busy protectin' my wife. Sure heard about it, though. Colton's been the talk of the town since then."

"You know him?" Luke sipped his warm beer and leaned closer.

"Sure, everybody does. Owns the first saloon this one-horse town had, The Buckhorn. Hell, he helped me get started with this place. Even though I was competition." The man wiped the inside of the glass and set it back on the counter behind him. "Said there were enough thirsty fellas for two establishments." He chuckled. "And he was right."

Luke raised an eyebrow. Sounded like his brother. "Know where I can find him? Like to meet this man."

"Not rightly sure. But I heard he's still in town. His brothers got all shot to hell by them Apache and when he's not tending them, he's putting his house and saloon back together."

"Where's his house at?"

The bartender raised one shaggy eyebrow. "Ain't a good idea to go askin' too many questions. Can get yourself killed askin' the wrong one."

Running down a quick list of reasons why not to reveal his identity then another list of explanations, Luke held up a hand. "Reckon so. I'm Luke, James' brother. Number three of four."

Tossing his rag on the counter, the man grabbed Luke's hand and pumped it. "Well, I'll be go to Hell. Good to meet ya. Why didn't you say so earlier?"

Luke shrugged.

The barkeep leaned back. "Lookin' at you now, you two do look alike." He grinned.

"Mustache there kinda hides the resemblance at first." He pumped Luke's hand again then released it. "Got a helluva brother there. Helluva brother."

"Thank you. We're all proud of him, too."

"Can't remember him sayin' he's expectin' you," the man said.

"He doesn't know," Luke put a finger to his lips. "Hoping to surprise him. I'm the last person he'd be looking for right now." He asked the question which had been on his mind for days. "How are my other brothers?"

"Go see for yourself. They're down the street, 'round the corner at Mrs. Durris'." A quick grin flitted across the bartender's face then disappeared. He dropped his voice. "She's a midwife, but closest thing we got to a doctor right now."

Luke nodded.

"She knows a lot more about doctorin' than birthin'

babies." A hint of red glowed across the bartender's cheeks.

"Sounds like they're in good hands. But how bad hurt are they?"

Picking up the limp rag, the barkeep wiped an imaginary spot at the end of the bar. "Can't say." He stopped and stared at Luke. "Afraid of what you're gonna find? I hear they're still in one piece."

Luke spun the empty glass on the bar.

"Tell you what, Mr. Colton." Leaning closer, the saloon owner picked up Luke's glass. "You go see those brothers of yours, come back in here and next beer's on me."

* * *

STEPPING down the rough boardwalk toward Mrs. Durris', Luke rehearsed the scenario. He opens the door and pushes his head into the room. James and Trace jump up, grab their long-lost brother while Andy bolts in, that wide grin plastered on his face. Four pairs of brown eyes glisten as the brothers embrace. They spend hours getting reacquainted, glasses hoisted, stories spun.

His long legs took him to the midwife's sooner than he'd expected. Luke removed his hat, smoothed his brown hair and pushed a hank of it out of his eyes. Like a spoiled child, it defiantly fell back into place over his right eye. Securing the errant hair under the crown and resetting his hat, Luke marched up to the door and squared his shoulders. The air prickled with hesitation.

Nausea threatening to take control, Luke touched the doorknob.

"Luke?"

The voice behind him spun him around. He glanced

across the road toward a man standing there, mouth open.

"James?" Luke's palms grew clammy, feet froze to the ground as the brother less than two years older loped across the street.

"Good Lord almighty, Luke. What the hell're you doin' here?" James wrapped his strong arms around his brother and squeezed.

Tension and doubt drained as Luke returned the embrace. Damn it felt good. He'd forgotten how much he missed his brothers.

"Damn, boy, you put on a few pounds there." James thumped Luke's belly. "Proves Sally's a fine cook." He held his brother by the shoulders. "Damn good to see you again. But, how'd you know we were here?"

"Thought I'd surprise you in Mesilla, but the joke was on me. Waited around 'til I knew where you were for sure, then came soon as I could." Luke peered into eyes he knew so well, yet detected a man he'd never know.

Healing scrapes down James' right cheek stood in contrast to the silver pink scar running across the left. The scar hadn't faded much since he'd last seen his brother back in Kansas. But the scratches were new, judging by the puffy redness, and probably still plenty tender. Luke pointed to the marks. "What happened?"

"Standing Pony."

"How—"

"Long story. Tell you later. Maybe over a beer or two." James slapped Luke's back.

"Fair enough."

"What the hell're we standing out here for? Andy and Trace are inside." James' smile reached both edges of his face and lit up his surprised eyes. "Wait 'til they see you. They'll think they're hallucinatin' from Mrs. Durris' pain killer." He grabbed the doorknob and turned around to Luke. "How'd you know we needed you right now?"

Luke's planned reunion evaporated as James pushed open Trace's door. There lay his oldest brother, looking small under a down quilt. His ashen face turned toward Luke.

James planted a hand on Luke's back and nudged. "Go on in."

Willing his feet forward, Luke held his breath, as if letting out air would somehow crush Trace. A quick sweep of the room. No Andy.

Rocking Trace's shoulder, James pointed. "Look who I found out wandering the street."

Trace's eyes narrowed then widened. "Luke?" He pushed himself up on one elbow. "That really you?" He rolled onto his side.

Luke swallowed the last bit of moisture in his mouth and inched forward.

James shoved a second pillow under Trace's head. "Thought he should come in and say howdy."

Glowing bruises on Trace's cheeks, the swollen lip complete with a pink scar that matched James' lip scars. Inwardly, Luke cringed.

His brother held out an arm. To shake hands or to embrace? Wide silver scars around Trace's wrist sent shivers through his entire body. Hell, it wasn't a dream, stories made up. Trace carried scars, too.

Luke eased backward then turned away. Everything James had told him about Trace and his captivity was true, no matter how much he hoped James had lied. Trace really *was* a hero like the newspaper editor had claimed. Even though Luke had saved Morningstar from certain shame, possibly even death, he knew his accomplishments paled in comparison. Again, the left-out brother.

"What the hell's wrong?" James' breath in his ear brought Luke's thoughts back.

No way he'd let on. Instead, he allowed a shrug.

"Whatever it is," James draped an arm around his brother's shoulder, "after you say a proper howdy to Trace and Andy, I'll show you my saloon." He thumped him on the chest. "Hell, boy, if you ask right, I might even buy you a drink."

CHAPTER FIFTY-SIX

NOT A GOOD IDEA, LUKE THOUGHT. TAKING TWO injured brothers to a saloon merely days after the Indian attack—not a good idea. Would they be strong enough? Trace had insisted he was good to go, and besides, who could resist those eyes ringed black and blue? Certainly not Luke. Even stubborn brother James had relented after Trace's second *"please."*

The trek from Mrs. Durris' to the Red Horse Saloon had been arduous at best, but Luke, had a firm grip around Trace's shoulders, while James did the same with Andy. Like drunken marionettes, the four brothers wobbled down the boardwalk.

"Howdy again!" Luke waved to the bartender as he pushed open the doors wide enough for he and Trace to maneuver through. James and Andy followed.

The barkeep, Billy, his white duck jacket covering an ample belly, waved back. "Usually, we gotta help men outta here—not in!" He grabbed Trace under the arm, guiding him to the nearest chair. "You must be the sheriff brother."

Easing down, Trace winced. "I am. Good to be out and about. Things going good enough.?"

"Fair to middlin', I reckon. Not much business lately. Hell, you boys are the most I've had in here all day!" The mixologist surveyed his crowd. "Nice family reunion. Like I told Mr. Colton here, first drink's on me!"

"And second's on me!" Luke pulled out a chair. It screeched against the rough wooden planking. He eyed James. Would he wheedle certain information out of Luke? Make him talk about Morningstar more than they already had?

So far, he'd been able to alter the conversations' paths when it came to James' wife, but would he always be able to avert catastrophe? A beer or two, and he could keep his mouth shut. More than two…

Reflecting on the last couple of nights, he and James had talked past midnight. Even this morning at James' house where they slept, James had spent hours talking about his saloon, the people of Pinos Altos and of his beautiful wife. Other than telling him about shooting the Waco Kid and that Morningstar had summoned a doctor, that was all he'd told his brother. Luke knew the best defense was to stay quiet.

Luke sipped his beer, listening to Andy go on about his latest foray into the world of mining. Trace interjected with a story or two about sheriffing and how glad he was the army had finally left town. Their martial law was rescinded, partially thanks to James and his campaign to get the army to quit eating the citizens' food and get the hell out of Mesilla.

Although James spent two months in jail when the army found him guilty of inciting a riot and civil unrest, then asked to leave town, Trace acknowledged the guilt he held for arresting his brother. Throughout Trace's explanations and further conversation, James stayed quiet, nodding on occasion, but mostly staring at his glass. It remained full.

Andy downed three to Luke's one, but Luke figured the healing jaw, knife slashes as well as that arrow wound in the arm pained him a great deal. Trace finished his second, called for a third when James coughed and spit. He clutched his neck and jumped to his feet, shouting, "God, no! No! Trace, get him off me!" Chair clattering to the floor, James backed to the corner of the saloon like a snared animal. Arms flailing then covering his face, James slid to the floor whimpering. "Don't! Don't! I'll be good...I'll be good..."

With a low groan, Andy pushed away from the table and hobbled across the sawdust-strewn floor to James. Andy knelt, embracing James crouched in the corner. Andy dragged him

into a tight cocoon, keeping his voice calm. "It's all right, James. Indians're gone. You're safe."

James fought, clamping his frantic hands around Andy's. Shirt material ripped.

"James...James," Andy said. "You're safe. No Apache. I'm your brother."

Luke eased across the room toward James and Andy, afraid if he rushed, James would...well, he wasn't sure what would happen. He knew, though, that James was crazed enough to injure Andy seriously. He glanced back at Trace still at the table. A gentle wag of the head and downcast eyes.

As he reached his brothers, James flailed once more, and then froze. From his corner on the floor, James' gaze roamed the room while his chest pumped like a steam engine's pistons. Luke had seen James hallucinate a few months back in Lawrence, Kansas. But that was when Quantrill was trying to kill them. In an odd way, Luke understood that trigger. But tonight?

James let out one loud breath, wriggled out of Andy's grasp, shoving him aside into the sawdust. James clambered to his feet, glaring. He rocked back and clenched his fists. "Dammit! Dammit to hell!"

"James?" Luke stepped in close. "You good?"

Without answering, James strong-armed Luke backwards and stormed through the swinging saloon doors. Light snow fell as he disappeared into the dark.

Offering Andy a hand, Luke pulled his brother to his feet and picked up his knocked-off hat. The brothers returned to their seats. A few sips of beer, several deep breaths, Luke smoothed his mustache. "What—?"

"He coughed just now. Reminds him when One Wing forced sand down his throat." Trace said. "Haunts James at odd times."

Luke massaged his own throat, imagined swallowing rough rocks and the panic it causes. He cringed at the thought. He studied his beer glass, now empty, then pointed to it as he caught the bartender's gaze.

More silence. Neither Andy nor Trace offered suggestions or further explanations.

Luke regarded his brothers. "Should one of us go get him?"

Both shook their heads. "He'll be back," Trace said.

"When?" Luke nodded at the new beer glass, now full.

"When he's ready," Andy said. "Might be tonight. Tomorrow. Or hell, even the day after that." He raised one shoulder. "Just takes time."

Despite the light tone of their voices, his brothers were worried. But what could they do that hadn't already been done? Or said?

Conversation between the three picked up after a long silence. Andy rubbed his shoulder and continued his tales of mining and the various prospectors he'd met. Luke's healing head wound throbbed. Two beers later, the brothers looked up as the saloon doors squeaked open, James sauntered in.

Andy halted mid-sentence, Luke picked up his half-empty beer glass, holding it to his lips, more for something to do than needing a drink. Trace nodded.

As if nothing had happened, James sat, picked up his glass and drained it. Half an hour passed while the brothers continued their unexpected reunion.

Luke regarded each brother. Trace's eyes closed then snapped open. James spoke louder than the others. And Andy rubbed his shoulder as he finished his fifth beer. A red stain spread from under Andy's hand.

James frowned and pointed his chin toward Andy's wound. "You're bleeding."

Andy shrugged at the red smear in his hand. "Probably tore out those stitches when—"

"Dammit!" James' voice sparked. "God, I'm always hurting one of you. Dammit!"

"Hell, James, don't worry." Andy covered his shirt with his coat. "Take more'n an arrow to hurt me."

Again, awkward silence. Trace broke it. "Yeah. Only thing that'd take you down is a woman. Right one comes along and you're putty in her hands. Melt all over this table." He hoisted an empty glass in his direction.

A red streak cascaded across Andy's bruised cheeks. "No way."

The three others clinked empty glasses at Andy.

"Before we go, I have something to say." James took his time making eye contact with each brother. "When I was outside screwing my head back on and trying not to freeze to death, I made a decision."

Luke's patience had worn thin. Could James make things even more dramatic? "Which is?"

"I've already talked to Trace about this, but tonight I'm sure." James scooted his chair back. "I'm gonna sell the Buckhorn—"

"What?" Luke and Andy spoke in unison.

"I think it's best." James nodded. "And take Star to California. See the ocean. Try to start over."

Shocked silence blanketed the brothers. James leaving? Luke couldn't imagine saying goodbye to Morningstar and, of course, James. Would they come back? How would his brother make a living? How could he sell his saloon?

After several stops and starts at conversation, Trace clasped James' shoulder. "You know we'll help however we can."

"I know." James flashed the famous Colton family grin. "And thanks. But it's been an interesting evening, and big brother here needs his beauty rest."

"Ah hell, James," Andy said. "It's much too late. No amount of rest—" He grimaced as he moved but turned the frown into a smile. "You grab one arm, I'll get the other and we'll help our ancient, decrepit brother to bed. After all," he thumped Luke on the chest, "sun's already down."

Luke stood and stretched. "Yep, past his bedtime." Gripping one arm and hoisting Trace to his feet, Luke caught his oldest brother's gaze. "Remember when Pa'd tell those stories at night and I'd struggle to stay awake, but couldn't? You'd pick me up to carry me to bed and instead tickle me."

Trace nodded. "And I'd get in trouble."

"As you *should* have." Luke held the door open and, waving to the bartender, followed his brothers into the frosty mountain air.

CHAPTER FIFTY-SEVEN

THE SIGHT OF ADOBE HOUSES ON THE outskirts of Mesilla brought a racing heart and anxious breath to James as the four brothers topped a hill northwest of town. A long sideways glance at Trace. He had been uncharactistically quiet in the three-day ride back, but his brother's pride had taken a beating by being captured by those Apache a second time. His own guilt tore at him. After all, he'd promised Trace they wouldn't be taken alive again. He'd let him down.

On the other hand, maybe Trace was upset at James' announced plans. They were close, he and Trace. Leaving would be tough. But it was something he *had* to do. Something to keep his sanity intact. Something to keep him from killing himself.

Or would it?

James topped a hill, pulled back on his reins, and stretched, waiting for his brothers to join him to enjoy the staggering view. Below, late afternoon sun drenched the Mesilla Valley in gold and orange bands. To the east, the spiked Organ Mountains were turning dusty rose.

"Good Lord, it's beautiful!" Luke's words snapped in James' ear. "Don't get views like this back home."

He had to agree. Thoughts turning to his wife, James envisioned their reunion. There'd be hugs, kisses freely exchanged, an hour of talking with Morningstar and the others, then he'd head over to the barber's for a much-needed shave, haircut and bath.

He and Morningstar would move over to the Corn Exchange Hotel where they could say hello as husband and wife—properly. Guilt stabbed James' soul. If he had been the lover, the husband Star deserved, by now she would have had good news. If she had, he and Trace would be busy building a cradle. But she wouldn't have news like that. Probably never.

More guilt.

California and the ocean. Maybe *that* would change things.

He gigged his horse into a trot and aimed for Mesilla.

* * *

JAMES and his brothers rode into Mesilla shortly before sunset and reined up in front of Trace's house. Swinging out of the saddle, James enjoyed the euphoria of home-coming. He twisted his torso listening to the snap of vertebrae popping back into place.

Morningstar and Teresa, toddler Faith in tow, rushed out the front door and into the arms of their tired men. Luke hugged his hellos and led two of the horses around back and into the barn. Following a long hug and quick kiss, James released Morningstar and led the other two horses. Walking beside him, she tossed a thousand ques-tions in his direction. James smiled, nodded, savoring the moment.

Horses rubbed and fed, James and Luke brushed off trail dust and sauntered inside to join their family. Trace, still painfully sore from his ordeal, leaned into the end of the sofa while Faith snuggled into her daddy's warm chest. Teresa handed Luke a cup. He blew on the freshly boiled coffee and settled into the other end of the sofa. Stifling a groan, Andy set his coffee cup on the end table and sagged back into the rocking chair opposite Trace.

In the kitchen, James wrapped his arms around Morningstar's waist as she stood at the stove, stirring a pot of red chile stew. Cuddling her, he nuzzled her neck and breathed in homey aromas. "So good to be here. Missed you."

Morningstar twisted around in his tight grip and faced him. "This has been the longest four weeks of my life." She smiled as their lips met. The kiss was deep.

Pulling back, James searched her eyes. Was something there? Something she wasn't saying? No. Had to be his imagination. His nervousness about his plans for later tonight. His anxiety trying to take over again.

"If you'll help me get plates and the table set, we can eat, Mr. Colton." Morningstar's soft voice brought James' focus back to the kitchen. He gazed at her face, the dark Indian eyes and high cheekbones radiating exotic beauty. She nodded to the stove. "Teresa and I've been working all day on a special supper."

He peeked into the stew pot. "Looks almost as good as you." James kissed her again then whispered, "Won't taste as good, though."

Morningstar giggled and playfully swatted his arm. "Mr. Colton. How you talk."

He smiled at his wife's pinking cheeks and gave her another quick kiss. "All right, I'll be good. Where're the plates?"

* * *

FULL DARK FOUND ALL four brothers lifting beers to each other at *Sam Bean's Saloon*. This hangout, located on the south side of the plaza and next to Butterfield's vacant office, was their favorite. Usually, the beer was colder than other places despite the lack of ice, and the piano player was acquainted with more than one tune. A real plus in James' mind.

At the insistence of the two women, the brothers left dirty dishes on the table as they were shooed out the door and told not to return for a couple of hours. As tired as he was, it was fine with James. He sat, beer glass in one hand and thought: life just doesn't get any better. All the brothers back together—alive, in one piece. And Star. More beautiful than he remembered.

James grinned at Morningstar's whispered words as he kissed her goodbye. *Tonight'll be a night to remember.*

"I'll ask again, James. What're you grinnin' at?" Andy's words in his face melted James' lustful thoughts. "Look. If you want to go back, we'll understand."

Luke smacked James' arm. "Hell, you're purrin' like a kitten in a creamery."

Andy reached across the table and slid his brother's beer glass away. "You're downright pathetic. You won't be needin' this where you're goin'." He held it up, his lips stretching for the glass.

James wrestled it away. "Thanks for mindin' your own business. I paid for this beer, and I intend to drink it. All of it." He glanced from brother to brother. "Besides, you heard what the women said. At least an hour."

"You two don't know our wives." Trace sipped his beer as he turned from Andy to Luke. "When they say an hour, they mean it." He glanced at James for confirmation. He grinned.

Conversation continued while Andy grew quiet, twirling his glass and staring into the liquid.

Worried, James elbowed Andy. "What's wrong? Figured you'd be tearin' up this place by now."

"Nothin'. Just thinkin'. Wish I didn't think so much sometimes." Andy met James' stare.

James set his glass down and faced his youngest brother. "What?" Trace and Luke were engrossed in their own conversation about the newest Henry repeating rifle. James knew the time was right for Andy to talk about whatever was on Andy's mind. Probably be hard for him.

Andy took a deep breath. "When I was bein' held by that Apache, Standing Pony, and you were tryin' to find me, he said something about you...well, about you and that captive Pima woman. He said...you...raped her."

James squeezed the glass.

Continuing, Andy glanced toward his other brothers deeply involved in their own discussion and lowered his voice. "Did you? You told me you married her. In my book there's a big difference. Hell, James, we marched side by side across that Sonoran Desert and back again last year and you never said more than that."

James stared into the past. "I *did* marry her. By an Apache shaman, a medicine man."

"What did you tell Morningstar?" Andy bent closer.

Trace and Luke stood, empty glasses in hand. Still engrossed in conversation, they sauntered toward the bar. James shrugged. "Nothing."

"You going to?"

"Dark Cloud's dead. Killed by Standing Pony and his brother, One Wing." James picked up a glass, its contents sloshing as his hand shook. "I told you before, she was so young...*I* was chosen because her people, the Pima, were even more dishonored by her being forced to marry a captive white man. Apparently, there was no disgrace lower than me."

"I had no idea." Andy's glass hovered halfway between his lips and the table.

James paused. "I thought she'd be allowed to live if we...well, she and I—"

"Got the picture." Andy caught his brother's downcast stare. "Did you?"

Nodding, James took a deep breath and studied the nicks and scrapes on the table.

"So, it wasn't rape."

James' hands trembled harder as he shook his head.

"But they didn't let her live?"

James buried his head on the table.

Andy patted his shoulder. "Sorry. Didn't mean to dredge up the past. But I had to know."

Turning his face to his brother, James' anguish edged each word. "I could make love to her, but not Morningstar." He sat up and squared his shoulders. "Now you know."

Easing back in his chair, Andy glanced over his shoulder. "Trace know?"

A quick nod signaled the end of James' discussion. Desperate to bury old memories and feelings, he stood so quickly the chair scooted out behind him.

Luke plopped a full beer glass in front of James. "Where you goin'?" Trace did the same for Andy.

"Just need some air. I'll be back." James zigzagged around tables and stepped into chilly night air. As he walked, he thought. *Why the hell did Andy bring her up?*

Tonight, of all nights. And why do I have to react like this? Dark Cloud is dead and buried. But not gone. Never gone.

Shivering, James realized he'd been outside probably a quarter hour. *I did it again. My brothers think I'm crazy and now I'm proving it.*

Stepping back into the saloon, James spotted Luke now up at the bar talking to the bartender, Slim. There was nothing slim about him, but everyone used that moniker, and he didn't seem to mind. James realized he'd never heard Slim's real name in the years he'd known him.

While James waited next to his brother at the bar, the stench of one too many beers on Luke surprised him. Was Luke a drinker? None of the brothers had ever acquired a real liking for the amber liquid. Except for him. James remembered his months being a drunk and cringed at the memories. He hated himself for wasting time.

Slim pushed four newly poured beer glasses across the wooden bar. James grabbed two while Luke picked up the others. Halfway across the room, a voice boomed.

"Well, I'll be gawd damned! Those Colton brothers finally managed to drag their flea-bitten hides back home!" Thomas Littleton drowned out conversations throughout the saloon. Even the piano player stopped mid-measure.

James spun around just in time to be knocked back by a bear hug from the newspaper editor.

"How the hell are you?" Littleton dumped James back on his feet then tried to shake hands with Luke. Waving to Trace and Andy, he marched across the saloon where he thumped Trace on the shoulder and knocked off Andy's hat. "What's wrong? No street signs pointin' the way home?"

"Join us, Tommy." James set down his glasses, grabbed a chair from a nearby table and offered it to his friend.

"Hell, yeah. Least you can do is buy me a beer for babysittin' your brother, here." Littleton gestured toward Luke. "Kept his sorry ass outta trouble more than once."

Trace smacked Luke on the chest as he sat. "He told us about shooting that gunfighter. Pretty exciting. Was that man, Waco Kid, really as dangerous as all that?" Trace leaned closer to Tommy.

Littleton gulped half his beer then wiped his mustache. "Sure was. Dangerous, mean hombre. Your brother defended Morningstar's honor by drillin' that devil in the head." Enjoying the attention, he continued. "'Course, Luke got grazed in his own head, but he's got that thick Colton skull just like the rest of you. Nothin' damaged."

James lowered his glass and stared at Luke. "Wait a minute. You never said Star was involved. You said she walked by afterwards and helped you. You said she went for the doctor. Somebody gonna tell me what *really* happened?" He searched his brother's paling face. Swinging his gaze to the editor, a poker face emerged, its plain wrapping covering any hint of additional information. Ice shot up and down James' spine as he set his jaw and asked Luke the question again. "What was your involvement with my wife?"

Stuttering, but trying to cover with a faceful of beer glass, Luke spoke over it. "She was in an alley near the plaza, that bastard come on to her, she resisted. I just happened to be in the right place at the right time, James. I killed him. But, like I told you, her honor's still intact."

Luke shot a warning glare at Thomas Littleton.

James caught the look. Something didn't feel right. Normally Tommy would be retelling the event, but he kept quiet, eyes fixed on the contents of his beer mug. Something was wrong, definitely wrong.

"Appreciate you defending her, Luke. But I'd like to get Morningstar's take on this." James glanced at Trace who seemed as surprised as he was.

Luke raised both eyebrows, his lips rose on one end. "Good idea."

Maybe he was wrong. Maybe nothing had happened. James trusted Morningstar, but Luke could be persuasive. He vowed not to let his suspicion spoil the evening. He forced himself to relax.

"Finish your beer, James." Trace ran his hand along a fading bruise on the right side of his face. "'Bout time to go."

Littleton peered at Trace's face. "Got a jim-dandy shiner there. Gotta be a helluva story to go with it. Mind if I come by tomorrow, do a feature on you brothers? You all got a rip-snortin' reunion goin' on. Hell, it's not every day this town sees something like this."

Trace thumbed over his shoulder toward the door. "Andy's gotta see the doc tomorrow, some stitches need lookin' after. James got a faceful of Apache claws. Sliced him pretty good, too. We ran outta string before we got him sewed up."

"Hell, Trace," James ran his fingers across his cheek. "I'm fine. Just scratches. You're the one who needs to be checked." He caught the respect in his brother's eyes. He hoped admiration for that brother reflected in his own eyes.

"Before we go, a toast to the Colton brothers." Andy, who'd been quiet for too long, raised his glass.

All eyes turned to Trace—the oldest, the sheriff of Mesilla, the leader. The one to make the toast.

"Damn right." Trace took a breath and held up his glass. "Here's to the Colton Clan. May we stay outta trouble."

"Here's to us!"

"To good friends!"

"To beautiful wives!"

Luke choked on his beer. Andy slapped his back while Luke spit brew all over the floor. Wiping his face, he pushed back and unsteadily found his feet.

Luke wobbled toward the bar while the other men laughed and saluted each other again. There had to be more to the story. Not letting it rest, James joined Luke leaning on the bar while Slim poured another glass.

"So let me get this straight," James said. "You and Star met in an alley. A gunman tried to…well, assault her. You killed him. That true?"

Luke nodded.

"And why were you meeting my wife in an alley?" James moved in close.

Backing up, Luke glanced at Littleton, still at the table with Trace and Andy. "She was walking there. I was walking there. Hell, James, it's a free country. I can walk anywhere I damn well please."

Knowing he should back down before things got out of hand, James lowered his voice.

"Guess I should thank you for saving her. You should've told me the whole story up there in Pinos Altos." James paused letting his temper calm. "Should've been me protecting her, though."

"Bet your ass it should've. But, thanks to me," Luke slurred his words, "she's still in one piece. Safe, lovely and silky soft."

"Silky soft?" Temper flaring, James gripped Luke's arm. "Meaning what?"

Luke grinned. "Huggable. Melts right in your arms. She has a real thing for men who protect her. A man who was there when she needed help. A man who jumped into the face of danger to save her. Willing to sacrifice his life for hers. You know—like a hero. Well, this hero made five hundred dollars just by killin' that sonovabitch!"

James spun his brother inches from his face. "You're drunk. Sober up before you make up stories, say things you'll regret."

"She's lonely, James. Everybody knows that. Just ask 'em." Luke swept his arm around the entire room as if presenting royalty. "But if it hadn't been for me, Luke Jeremiah Colton, number three brother, she'd be sweet meat by now."

Grabbing his brother's arms, James pulled him toward the doors. "Let's get outta here. You've had enough for tonight."

"Can't ever have enough, brother. Love's just like beer. One ain't enough, two's even better." With his elbow, Luke nudged James and winked.

"You talking about Morningstar?"

Luke shrugged. "Just talkin' in general. But, that Morningstar's a looker. A real beaut. Wouldn't mind gettin' her again—"

"You slept with my wife?" James' voice rose above the crowd. The piano player stopped, conversations hushed. Trace moved to James' right, Andy on Luke's left. James focused on the man who resembled him, the man he thought he knew. A man he could trust. "How could you? Is that why you've been quiet about her?"

Dropping his voice to a slurred whisper, Luke stared into James' angry eyes. "You'll have to ask your *wife*."

James clutched the front of Luke's shirt and shook him. "I'm askin' you, *brother*. Did you?"

Luke gazed at the ceiling and shrugged. "She's a desirable, lovely woman. Neglected, lonely, but full of spark. She needs a *man*. Someone who can give her babies. A real man like me. You know...a hero."

James drew back his clenched fist and punched Luke in his face. Blood spurted over both men's shirts and ran down Luke's chin. Trace pinned James' arms behind him as Luke sagged against the bar. Luke recoiled, sprung to his feet and head-butted James. Trace, James and Luke crashed to the floor, a tangled pile of arms and legs.

Pinned under Luke, James gasped for breath with his heavy brother flailing on top, Trace underneath. Sandwiched, he spotted swirling fists, legs, an arm or two. Was that Andy still standing? Were those Littleton's legs?

Luke rolled off as Trace pushed James over. The brothers wobbled to their feet. James struggled to stand, his world blurring black and white. A fist to his face rocked him back down to his knees. Brilliant white stars spun. Shaking his head brought only pain. Locating the bar, he crawled toward it. He pulled himself up and leaned against the wooden bar top, pulling in air.

Cowboys, ranchers, even businessmen swung fists and beer bottles. Fists plowed into flesh. Glass crashed. Men shouted.

"James!" He turned in time to receive Luke's fist. The power knocked him sideways against the bar then ricocheted him into a table. It screeched across the wood, the chairs crashing into others. James grabbed the closest chair and threw it toward Luke.

Luke ducked as the chair sailed across the bar and crashed into the mirror. Both splintered, raining glass and chair on the bar and bartender. Slim grabbed a chair leg and held it up, brandishing it like a sword. He hollered, but his words were lost under the chaos.

Before James could apologize, Luke lunged at him. Gripping Luke's shirt front, James spun him around, slamming him against the bar. Luke sank.

From behind, someone collided into James, both men reeling to the floor. James tasted sawdust and rolled, hoping to find his knees, feet and then brothers. Managing to get to his knees, a boot to his face turned his world black.

* * *

"JAMES? WAKE UP NOW." Someone shook his shoulders. "James, you all right?"

The voice. Too masculine to be Morningstar. Who, besides her, was here in his bedroom? James fought the hands gripping his shirt, pulling him upright. And why was his bed as hard as a wooden floor?

"Come on, you're fine." The voice sounded strained. "Let's get your feet under you."

Eyes blinking, James' thumping head refused to allow the eyes to focus. A firm hand under his arm tugged as he wobbled to his feet and gazed into an alien world. Intermittently, blurred images, some far away, some close, melded into some sort of black and white tableau. Without warning, his knees weakened, but the tenacious grip on his arm kept him upright.

"On second thought, better sit down."

He sank, hoping a chair would appear under his rear end. It did.

Deep breaths cleared his vision. The hand pressing on

his shoulder belonged to Sammy, Trace's deputy. James frowned up at the lawman. "Where's Trace?"

"Over there," Sammy pointed with his chin. "Helping your brothers."

On the far side of the saloon, bathed in yellow glow from the kerosene lamp, the three Colton boys stood, wiping glass, wooden furniture parts and sawdust from their clothes. Trace gripped Andy's arm.

"I'll go help." James pushed off from the chair, but Sammy's hand kept him down.

"Sorry," Sammy said. "You're stayin' right here."

"Why?"

"You're under arrest."

"What?" James rubbed his eyes.

Sammy bent closer to James' ear. "I said you're stayin' right here."

"Why?" James squirmed, but knew he lacked the strength to do much more than ask questions.

"Slim's pressing charges." Sammy touched the butt of his holstered Colt. "I gotta take you in. Sorry."

"What?" James rose, but the deputy pressed down forcefully, keeping him in his seat. Was that all he could say? None of this made sense. Maybe Trace would have the answers. But he couldn't sit and wait all night. His brothers needed his help, and from the looks of the destroyed saloon, Slim did, too. Shattered mirror, glasses scattered everywhere, cards strewn around, faro table sitting lopsided, tables upended and in pieces, chairs torn apart— a tornado couldn't have done this much damage. It would take long days to put *Sam Bean's Saloon* back together.

Thomas Littleton, notebook in one hand and pencil poised in other, wound his way across the room. He shouted at James. "*Helluva* reunion here. *Helluva* reunion.

Paper's gonna sell out with this story!" Littleton turned to Sammy. "Might even make New York papers!"

"Bully for you, Tommy!" James leaped to his feet, pushing away Sammy's hand. "Bully hell for you. Hell, sell it to England. To Paris. Blab it to the whole world! You'll be famous while I'm rotting in jail," he shouted. "Again!"

From behind James, bartender Slim shouted back. "You deserve jail and then some! What the hell were you thinking? Tearing up the place like this?" Brandishing a chair leg like a club, he stormed toward James. "Sam's gonna be furious!"

Slim reached James the same time as Trace, Luke and Andy. They stood next to James.

Littleton, still writing, moved back giving room for the brothers.

Slim waved the wooden leg toward the piano. "You know how much it's gonna cost to fix this mess? How much you're gonna have to pay?" Shaking the leg at James, he glared. "Hell, I oughta take it outta your hide."

"Whoa, settle down there, men." Sammy stepped between James and Slim and held up his hands. "We've had all the fun there is for one night."

"Shouldn't have to go to jail for it!" James struggled to reel in his temper. "Not tonight. Especially not tonight."

Slim moved in closer, his words dropping to icy. "You should stay in jail 'til you pay for the damages. All of them!"

"How the hell can I do that from stinkin' jail?"

"Enough." Sammy pushed James down to the chair, again firmly pressing on his shoulder.

"What're you waitin' for, deputy?" Slim hollered. "His sorry ass's supposed to be in jail."

"Now Slim, you settle down, too." He wrestled the chair leg from the barkeep and tossed it onto a pile of debris. "It'll get there soon enough. I'll take these boys to jail and the court'll work out payment." He turned to Trace. "I'm sorry. Your brother's gotta go, too."

Trace huffed.

Slim shot another glare at James, spun and stormed toward the bar. He tossed curses over his shoulder. "This ain't over yet, Colton."

His face hurting, James cradled his chin. Warm liquid pooled in his hand.

Without saying a word, Littleton dug into his pocket and handed over a handkerchief. James pressed the material against a gash while the newspaperman sketched the wreckage and scribbled cryptic words on his small pad.

Muttering, Littleton wandered off toward Slim.

Temper now under control, James eyed Trace still standing by him. A new bruise glowed on his right cheek. Andy, on Trace's left, swayed, sagging against his brother while Luke kept his back turned to James.

A tug on his shirt brought James to his feet. "Let's go," Sammy said. "I won't use cuffs but come along peaceful and we'll get on fine." He tugged harder and aimed for the door.

"Wait," Trace held up a hand. "Don't lock him up. You know how he'll get. Release him to me and I'll see he makes it to court."

"Ah hell, Trace. The law's the law," Sammy said. "You know that even better than I do. Besides, Slim's pressing charges. He insists on jail."

Over his throbbing head and chin, James fought to make sense of things. "What exactly are the charges?"

"Let's see." Sammy ticked off on his free hand. "Disturbin' the peace, destruction of property, assault on a peace officer, that's you, Trace. Drunk and disorderly conduct—"

"Then you'll have to take us all in, Sammy." Trace glanced beside him at Andy.

"Only your brothers, Trace. Can't arrest you—you're the *sheriff*. Besides, Slim pointed his finger at them. Said James here started it. Two other cowboys said the same thing."

James sighed, inspected the red-stained handkerchief in his hand, and shrugged. "What the hell're we waiting for? Let's go." He glared at Luke's back then pushed him. "You, too."

Luke spun around, blood drying on his face. "What the hell—"

"You slept with—"

"Enough!" Sammy shoved James forward who stumbled around the piles of cowboys and debris. Both men stepped into cold night air. As they marched across the plaza, the grip on James' arm increased until all feeling was lost. How could he enter a jail cell again? Set foot into that dreaded cage?

His stomach knotted sending supper upward. But he wouldn't throw up. No, he'd keep his supper and dignity intact. What was left of it.

The key clicked in the closed door's iron lock. Sammy stood back shaking his head. "More for your own protection than anything else. Don't want somebody coming in here and...well, assaulting your person." He thumbed over his shoulder. "Tell Trace I've gone for the doc."

Alone, James eased down to the lumpy cot and sat, head in hands. Within minutes, Andy and Luke occupied the adjacent cell, theirs conspicuously left open and unlocked. Trace stood on the outside, between them.

Trace wagged his head, his gaze sweeping across his brothers. "We'll get this figured out. Don't worry." Receiving nothing but groans, he stepped into the open cell.

While Trace tended to Andy, James sagged against the stone jail wall and contemplated life. What the hell had gone wrong? Had Luke really bedded Star? Was she a willing participant? Couldn't blame her if she did. James hadn't been able to love her like a man. A real man. Isn't that what Luke said?

Eyeing Luke in the other cell, James studied the bruised brother who also sat on a cot, slumped against the hard wall. Luke's eyes were closed but James knew he was awake. Icy silence hung in the jail like pall over a funeral.

"Heard about the fight. Quite a doozey." Dr. Morgan, black instrument bag in hand, bustled through the hallway door and into Andy and Luke's cell. "Let's take a look and see what happened."

He harrumphed and muttered, turning Andy's face this way and that. Peeling off Andy's shirt, the doctor inspected the healing arrow wound, now bloody. More muttering, he opened his bag and dug through tools.

"What d'you think, Doc?" Trace held Andy's shirt.

"Upper arm was healing nicely 'til he pulled out those stitches. Reopened that gash. Took a bad beating to the face tonight, too. Looks like he broke that jaw again." He looked up at Trace. "Might be some time before he does any kind of talking."

James launched himself to his feet and peered through the iron bars. "He gonna be all right?"

The doctor turned in his chair and faced James. "Right enough. Enjoy the peace and quiet while you can." Doc's dark blue eyes gleamed. "Now, let me come over and take a look at you. Your other brothers are in good enough shape."

Sammy unlocked the door. For a split second, James considered rushing through the unlocked door and bolting out into freedom. But what would that buy him? Instead, he sat while Doc Morgan maneuvered his way into the cell.

Jerking at the eye-watering liquid Doc swabbed across his face and chin, James thought about his future. How long would he be jailed this time? And what about Morningstar? Now, she'd leave him for sure. As it was, she'd stuck by him too many times. She deserved someone better.

While he tried not to feel the tug and pull, the sting of Doc's stitches, he ignored his brothers' watchful gaze. James couldn't fight the weight on his chest, in his heart. He squeezed his eyes shut. He listed the setbacks: his own saloon burned down, his house ransacked, Star wanted to go off to medical school, Luke seduced her... the list grew. Maybe when he opened his eyes, he'd be dead. Or at least somewhere else. Anywhere else.

"Been thinkin', James." Luke sat on the end of James' cot.

James opened his eyes and frowned at Trace and Sammy. Why'd they let Luke into the cell?

"Thinking? That's new for you." James glared at Luke, but the look on his brother's face he'd never seen before.

"Hold still, James." Doc pulled on the string. "Got enough scars as it is."

James sat stock still.

After more tugs and pulls, Dr. Morgan clipped the end of the final stitch, arranged the various instruments back into his bag, snapped it shut and stood. "Finished.

Now all of you. Listen to me. No more fighting. Take time to heal up." His eyes sparked. "Will you do that? Please? For me?"

"I'll see to it." Trace said.

"Uh huh." Doc patted Trace's arm. "I want to see everybody in my office first thing tomorrow morn—" His eyes swept across both cells. "Well...soon as you can." He marched through the door mumbling and muttering.

Turning his attention back to his brother, James wondered what was on Luke's mind.

He loved this brother, but if he'd really slept with his wife, could he ever forgive him?

"About Morningstar."

James clenched both hands.

Luke dropped his voice. "Hell, James, I'm full of hooey. Too damn much beer. Morningstar's a beautiful woman, and you're lucky to have her."

"I agree." James looked at Luke and let his gaze trail over to Andy and Trace, neither giving any hint of what Luke was about to say.

Luke continued. "To be honest, I tried to seduce her. My own wife's...well, unless something changes...let's say we probably won't have three kids. Morningstar was warm and lonely. I needed somebody to hold. But, dammit, James, she loves you. Not me—*you*. I hate to admit, I tried to...I *really* tried. But *she loves you*."

"She really does, James." The feminine voice floated across the cell.

James peered around Trace standing in the open cell door. Morningstar stood next to a grinning deputy sheriff.

"I came as soon as I heard." She looked at Trace. "Teresa's home with Faith, but she's as worried about all of you as I am."

Trace moved aside allowing her to step through the iron door. She knelt by James. "Are you good?"

Now he was. James grinned, the crushing weight on his chest gone.

He stood, bringing her with him. He enveloped his wife in his arms, her soft body melting into his. He spoke to her and her alone. "Ever seen the sun set over the Pacific? I hear California's beautiful."

HISTORICAL NOTES

Pinos Altos (Tall Pines) is located six miles north of Silver City, New Mexico, and sits at an elevation of 7,040 feet. The town began in May 1860 when three 49-ers stopped to drink at Bear Creek and discovered gold. Needing supplies, the men ventured into Santa Rita where they shared their discovery with the Marston brothers. News spread like wildfire and by September 1860, seven hundred men were clamoring for that gold.

However, the area was populated long before 1860. Mimbres Apache have called this area home for centuries. In addition, an early Mexican settlement, also called Pinos Altos, sent gold to Chihuahua as early as 1837.

Pinos Altos was officially incorporated in 1868 with a population of seven hundred people, about one hundred twenty houses, two hotels, one school and several mercantiles, and of course, The Buckhorn Saloon.

The **Buckhorn Saloon**, located on the main street of Pinos Altos, opened its doors as a saloon in 1860 and has operated as such ever since. Original furnishings decorate the saloon now doubling as a restaurant.

Mangas Colorado, a Mimbreno Apache chief, was killed near Pinos Altos in January 1863. The California Volunteers were told that the Apache must be subdued. Mangus Colorado (Red Sleeves) was to be brought in by strategy or force. Mangus, a relative of Cochise, sought peace with the Americans and was willing to negotiate. Offering a flag of truce to Mangus, the army captured and eventually killed this Apache leader. He was buried in the nearby hills, but later exhumed and sent to Washington where they found his skull to be larger and weigh more than Daniel Webster's.

Two of the oldest graves in the Pinos Altos cemetery belong to the **Marston brothers**. Captain Thomas Marston was fatally wounded by Apache on September 22, 1861. His marker under a large juniper tree reads:

<blockquote>
Capt. Arizona Scouts
Thomas J. Marston
Sept. 13, 1839
Sept. 27, 1861
Died of fatal wounds recd. in action as he led the settlers
in defense and repulsed 400 Apache led by Chief
Cochise.
</blockquote>

His brother, Virgil, was also killed by Indians in 1870 and is buried beside his brother.

A LOOK AT: TRAIL TO TIN TOWN

The exciting action and adventure western series from award-winning author Melody Groves and starring the Colton Brothers continues!

Despite battling a frenzied horse, poisoned water, aggravated Apache, a fanatical Army officer, along with other life-threatening trials, the four Colton Brothers—Trace, James, Luke, and Andy—refuse to turn their three thousand longhorns around and head back to Mesilla, New Mexico.

Determined to deliver the contracted beeves to Tin Town, California, on time, James Colton drives men and cattle as hard and as fast as he can. The brothers hope to celebrate the end of the Civil War and the cattle drive by hoisting a beer in Tin Town.

But Whid MacGilvry has other ideas. Killing James is not enough to exact his revenge for incorrectly perceived injustices. Destroying the entire Colton family will have to do. And where better than out on the range?

AVAILABLE NOW

ABOUT THE AUTHOR

Melody Groves is author of NM Press Women's Zia Award-winning *She Was Sheriff*, set in 1872 northern California, prequel to *Lady of the Law*. She also penned the Colton Brothers Saga: *Border Ambush, Sonoran Rage, Arizona War, Kansas Bleeds, Black Range Revenge,* and *Trail to Tin Town*.

Her non-fiction books include: the New Mexico Book Award winner, *Hoist a Cold One! Historic Bars of the Southwest*. Also, Zia finalist *Butterfield's Byways: The First Stagecoach Line and Overland Mail Route Across America* and *Ropes, Reins, and Rawhide: All About Rodeo, When Outlaws Wore Badges,* and recently, *Before Billy the Kid: The Boy Behind the Legendary Outlaw*.

Melody writes for national magazines. She won the prestigious National Press Women's Award for her article in *True West Magazine*.

When not writing, she plays rhythm guitar with the Jammy Time Band.